The Man Who Could Not Kill Enough

The Secret Murders of Milwaukee's Jeffrey Dahmer

by Anne E. Schwartz

A Birch Lane Press Book
Published by Carol Publishing Group

A Birch Lane Press Book
Published by Carol Publishing Group
Birch Lane Press is a registered trademark of Carol Communications, Inc.

Editorial Offices: 600 Madison Avenue, New York, N.Y. 10022
Sales & Distribution Offices: 120 Enterprise Avenue, Secaucus, N.J. 07094

In Canada: Canadian Manda Group, P.O. Box 920, Station U, Toronto, Ontario M8Z 5P9

Queries regarding rights and permissions should be addressed to Carol Publishing Group, 600 Madison Avenue, New York, N.Y. 10022

Carol Publishing Group books are available at special discounts for bulk purchases, for sales promotions, fund raising, or educational purposes. Special editions can be created to specifications. For details, contact: Special Sales Department, Carol Publishing Group, 120 Enterprise Avenue, Secaucus, N.J. 07094

Manufactured in the United States of America
10 9 8 7 6 5 4 3 2 1

Library of Congress Cataloging-in-Publication Data

Schwartz, Anne E.
    The man who could not kill enough : the secret murders of
  Milwaukee's Jeffrey Dahmer / by Anne E. Schwartz.
      p.   cm.
    "A Birch Lane Press book."
    ISBN1-55972-117-0
      1. Serial murders—Wisconsin—Milwaukee—Case studies. 2. Sexual
  deviation—Case studies. 3. Dahmer, Jeffrey. 4. Murderers—
  Wisconsin—Milwaukee—Biography. 5. Insane, Criminal and
  dangerous—Wisconsin—Milwaukee—Biography. I. Title.
  HV6534.M65S38   1992
  364.1'523'0977595—dc20   92-6662
                                                              CIP

For Robert Enters, the love of my life, my best friend, and the best damn cop I know.

And to the memory of my mother, Jean Hanson Schwartz.

Their unwavering faith and support made my first book possible.

Contents

Acknowledgments

Actually sitting down and writing *The Man Who Could Not Kill Enough* was a solitary and lonely effort, but a great many people made invaluable contributions to the preparation of the book and deserve my public thanks:

The men and women of the Milwaukee Police Department, whose cooperation with a reporter has always been at a considerable risk to their jobs: You are my heroes and I am grateful for your trust.

Kris Radish, who took time out from writing her own first book to alternately commiserate and rejoice with me and become my friend.

Marty Burns Wolfe, who, as Ethel to my Lucy, did not forget how to be a best friend while also being a top television news anchor.

Reporters Leonard Sykes, Jackie Gray, Eugene Kane, and Jack Norman; and sports editor Chuck Salituro and his staff, who consistently supported me at the *Journal* and in this effort. Jackie Loohauis, who believed in me and gave me my first daily newspaper job.

I have a special place in my heart for the faculty of the University of Missouri–Columbia School of Journalism, especially Hal Lister and Hal Cordry, who taught me how to make something of my life. And Dr. Don Ranly, whose grammar drills in J-School helped me forever to irritate my colleagues.

My bosses, Fred D'Ambrosi, news director at WISN-TV in Milwaukee (and a Missouri grad), and Maryann Lazarski, who hired me to cover the Dahmer story and gave me access to the photos in this book. Photographers Mary Jo Walicki, Bobby Vermiglio, and Jack Orton, who accepted payment in homemade cheesecakes for their invaluable photography services.

My family, Duane and Gloria Dunham, who swore I would do this one day.

In the last but definitely not least category, I am grateful to my editor, Hillel Black, for making my dream come true.

1

The Discovery

July 22, 1991, 11:25 P.M.

Police Officers Rolf Mueller and Robert Rauth were finishing their four P.M.-to-midnight shift in Milwaukee's Third Police District. They had been driving along the 2600 block of West Kilbourn Avenue, a grimy neighborhood on the fringes of the downtown area near Marquette University, the highest crime area in the inner city. To the north, the main thoroughfare was peppered with strip bars and small, corner grocery stores. Faded, tattered signs in the windows advertised: WE TAKE FOOD STAMPS.

The neighborhood included drug dealers, prostitutes, and the unemployed mentally ill, who collected state aid because they managed to live on their own or in one of the area's numerous halfway houses. They would carry their belongings in rusty metal grocery carts and sleep in doorways. There was evidence of the area's glory days: expansive turn-of-the-century Victorian homes, rambling apartment complexes, and stately cathedral-style dwellings. For the police, the district has the dubious distinction of being the place where more than half the city's homicides have occurred in the last five years.

That Monday, July 22, felt oppressively hot and humid, the kind of heat that would cling to the body. For cops on the beat, the sweat would trickle down their chests and form salty pools under their steel-plated bulletproof vests. Their gun belts would hang uncomfortably from their waists, and the constant rubbing chafed their middles. The squad cars they patroled in reeked of burning motor oil and the body odor of the last prisoner who sat in the back seat. It was on nights like this that they could not wait to go home.

Anxious to see his wife and daughter, Mueller hoped to make it to the end of the shift without stumbling into any overtime. Mueller, thirty-nine, was a ten-year veteran of the Milwaukee Police Department. Born in Germany, he had moved to America as a youngster but he spoke a little German at home with his daughter to preserve his heritage. He sported a mass of perpetually tousled blond curls on top of his six-foot frame. Mueller enjoyed horror movies and always talked about how much he loved a good scare.

Mueller's partner, Bob Rauth, forty-one, had spent thirteen years in the department. His strawberry-blond hair had begun to thin, exposing a long scar on his forehead from a car accident that pushed his face through the windshield. His stocky build seemed more suited to a wrestler than a policeman. Like many police officers, Rauth was divorced. His fellow officers knew he consistently took as much overtime as he could get, anxious to find an assignment so he could squirrel away some extra money for a couple more hours' work, something cops call "hunting for overtime." To work with Rauth was to "work over." Other cops described Rauth as one of those guys to whom all the strange, almost unbelievable things happen on the job. Fortunately, Rauth had a self-deprecating sense of humor and would frequently keep the station in stitches about something that happened to him on an assignment or "hitch."

Sitting in their squad car waiting to take a prisoner to jail, Mueller and Rauth were approached by a short, wiry black man with a handcuff dangling from his left wrist. Another summer night that brings out the best in everybody, they thought.

"Which one of us did you escape from?" one of the officers asked through an open window in the car.

The man was thirty-two-year-old Tracy Edwards. While someone coming down the street with a handcuff dangling from his wrist would be an attention-grabber in Milwaukee's posher suburbs, on 25th and Kilbourn it's nothing out of the ordinary. Police calls in that area can range from a man with his head wrapped in aluminum foil spray-painting symbols on houses to a naked man directing traffic at a major intersection. The area is filled with "MOs," citizens brought to the Milwaukee County Mental Health Complex for "mental observation" rather than taken to jail when arrested.

Rauth and Mueller were hesitant to let Edwards go on his way in case he had escaped from another officer, so they asked whether the scuffed silver bracelets were souvenirs of a homosexual encounter. Cops practice the cover-your-ass motto with every shift they work. They don't want to stand in somebody's glass office the next day, trying to explain their way out of a situation that went bad after they left and citizens called screaming their name and badge number to the Chief.

As Edwards stood next to the squad car, he rambled on about a "weird dude" who slapped a handcuff on him during his visit to the dude's apartment. After initially rebuking Edwards, telling him to have his "friend" remove the handcuffs, the two officers eventually listened to Edwards's story. It would not have been unusual for the two men to write the incident off as a homosexual encounter gone awry, but Rauth sniffed overtime and asked Edwards to show him where all this happened. That's how close Jeffrey Dahmer came to not getting caught that day. Criminals sometimes escape arrest because they are stopped at the end of a cop's shift or because an officer, tired from working late the night before, does not want to spend the next day tied up in court and then have to report for work.

The two officers decided to go with Edwards to apartment 213 in the Oxford Apartments at 924 North 25th Street. They were not familiar with the building, a reasonably well maintained three-story brick structure. They were rarely called there because most of its occupants held jobs and lived quietly. Once inside the building, the officers were struck by the rancid odor hanging heavy in the air as they approached the apartment.

But all these places stink around here, they thought. A variety of smells greet the police when they are sent to check on the welfare of an apartment full of children who, officers discover, have been sitting alone for several days in their own feces and who have been using the bathtub and the toilet interchangeably while their mother sits at a tavern down the street. Foul smells are as much a part of the inner city as crime.

"Milwaukee police officers," Rauth shouted for all to hear as he rapped loudly with his beefy hand on the wooden door of apartment 213.

Jeffrey Dahmer, thirty-one, an attractive but scruffy, thin man with dirty blond hair and a scar over his right eye, opened the door and allowed the officers and Edwards to enter.

Inside, Mueller and Rauth talked to Dahmer about the incident with Edwards and asked him for the key to the handcuffs. This way, if they got the right answers, they could "advise" the assignment, meaning they could handle the problem and leave without writing a ticket or making an arrest.

Dahmer talked to the officers in the calm voice that, we would later learn, had manipulated so many victims and officials in the past. He told them that the key was in the bedroom. But before Dahmer left the room, Edwards piped up that they would find there a knife that Dahmer had used to threaten him.

It did not appear that Mueller would get home on time, but maybe they could still "advise" the situation if they discovered no knife. Mueller told Dahmer to stay put and went into the bedroom.

Mueller peered into an open dresser drawer and saw something he still describes with difficulty: Polaroid photographs of males in various stages of dismemberment, pictures of skulls in kitchen cabinets and freezers, and a snapshot of a skeleton dangling from a shower spigot. He stopped breathing for a time as he stood frozen, staring at the gruesome Polaroids that barely seemed to depict humans.

In a tremulous voice Mueller screamed for his partner to cuff Dahmer and place him under arrest. "Bob, I don't think we can advise this any more," he shouted, with that gallows humor cops use to keep a safe distance from the stresses of their jobs.

Realizing he was bound for jail, Dahmer turned violent. He and Officer Rauth tumbled around the living room floor until Dahmer was safely in handcuffs. Mueller emerged from the bedroom clutching several photos in his hand.

"You're one lucky son of a bitch, buddy," Mueller told Edwards. "This could have been you," he added, his hands shaking as he waved a photo of a severed human head at Edwards.

Edwards looked wide-eyed at Mueller and told him how Dahmer "freaked" when he went toward the refrigerator to get a beer. "Maybe he's got one of those heads in there," Edwards said uncomfortably. "Yeah, right, maybe there's a head in there." Mueller laughed at Edwards's fear.

Mueller opened the refrigerator door to taunt Edwards, then let out two screams from deep in his gut that neighbors would later recall had awakened them. Mueller slammed the door shut and shouted, "Bob, there's a fucking head in the refrigerator!"

One cop realized this was going to be one hell of a story for some reporter.

Milwaukee police do not talk much with the media. Milwaukee Police Chief Philip Arreola believes that the press should print good news and the funnies. Arreola does not want his patrol officers talking to the press at crime scenes, and he ardently objects to a cop breaking a story to the media. Some officers tip off the press for the satisfaction of screwing the chief.

The late-night call from a source is every reporter's dream, which occasionally turns into a nightmare. Awakened by the ring of the telephone a little before midnight on Monday, July 22, I reached for the pad and pen I always keep at my bedside so I can jot down what the caller tells me.

Without giving a name, the excited voice of one of my police sources said, "Rauth and Mueller found a human head in a refrigerator at 924 North 25th Street, apartment 213. There are other body parts in the place, too. You aren't gonna believe what-all's in this goof's apartment. He was cutting up black guys and saving their body parts. You'd better get over here before all the brass shows up and all you get is a bullshit press release."

Cops! What kidders. But what if it was not a joke? Bob Woodward from the *Washington Post* got whispered tips on the Watergate story from Deep Throat in parking garages. That was national news involving the President of the United States.

But this is Milwaukee. Nothing ever happens here.

I dialed the lieutenant in the Criminal Investigation Bureau at the Milwaukee Police Department who chides reporters for wasting his time with what he considers stupid tips and worthless stories that editors demand their reporters pursue. When on duty, he sits at a desk for his entire shift and dispatches detectives to crime scenes, keeps tabs on the progress of all investigations, and handles calls from the media, the latter being the least favorite, hands down, of any of his duties.

"Lieutenant, what can you tell me about something in a refrigerator on North 25th Street?" I asked in a just-awakened voice and waited for the inevitable response.

"How in the hell do you know about that?" he barked. "Jesus Christ, you reporters! Do you guys mind if we ever get there first and find out what's happening before you tell the whole world?"

The average person takes about an hour to get ready for work. But a reporter eager to be first on the scene will grab clothing closest to the bed. I didn't know what I'd thrown on until much later, when television camera lights set up at the scene revealed that I had chosen two mismatched sneakers and black underwear beneath white shorts.

I hopped into my brown 1979 Chevy Caprice and, pushing the accelerator to its limit, drove from my neighborhood of manicured lawns into the bowels of the city to my reporting beat of darkened tenements, burned-out streetlights, and wary looks from the locals. When a white female cruises slowly down a block in the inner city, residents are most likely to peg her for a cop or a social services worker coming to transplant someone's children to a foster home.

I was familiar with the area surrounding the Oxford Apartments. There I had reported on scores of stories about shootings, stabbings, armed robberies, and arson. I knew the drug houses by sight after spending hours waiting for narcotics officers to hit the doors and then spill out, preening with their arrests. When I pulled up to Dahmer's building, there was no crowd of onlookers and television cameras and no other reporters. Maybe it was all over. Out in front, a fire engine's red strobe lights pierced the darkness, not an unusual sight, because firefighters are the first responders to any emergency.

I noticed a large black woman sitting on the front stoop of 924 North 25th Street, probably seeking some respite from the heat in the building. Pamela Bass, in her thirties with her hair pulled severely back from her face, looked up and opened the locked glass door that led to the lobby.

"I don't think you want to go up there," she said, obviously shaken and struggling to pull her maroon nylon robe tight around her body. "The man was my neighbor, you know. I had no idea, no idea at all. They found a head in the refrigerator, you know."

I scribbled furiously in my notebook and extracted a promise from Pamela Bass that she would talk to me later about what she knew. I knew I had to get upstairs before anyone else did.

The building was cheap-looking outside but clean inside, which set it apart from most multiple-unit dwellings in the inner city. Sprinting up the carpeted steps to the second floor, I took just one step into the second-floor hallway before the sickening smell made my legs buckle. A combination of something chemical and rotten. But it was not the smell of death. Ask a veteran cop what death smells like and he or she will say, "Once you've smelled it, you'll never forget it. There's nothing else like it."

I have smelled death on a number of ride-alongs with the police department, and they are right. This smell was different, however, a fact which would become important when police who had been in the apartment in the months before the discovery were asked why their trained noses had failed to detect a deathly odor.

I approached the open door of apartment 213 and stepped cautiously inside. Because most officers know me from three years of covering crime scenes, they have often beckoned me inside when other reporters were kept away by yellow tape that reads "POLICE LINE. DO NOT CROSS." The police have often shared details of a case with me because, although I could not print it because I worked for a family newspaper, they knew the information would fascinate me.

The stench inside Dahmer's apartment was not of death but of something more, just as those killed there were not merely murdered but had their lives unspeakably ended.

I was poised to take copious notes, but in the few minutes I was inside Dahmer's one-bedroom apartment, I found it quite unremarkable. The kitchen, dining area, and living room were all one, and, for a single man's dwelling, it was tidy. When police came Tuesday afternoon to haul out the furniture and tear up the carpeting, they discovered extensive dried blood-stains on the underside of the carpeting that had soaked right through and heavily stained the wood floor beneath.

I thought it odd that Dahmer had mounted a video camera on the back wall of his apartment. Much like the surveillance cameras used at banks, it was aimed at the front door. (Police later discovered it was a dummy.) As I stood just a few steps inside the front door, I craned left around the corner to look into the kitchen. Because I didn't want my fingerprints to smear the evidence, and because I did not know what horror would haunt my sleep later, I did *not* look into the refrigerator that contained the perfectly preserved head or into the deep freezer with a lift-top that I later learned contained heads in plastic bags. Later, my foray into the apartment would become the talk of the local newsrooms when, around various water coolers, reporters debated, "Would *you* have looked in the refrigerator?" Suffice it to say, I felt participatory journalism had its limits.

Between the kitchen and living room was a table containing beer cans, an open bag of potato chips, supplies for Dahmer's aquarium, an ashtray with cigarette butts, and a man's porno-graphic magazine. On the walls of the living room hung black-

and-white posters of the torsos of male bodybuilders striking muscle-man-type poses. A print by surrealist painter Salvador Dali, depicting a netherworld scene, hung on another wall. A blue lava lamp was in one corner of the room. A fish tank on a black table had several fish swimming about, and all appeared to be well cared for. Near the nubby, neutral-color sofa was a bleach container and a tool resembling an electric drill. On a cheap brown end table sat several more beer cans, an ashtray, an electric toothbrush, an empty tissue box, and a spray can of Lysol disinfectant.

A dead-bolt lock was mounted on the outside of the sliding door that led to the bedroom, bathroom, and closet. Police officers whispered to me, nearly inaudibly, of what lay in the next room. On the floor of the bedroom closet were various tools and loose wires, but in back of the closet was a metal stockpot, the size of a lobster pot, that contained decomposed hands and a penis. On the shelf above the kettle were two skulls. Also in the closet were containers of ethyl alcohol, chloroform, and formaldehyde, along with some glass jars holding male genitalia preserved in formaldehyde. In the bathroom, where, Dahmer confessed, he had dismembered many of his victims, a picture of a nude male was taped next to the mirror.

In the bedroom, on top of a dresser, were a television, a beer can, and a pornographic male homosexual videotape. The top dresser drawer contained about thirty Polaroid photos taken by Dahmer at various stages of his victims' deaths. One showed a man's head, with the flesh still intact, lying in a sink. Another displayed a victim cut open from the neck to the groin, like a deer gutted after the kill, the cuts so clean I could see the pelvic bone clearly. I was jolted by a photograph of a bleached skeleton hanging in the closet—the flesh on the head, hands, and feet jutting from the bones were left perfectly intact.

Many male bodies were cut open and displayed in various positions on the bed. One photo showed hands and genitals placed in the stockpot in the closet. Possibly fancying himself an artist, Dahmer arranged the body parts so he could photograph them. He placed a severed head—the skin and hair intact and the face recognizable—on top of a white cloth. He put the hands on a folded cloth next to the head and the genital organs on a cloth on the other side. Dahmer photographed two skulls side by side on a plate next to various condiments in what appeared to be a kitchen cupboard. He also took pictures of two skulls in the freezer. One corpse was carefully skinned and photographed.

Along with the unspeakable pictures of his deadly handiwork, Dahmer took snapshots of his victims while they were still alive. They assumed various sexually explicit positions, including wearing handcuffs for bondage photos, and one victim, fourteen-year-old Konerak Sinthasomphone, posed in his black bikini briefs in a muscle-man stance.

On top of the bed was a Polaroid camera, while underneath was a beer can and the hunting knife Edwards mentioned to Rauth and Mueller.

Also in the bedroom was a computer box with two skulls in it and a photo diary of the dismembered corpses. The photos were mounted the same way most people mount vacation pictures in a book so they can look back and fondly remember the time. Jeffrey Dahmer later told police that he wanted to keep his victims with him always. On his bedroom walls hung more photos of male bodybuilders. Resting on a two-drawer metal file cabinet were a clock radio, television remote control, and an ashtray filled with cigarette butts. The top drawer of the file cabinet contained three skulls, and the bottom drawer contained various bones. Several pornographic homosexual videotapes were strewn about the floor.

In the corner of the bedroom sat an ominous, blue, fifty-seven-gallon barrel with a black lid holding decomposing body parts in a sludgy chemical bath. Just to look at the barrel and know what was inside made me nauseated. In all, seven skulls and four heads with flesh still on them were recovered from the apartment.

The horror of what Dahmer had done, combined with my amazement that these crimes went undetected in an apartment building in the middle of a metropolis, seemed overwhelming. My head ached and my heart pounded as I stood in the apartment. I thought about my neighbors and about what my apartment building smelled like. Dahmer was safely in police custody, but I nevertheless stepped back out into the hallway.

I have always felt a little uncomfortable standing in the place where a crime has been committed, but I felt more than simple discomfort that night. During my adventures as a police reporter, I have had a gun held to my head and my face slashed by gang members. This time I was more frightened. In the hallway, as I looked at the hieroglyphics in my notebook, I struggled to write what I had seen and been told. It was clear that Jeffrey Dahmer was not only a man with a human head in his refrigerator but almost certainly a mass murderer.

I wanted to know who Jeffrey Dahmer was and what sort of incident in his life triggered such actions. I wondered how the police would explain to the families of these men how their sons and brothers died. It may sound unfeeling, but I knew then that this was the story of a lifetime, an awareness that allowed me to process all that I saw. This is what I had been trained for. I realized I was the last person who was not a police official to leave the apartment alive, and I was the only one who could really ever tell the story from a point of view different from all other reporters because I was the closest to the actual scene of the crime. Others would come to the building, but the experience of seeing the apartment and witnessing the horror of the residents that night was mine alone.

The air outside the Oxford Apartments felt good and clean, even though it was hot and humid. But the heavy odor, like meat left to rot in an unplugged refrigerator, would not go away. It clung to the inside of my nostrils, and the scene inside remained etched on my mind. Ask me today to remember that night and I can still recall the smell and the photographs. Hours, even days, later, the memory of what I had observed would take me back to the scene, usually when I was doing some household task.

But at that moment, there was work to do. At the back of the building, the familiar crime-scene onlookers were gathering, and I was in my bailiwick. I recovered my composure and I knew what to do. Who lived in the building? And how did the residents go on about their lives while such stench lurked in the hallway right outside their doors? Did anyone know Jeffrey Dahmer?

At the end of the darkened cobblestone alley, in the rear of the building, the fire department's Hazardous Materials Unit had arrived. I wondered if they knew what their cargo would be as they dressed in their spacesuit-like gear. Sitting in the back of the truck waiting for orders from his chief, one of the firefighters told me, "We were told there is a barrel in there containing an unknown chemical substance."

"Unknown," he had said tersely as I dutifully scribbled his innocuous quote in my notebook, but his ashen face and somber demeanor gave away that he knew what it was.

I looked at the open door leading to the hallway in front of Dahmer's apartment and spied Mueller staring at the ceiling, leaning up against the wall for support. Rauth was standing next to him, his hands shoved deep into his pockets. The two were visibly shaken. Mueller came down and sidled up to me. He said in subdued tones, "You think you've seen it all out here, and then something like this happens."

I asked what happened when he discovered the head, just an hour before. After a lengthy pause Mueller said, "I screamed, Annie. But don't write in the paper that I said that, okay? I've got a feeling I'm going to take enough grief from other cops about this as it is."

Their grief was just beginning. The two officers requested three days' administrative leave to deal psychologically with the trauma caused by what they had seen. Chief Arreola denied their request. When a police officer is personally involved with death or great bodily harm, the department routinely grants them three days off and supplies them with counseling. Mueller and Rauth would have had to shoot someone to get that. They were offered neither counseling nor time off and were back at work the next night.

Stepping away from Mueller, I scanned the crowd. In a neighborhood inured to the nightly blast of gunfire and to tragedy openly played out in the streets, residents of the Oxford Apartments stood by incredulously, almost reverently, as they took in the scene in their backyard in the early morning hours of July 23. By this time, rumors as well as facts had spread among the tenants and newspeople there.

Crime scenes or spectacular fires in the city are not, as a rule, somber occasions. Onlookers prance about for the television cameras and wave to Mom behind reporters trying to be oblivious as they do their live shots. Young boys ride past on bicycles or skateboards, claiming to have seen everything, as newspaper reporters take down their accounts and television cameramen shove microphones in their faces. Young men with huge boom boxes perched on their shoulders often pump out rap music, the words indiscernible, loud enough so passersby can feel the strong bass beat in their chests. But not on Tuesday, July 23.

About twenty residents huddled in the alley behind the Oxford Apartments, silent, unlike the usual crime-scene crowd. They had rushed from their homes in various stages of dress—nightclothes, loose cotton shifts, and hastily assembled outfits, like that of the woman who pulled on gym shorts under her robe and dashed outside in frayed, dirty, terrycloth slippers. It was about one A.M. and it was still hot, hovering around eighty degrees.

Pamela Bass was there with her husband, Vernell. She held one hand over her mouth and clutched her husband's hand in the other, her eyes wide and wet. For the last year, the Basses had lived directly across the hall from Jeffrey Dahmer, and they were already talking about moving.

"This is a good building. You know, good people, working people," Vernell Bass told me. "But I can't stay here knowing that this happened under my nose. I'll never forget it and I'm certainly not going to stay somewhere that reminds me of it every day."

Like many other residents, the Basses remembered some of Dahmer's oddities. "We used to hear sawing coming from his apartment at all hours," Pamela Bass recalled. "I said to Vernell one night about two in the morning, 'What in the world is he building at this hour?' I knocked on Jeff's door to ask him to do that during the day, but he didn't answer."

She closed her eyes, shuddered, and continued. "And then there was that smell. I put a note under the door several times asking him to take care of the smell, but he just told me he had some meat that went bad in his refrigerator. Once he told me it was his fish tank. But I tell you, those would have had to have been some pretty big fish. It was a strong stench, you know, like a lot of meat went bad in your refrigerator."

Most residents said they noticed the smell invading their hallways but did not report their concerns to anyone. The building manager, an African immigrant, on one visit to the apartment helped Dahmer clean out his refrigerator in hopes of alleviating the odor. The manager even told one resident the day before the discovery that if the smell didn't stop, he was going to call the police to investigate. Residents characterized Dahmer as "that weird white dude," and many said they knew he was gay. Dahmer was the only Caucasian in the building; the other residents were black.

His neighbors recalled the man with the strange habits. They spoke of a man who took a lot of garbage out but was never seen coming in with groceries.

Twenty-year-old Doug Jackson, who lived in the apartment below Dahmer's, remembered frequently seeing Dahmer at the huge, green, steel dumpster in the back yard with a horde of cats gathering at his feet when he dumped his human refuse inside. Jackson told me, "Those cats would go crazy trying to jump up to get into that can to get at his garbage. I don't mean a couple of cats, either. I'm talking twenty some cats!" He figured Dahmer threw away a lot of fish products.

An attractive, short black man with curly hair, Jackson was more shaken up by the night's news than most of his neighbors. A little over a week earlier, Dahmer had invited Jackson to his apartment for a beer. "I thought, 'Yeah, why not?' I mean the dude was being friendly and all. But my girlfriend said I shouldn't go. She thought I was crazy to go into somebody's apartment I didn't know, especially that white guy's."

Reflecting on the invitation, Jackson remembered how he and Dahmer were outside on the rear landing, Dahmer on the steps going upstairs to the second floor while Jackson was below. Dahmer stared straight ahead, transfixed, never looking at Jackson when he extended the invitation.

"My head could've been in that refrigerator," Jackson said quietly, his eyes downcast.

Another resident said Dahmer always "sneaked" into his apartment by opening the door just enough to squeeze his body through and then immediately shutting the door. The neighbor thought Dahmer had a messy apartment and didn't want anyone to see it. In hindsight, it was strange behavior, but not so strange that anyone suspected anything was amiss.

The residents fell silent—with reporters and with each other—as a huge truck, with TJ ENVIRONMENTAL CONTRACTORS emblazoned across it, pulled into the alley about 4 A.M. Tuesday. This company specializes in handling hazardous materials. Its owners, brothers Tom and Joel Jacobson, were dressed in oversized, bright yellow jumpsuits that appeared to be made from rain-slicker material. They strapped on oxygen tanks, slid their hands into big black work gloves, and pulled rubber boots up over their feet. They covered their heads with the hoods of the jumpsuits and put on red hard hats. The cops were wandering in and out of the apartment in their blue cotton uniforms; one officer wondered out loud why they weren't told to get out if these guys were dressed for Three Mile Island. Because I, too, had been inside, I wondered if I would give birth to a two-headed child someday, to serve as a constant memory of the biggest story of my life.

The crowd parted to make way for Milwaukee County Medical Examiner Jeffrey Jentzen's white station wagon. Jentzen is boyish-looking for thirty-seven, with thick brown hair and wire-rimmed glasses that sit atop a snub nose. He is uncomfortable around television cameras and sports a generic, emotionless look at scenes where unnatural death is involved. He appeared no different that night, though officers said he was aghast once he stepped inside apartment 213. He and his staff took careful notes on the precise location of all the body parts to aid in later identification.

Jentzen later said he had never seen anything of that magnitude. "I'd heard about it. I hadn't seen it." In the coming days, the office's three full-time pathologists, a forensic dentist, and a forensic anthropologist would form a team that worked doggedly on identifying the victims.

In the apartment, Jentzen went about rounding up the various body parts. He took three plastic bags containing human heads found in the refrigerator's top-mounted freezer and put them into Dahmer's separate, chest-type deep freezer. Jentzen then moved the head Mueller had seen in the refrigerator into the separate freezer with the other heads. He noted that next to the head was an open box of baking soda and some catsup and mustard. The skulls from the closet were placed in cardboard boxes labeled Skull Parts with thick black Magic Marker. Jentzen sealed the freezer and the big blue barrel of acid bath with silver duct tape. He also sealed the cardboard boxes containing the skulls. The Jacobsons loaded the freezer and the barrel one by one onto dollies and hauled them out of the apartment and into their truck.

When the Jacobsons emerged from the building with the freezer, the crowd let out a gasp. "Oh, God, there's the refrigerator. Do you think the head is in there?" The crowd was mistaken: The refrigerator in which the head was discovered was not removed by detectives until later that day.

The crowd was so silent, the night so still, that the quiet was broken only by the eerie guttural hiss of the Jacobson brothers' labored breathing through their oxygen masks—not unlike the sound of Darth Vader's breathing in the Star Wars movies—as they slowly, deliberately, descended the stairs with their horrific cargo.

Then Jentzen and several of his staff came down the stairs toting the boxes labeled Skull Parts. It was too much for the crowd; the residents backed away to give the medical examiners ample room to move. But not the reporters. Television cameras zoomed in on the cardboard boxes in the station wagon, each hoping to get video that clearly showed the words *Skull Parts*. Through a hole in the side of a box, hair from one of the heads could clearly be seen. It is what the electronic media refer to as "good TV."

The crowd jumped back when one police officer, wearing hospital-type rubber gloves, opened the large green steel trash container, shone his flashlight inside, and poked through the debris with a long stick.

"I used to go in Jeff's apartment on occasion and always noticed a stench in there," Vernell Bass said to me, trying to regain his composure. "I saw that big barrel there in his apartment and I asked him how he carried it on the bus, because he didn't drive. He just evaded the question. But you never think of anything like this."

For the residents, it was beginning to sink in. For the first time in the city's history, a serial killer had been living in their midst.

2

Harnessing an Octopus

July 23, 1991

The Jeffrey Dahmer story soon revealed itself to be an oc-
topus, its numerous tentacles spreading in all directions. But
that first night, there was just one big crime story. The sidebars
on Jeffrey Dahmer's prom date and the ramifications of his
childhood habits would be spattered across supermarket tabloids, daily newspapers, and the electronic media later in the
week and for months after.

My editor, Paul Gores, was the lone person in the downtown
newsroom of the *Milwaukee Journal* when I called him shortly
after midnight after getting the tip at home. Gores was in his
early thirties, with wire-rimmed glasses and blond hair that had
begun to thin. He always spoke in a monotone; even when I
called him from a pay phone with some incredible story, his
voice never revealed shock or surprise. As the night editor, he

worked on stories so the morning editors could deal with the breaking news. Even if a big story broke at night, the first edition's eight A.M. deadline usually left enough time to get the nuts and bolts. The Dahmer story was anything but business as usual.

Gores and I were briefly the only two people, besides the police, who knew what had been discovered in a cheap, unassuming apartment building in the inner city. We had no idea of the magnitude of the Jeffrey Dahmer story.

"My first reaction to that phone call was a very vivid picture in my mind," Gores remembered. "It's such a weird thing to hear that my mind immediately painted this picture of this refrigerator swinging open and the head of a guy being in there. My instinct was to completely cover whatever this turned out to be. At the very least it was going to be a gruesome and bizarre story, but I didn't realize how big.

"It was bizarre," he added, "but not as bizarre as it might have been at any other time because we had the Dressler trial going on at the same time. So this idea of people cutting up a body, well, there was a precedent for it."

The Dahmer story broke at the same time as the trial of Joachim Dressler, forty-three, from Racine, Wisconsin. In August 1991, Dressler was convicted of first-degree intentional homicide in the June 1990 murder of James Madden, twenty-four. Dressler murdered and dismembered Madden when Madden was soliciting funds for an environmental group in Dressler's neighborhood. After he killed him, Dressler cut up the body and put it through his kitchen garbage disposal. Videotapes depicting death and torture were found in Dressler's home. Until Jeffrey Dahmer, the gory details of the Dressler case had mesmerized the public. Formerly front-page news, the Dressler story was relegated to the inside of the *Journal*; the front page now belonged to Jeffrey Dahmer.

I was lucky to have Gores on the other end of the phone that night. In 1978, as a reporter for the *Arlington Daily Herald* in Arlington Heights, Illinois, he stood outside the home of John Wayne Gacy, Jr., while investigators inside cut away the floorboards with power saws and later emerged with two dozen body bags. In the Gacy case, the bodies of thirty-three boys and young men were found, most of them at Gacy's suburban Chicago house.

Gores's reaction to the Jeffrey Dahmer story was atypical of most reporters because the Gacy case had toughened him up. He did not feel "it couldn't happen here," as others of us did. "When I heard all the details, saw the photographs, the vat with acid and body parts, I immediately started to think, 'Gacy. This is another Gacy,'" he said.

Once I had been in the apartment and had a chance to talk to some officers, I called Gores about one-thirty A.M. from the scene on a portable telephone and told him about the eleven skulls, the preserved body parts, and told him what I knew about the man who had apparently murdered at least eleven people. Police told me they had found inside Dahmer's apartment the identification of at least two people who had been reported missing. I told Gores about the photographs and about the Polaroid camera on the bed.

A couple of onlookers from the crowd behind Dahmer's building craned to hear my conversation. They stood and listened intently, oohing and aahing at the grisly information. In what became an almost comical situation, every time I went to call Gores the little band of eavesdroppers, who had figured out I was privy to what was going on, trailed behind me to get the latest tidbits. I resorted to crouching behind bushes and squad cars in hopes of being able to hold a private conversation with my editor. All I needed was for someone to overhear what I knew and call one of the television news tip lines.

Gores tried to call in other reporters from their homes to help with the story, specifically the police reporter who was due in at six-thirty A.M., but his calls were consistently answered by answering machines.

Several months earlier, *Journal* management had issued a memo to reporters telling us we were on call twenty-four hours a day, like doctors, but for only a quarter of the salary. Many reporters turned their machines on at night to ensure themselves some modicum of peace. So what if there's a homicide or fire that no one covers? What amused me as the story kept growing was those same reporters whose machines answered the night of the discovery pleading for some scrap of the story to cover. No one wanted to be left out of the biggest story of the decade.

Gores finally decided not to try to call in any other reporters until the next morning. "I think anyone else would have been hard-pressed to come up with more details," he wrote in a memo to the morning editors, explaining his decision to leave me on the story by myself. I would go it alone until the staff reported for work at six-thirty A.M.

I returned to the back of the building after I called Gores and spied Jack Orton, one of the *Journal* reporters' favorite photographers. Orton, an award-winning photojournalist, had already put in a full day. He had started at two P.M. Monday with a few color shots at Milwaukee's lakefront for the Metro news section. Then, at four-forty-five P.M., he had left for Chicago to shoot the White Sox–Milwaukee Brewers game for Sports. Exhausted from a day of extremely physical photography, Orton had walked into the newsroom at twelve-forty-five A.M. to write the captions for the baseball pictures.

Gores walked over to the photo desk, hands shoved deep in his pockets, and sheepishly told Orton I had called saying there was a human head in a guy's refrigerator. No one liked sending a photographer out on a job after he or she had put in a twelve-hour day.

I was delighted to see Orton at the scene. Most reporters usually are, because we know that the better the pictures, the better play the piece will get in the paper.

Orton shot a few "scene-setters," or photos of people standing around waiting for something to happen. This scene was not particularly visual, it was more something to be felt. When we overheard a detective say the hazardous waste removal company would arrive in a couple of hours, Orton decided to go back to the paper to edit his baseball film.

While I waited behind the apartment house and talked to the cops, a call came over a police radio about a convenience-store clerk who had just been gunned down during an armed robbery at an Open Pantry store. It was the second killing of a store employee in a week, so Gores and I decided to send Orton to the Open Pantry to shoot the homicide scene. While he was there, TJ Environmental Contractors arrived, and I shrieked over the radio for him to get back to Dahmer's apartment.

"Jack, they're going to bring out the body parts! Hurry up and get back here!" I didn't realize how loudly I was talking until I saw some of the residents eyeing me strangely. They were too preoccupied to care what I was doing.

Gores left the newsroom at 2:45 A.M., and I was on my own. "Although we had only one reporter on the story at that time, I was confident we had our bases covered," he remembered.

Once back at the scene, Orton was the only still photographer there, and his exclusive pictures would later be plastered across newspapers around the world. Jack went home at six A.M., but I still had a few hours' work ahead of me.

Two television crews from local stations were there, but they didn't have the information I did. I was the only reporter who had the story of what had really been discovered in the apartment and how many people were feared dead, making the *Milwaukee Journal* the first to break the story of what police knew but had not said officially.

I stayed behind Dahmer's apartment building until seven A.M., taking it all in. I decided to write the main crime story as well as another story strictly on the mood of the scene. The mood of shock and fear that night presaged the pall that would fall over the city in the coming months.

As I drove the twenty blocks down to the *Journal* offices, my mind was awash with details of what I had seen. I wanted to rethink and analyze it all so I would leave nothing out when I sat down to write. But journalists breaking news stories on deadline do not have the luxury of time.

Bursting into the newsroom, I was met by a cluster of reporters who besieged me with questions:

"How did you get the story?"

"I heard you got in the apartment. What did he have in there?"

"Was there really a human head in the fridge? Did you look? Why not?!"

It is widely disputed who are more insatiable for juicy gossip: reporters or cops. I placated them with snippets of what I had learned in the past seven hours and headed toward the Metro desk and a computer.

The *Journal* was the only afternoon daily in Milwaukee; the *Milwaukee Sentinel* was the only morning daily. Both were owned by the same company. As the story progressed, the two papers heatedly raced against each other to break any piece of news in the Dahmer case.

Most people cannot understand how two newspapers sharing the same parent company can become embroiled in fierce competition. But it's like intense sibling rivalry. Each paper has its own identification, and reporters are loyal to their paper, not the owners. It is not unusual for reporters from the two papers to laugh uncomfortably when bumping into one another while pursuing a story each thought the other did not know about. People being interviewed often think that by talking to a reporter from the *Journal*, they are also covering the *Sentinel*. They then shoo the later-arriving *Sentinel* reporter away, saying, "I talked to your paper already." People usually don't understand the explanation. One of Gores's first questions when I called him from the scene was, "Is the *Sentinel* there?" They were not. We were in the clear.

The reason I alone had the story is that phone tip from my source. Most newsrooms have police scanners—a scanner is a type of radio that picks up police-radio transmissions—that squawk around the clock. But no one was talking over the air about this case, so nothing could be heard over the scanner. With a scanner, you can always tell when something big goes on by an address being repeated over and over and lots of personnel being sent to the scene. Cops are usually pretty careful about what they say over a radio. They always tell me, "You never know who's listening." More often than not, the listener is a reporter.

As early as Day One of the Jeffrey Dahmer case, the story was a runaway train, with five editors and twenty reporters trying to catch it. The newsroom was in a frenzy. Everyone was clamoring for a piece of the story, and editors were trying to get on top of it. Nothing else was news. Gorbachev? Put him in the inside pages somewhere. Iraq? Old news. By the eight

A.M. morning-news deadline, we had only my two stories on the case, but we were chasing a dozen angles for the next four editions. By necessity, deadlines were thrown out during the first two weeks as we raced to get in the latest news.

(Later, Gores said, "What was incredible was that by morning, from just one reporter, we had all the nuts and bolts of this story nailed down. A lot of times when these things happen you hear all kinds of rumors that later don't pan out. But all these things checked out from the start to finish.")

I sat down to write, overwhelmed with frustration that I could not type as fast as I was thinking. I wondered if Tony Hughes, a deaf man who had disappeared earlier after going to a gay bar and about whom we had written several stories, was one of the victims. (He was.)

Linda Fibich, assistant managing editor, shouted for someone to get the suspect's name so we could check his criminal record and find his family. Several reporters tried unsuccessfully, so I volunteered. I dialed a source of mine. The editors clustered around the Metro desk, their ears perked up to hear what I said. It was like an E. F. Hutton commercial.

"Hi, this is Annie," I said to the officer on the other end. The editors commented aloud that I did not have to give my last name.

I asked how the officer's family was and commented on his play in a police softball tournament the week before. Then I asked for the name of the man who had the bodies of nearly a dozen people in his apartment. He asked if I would publish the name, and I said confidently, Of course not, the *Journal* does not print people's names until they are charged. "You're a sweetheart and you can expect a homemade cheesecake for you to take to your wife and the kids," I gushed to him.

I hung up and looked at Fibich. "D-A-H-M-E-R," I said.

Fibich shook her head. Not exactly *Journal* management's idea of a professional phone call to a source, but when it came to this story, they didn't care how a reporter obtained the information, just as long as the reporter got it. All of a sudden, my sources were beyond reproach because we were getting vital information.

I certainly had come a long way since being forced to write

a memo in 1989 explaining why I had joined a few cops after work for a drink. I was new on the beat then, and I was trying to cultivate sources. Not unlike other cops, the Milwaukee police don't readily let strangers into the fraternity. I knew I would have to work hard to get them to trust me.

My conduct was ruled "inappropriate," and I had to sit in a glass office and hear how a female reporter should not go with male cops for a beer. "Those people are not your friends," a senior editor told me. But when a male reporter wined and dined a source, he was "aggressive" and was "working his sources."

Now, during the early days of the Dahmer case, editors shoved expense vouchers into my hand when I left the newsroom and told me to take a cop for a drink or even dinner if I thought he or she had any information on the story.

As the editors looked over both of my breaking stories, I saw them write in *Dahmer* where I had written *the suspect*. Management ran a qualifier with the story explaining that the paper usually withholds the identity of criminal suspects until they have been charged in order to spare them publicly until the district attorney determines there is sufficient evidence to go to trial. They said that because of "widespread interest in this case and the certainty that the suspect's name will be published and broadcast nationwide, there is little chance that the suspect would be protected even if the *Journal* did not name him."

I immediately called my source to apologize. We were going with the name.

In the middle of the furor, some compassion emerged. Manny Mendoza, a general-assignment reporter, was sent to Dahmer's grandmother's home, after a neighbor at the scene told me Dahmer worked the night shift at Ambrosia Chocolate. We checked with the company and got the home address Dahmer gave them: it belonged to Catherine Dahmer, Jeffrey Dahmer's frail, eighty-seven-year-old grandmother, whom he had lived with when he started at Ambrosia.

When Catherine Dahmer answered the door, Mendoza explained that he wanted to talk to her about her son, Jeffrey Dahmer. She said, "You mean my grandson," and invited Mendoza in. As a reporter for the *Miami News*, Mendoza had covered the 1980 riots and the Mariel boatlift. But this one was going to be tough.

About fifteen minutes into the interview, it became apparent that Catherine Dahmer did not know her grandson had been arrested. When Mendoza told her, she asked why, but he said he didn't know. "I didn't want to be the one to break the news to her," Mendoza said later.

About then Catherine Dahmer got up to answer the phone. Mendoza overheard her say, "Oh, my God." A *Sentinel* reporter told her about the murders. When she returned she was too distracted to talk to Mendoza anymore.

Before the phone call, she told Mendoza her grandson had not looked well and was "terribly thin" when he came to see her recently. She had last spoken to him a week earlier, when Dahmer told her he lost his job at Ambrosia.

"He has an awful lot of love for me. He never left without giving me a big hug. He always wanted to do things for me. He's a boy who likes things I like. He loves flowers, roses. He doesn't hesitate to show his love for me," she told Mendoza.

There were many judgment calls made on the Dahmer story, like the one Mendoza made not to tell Catherine Dahmer of her grandson's crimes. Editors had to decide questions of taste, sensitivity, and tone, in stories as well as in headlines. They had to worry about rumor versus fact, details in numerous stories that had to agree with each other, and stories changing in every edition. Copydesk editor Brahm Resnik said the story generated more hard news copy than the *Journal* has handled on a single day in many years.

As the news spread, the paper received calls from around the country. We faxed our stories all over the world, and they ran in the *Los Angeles Times*, the *New York Times*, and the *International Herald Tribune*. We saw our bylines in French, Spanish, and German. Reporters from out-of-town papers called the newsroom and spoke to whoever picked up the phone, as if he or she were an expert on the case. If you worked for the *Journal*, you must know something about Jeffrey Dahmer.

"Who wants to do 'Larry King'?" a secretary yelled out. Reporters lunged for their phones. We got calls from *People* magazine, a producer from "Geraldo," a Canadian radio talk show, and a publishing company looking for someone to write a book in a month.

We were celebrities. We were dizzy with it.

One editor, irritated after a while, said we were doing the reporting for the other media: "A lot of the time, it was for information they could have checked out themselves. So I gave them numbers for police and other officials so they could do their own work."

Along with the media calls came the inevitable crackpot calls. People who claimed that they knew, talked to, or slept with Jeffrey Dahmer were as prevalent as those who sighted Elvis.

Astrologers called and wanted the exact date and time of Dahmer's birth so they could do his chart. A psychic said she could identify the unnamed victims; a handwriting analyst wanted a sample of Dahmer's writing so she could detect murderous characteristics from his scribbling. Psychologists, amateur and otherwise, called and offered to tell us why he did it. People who claimed they were experts on satanic cults called and said they had evidence that Dahmer fancied the devil.

Nothing could be dismissed. Everything had to be checked out. "You didn't want to be the reporter who missed something on the Dahmer story," said Tom Held, the police reporter who covered the story for the *Milwaukee Sentinel*.

We chased tips about Dahmer selling meat to his neighbors and tried to find out what he brought in his lunch when he worked at Ambrosia: one of his former coworkers had called the newsroom anonymously and said Dahmer always brought meat for lunch topped with what he called "my special gravy"; he refused to share it with the other employees, the caller said. We talked to the doughnut-shop employee who thought Dahmer was a regular and inmates at prisons nationwide who thought they knew Dahmer or had shared a cell with him once.

One night Gores got a call from a woman who said she had sat next to Dahmer in a bar and struck up a conversation with him. She told him about her son in the military and how he never called or wrote her. Dahmer was very offended that her son would just abandon his mother, she told Gores. We could not prove it was Dahmer. And the woman, like so many callers on this story, refused to leave her name.

"It was like she had an encounter with the guy and was just dying to tell somebody about it," Gores said. "It reminded me of the way the Gacy thing was covered. There were the 'I spent a night with Gacy and lived to tell about it' kinds of stories coming out of the woodwork."

So much could not be verified. Nonetheless, you could still read some of those stories. That's why we have supermarket tabloids.

The heartbreaking calls were from the relatives of missing people. The people who pleaded with us to see if any of the victims not yet identified could be their loved ones. They desperately left vivid descriptions and their phone numbers so we could call if we heard anything—at least they could be at peace. People who lived in cities where Dahmer had lived, traveled to, or was stationed in with the army, called and begged to know if authorities believed he had killed anywhere besides Milwaukee.

All the calls, interviews, and the deluge of information turned the normal running operation of the *Milwaukee Journal* to chaos. Night editors could not go over stories because there were developments virtually every hour in the first days after the story broke. Everything had to be done in the morning right on deadline, which made for a testy staff and management.

Milwaukee County Medical Examiner Jeffrey Jentzen held daily morning press conferences identifying the victims. Since they were typically given close to our deadlines, the paper sent several reporters, each alternately dashing out from the press conference to a pay phone to file what Jentzen had to say. The stories came together in pieces.

That first day—Tuesday, July 23—was a fiery baptism for all who covered the Dahmer story. High fives were exchanged when the last edition rolled off the presses and made its way to the newsroom. The Dahmer story commanded the top half of the front page, framed by Jack Orton's vivid photographs. I looked at the pictures and read the stories and felt as if it had all happened to someone else. The two other page-one stories that day were on President Bush easing sanctions on Iraq and about three boys who threw a rock from a highway overpass resulting in the death of a motorist. There was also a color photo of a giraffe at the Milwaukee County Zoo nuzzling her new baby. I wondered if anyone read them.

On the front of the city news section was the story about the Open Pantry shooting, accompanied by Orton's photo. He had a photo credit; he should have had a medal. I wondered how the family of the murdered store clerk felt when they picked up their *Journal* and saw that Jeffrey Dahmer eclipsed the death of their relative. In fact, it seemed all other homicides paled in comparison, and most blurred into the city's skyrocketing homicide count for 1991.

The circulation department sent newsboys out hawking editions of the paper emblazoned MAN HELD IN GRISLY SLAYINGS and BODY PARTS LITTER APARTMENT. I had stayed at the paper until shortly after noon, when the last edition went to press, in case anyone needed anything more from the police, and I passed one of the newsboys on my way home that first day.

I watched as people anxiously pressed fifty cents into the boy's hand and stared at the front page, their mouths agape at what they read. I was overwhelmed with a strange kind of pride that only other journalists could understand, knowing that I had set in motion the stories they were reading. I didn't need to stop and buy a paper. I had a stack of them on the seat next to me in the car.

As I left the *Journal* and drove three blocks to the freeway leading home, I looked to my left at the Police Administration Building where Jeffrey Dahmer was being held. I wondered what he had told police.

I wondered if anyone knew why it all happened.

3

Uncloaking a Sinister Soul

July 22–23, 1991

Jeffrey Dahmer left apartment 213 at one-fifteen A.M., Tuesday, July 23, and settled listlessly onto the stiff bench in the back of a paddy wagon for the short trip to police headquarters downtown. Detective Patrick Kennedy took a statement from Rauth and Mueller, surveyed the scene, and then accompanied Dahmer in the wagon.

A third-generation cop, the thirty-eight-year-old Kennedy had worked the midnight-to-eight A.M. shift since becoming a detective in 1989. Kennedy was an imposing figure at crime scenes, with his six-foot-seven-inch frame and a bushy brown handlebar mustache. In his off time he donned a furry dog suit and became the department mascot, McGruff, a trenchcoat-clad dog who taught youngsters crime prevention and cautioned them on the dangers of drugs. Kennedy played McGruff during presentations at grammar schools around the metropolitan area that combined drug awareness programs with musical performances by the Milwaukee Police Band. Kennedy was also the band's drummer.

At crime scenes, I often saw him shaking his head and marveling out loud at the things people did to one another. Like most cops, Kennedy had an acute wit and loved to joke about the book he might write when he retires from the department in twenty years. I've always felt that every cop I ever met on the job has at least one book in him, especially Pat Kennedy.

Kennedy came on the job when the city's homicide rate began to skyrocket. Guys who worked the third shift got to see it all. They picked up the pieces of cases left over from the previous shift and ventured into the dark recesses of the city to investigate crimes committed between midnight and eight A.M., the hours when, the late-shift detectives told me, a whole other part of the city that the hard-working citizen never sees comes out to play. The cops who work the third, or late, shift are permanently tired and always seem to end up investigating whatever ends up on the next day's front page. Not many reporters know the late-shift cops because most reporters are in bed after midnight, except on breaking news. I went on several ridealongs on that shift, and those are definitely the officers who have seen it all.

Kennedy never relished the media attention he got from the Dahmer case. When I interviewed him in 1989 for a story I wrote on the newest detectives and what they could look forward to, Kennedy constantly tugged at his collar and scraped his foot along the floor like a nervous schoolboy in the principal's office.

Because of his engaging nature, children always flocked to him, whether he was McGruff or just Detective Kennedy. But Kennedy now developed a new fan, one about whom his fellow detectives would rib him mercilessly for months and probably years to come. Five days a week for the next six weeks, Kennedy became Jeffrey Dahmer's confidant, the only person Dahmer cared to talk to, and the only one, besides his legal counsel, to hear the shocking details of his life firsthand. When Dahmer sat alone in his jail cell the next day on suicide watch, officers who guarded him remembered the only item he constantly kept with him was the creased business card Kennedy gave him in case he wanted to talk about the murders some more.

At police headquarters the night the murders were discovered, Dahmer was ushered into a tiny interrogation room in the Criminal Investigation Bureau, or the CIB, the nerve center of the police department. Kennedy advised Dahmer of his constitutional rights and took a seat in a plastic chair across the table from his prisoner. Beginning at one-thirty A.M., and for the next six hours, Dahmer sat in the stuffy little room on the fourth floor of the Milwaukee Police Administration Building and uncloaked his soul as Kennedy twisted the tip of his mustache and listened intently, at times, disbelievingly. Another officer, Detective Dennis Murphy, was also present.

As he spoke, Dahmer smoked numerous cigarettes, sipped four or five cups of coffee, drank two glasses of water, and had two cans of cola. The room was enveloped in a smoky haze as Dahmer recounted seventeen murders, providing minute details of the crimes but remembering his victims only as shadowy figures. He did not know any of them by name, but he could usually recall the bar, shopping mall, bus station, or adult bookstore where he had picked them up.

In his confession, Dahmer talked a little about his childhood in Ohio and about the hitchhiker he picked up when he was eighteen years old who became his first murder victim. After a two-year tour with the Army, Dahmer said he moved to Miami, but nothing of that nature, meaning murder, happened there.

Dahmer minimized his police record, which he said involved taking Polaroid pictures of a minor. The actual offense was second-degree sexual assault and enticing a child for immoral purposes.

Then, as easily as he talked about his childhood and being an atheist, he talked about being a murderer and a cannibal.

At one point in his confession, he told detectives that while living with his grandmother, he used a gray-handled sledgehammer he kept in her garage to break up the bones of his victims. In a search of Catherine Dahmer's home Tuesday morning, police had recovered a sledgehammer from her garage. He identified it as the one he used in the killings at his grandmother's home.

We in the media were anxious to hear officially that Dahmer engaged in cannibalism. We never did, officially. The information came out in a report a janitor stole from the District Attorney's offices and subsequently passed on to the *New York Times*. Even after it was published in the *Times*, police would not confirm the information. It would not be published in Milwaukee until I and other reporters managed to get a copy of the confession from our own sources and could read it for ourselves.

Dahmer admitted to cannibalism, but only on one occasion, according to the confession. The only time he ever consumed any body parts was when he ate the biceps of one of his victims, he told detectives, pointing to his own right biceps. "It was big and he wanted to try it," the confession read.

He also said he would masturbate in front of the body parts and skulls he had collected because it brought back memories of the victims. The reason he gave for killing the homosexuals—and he emphasized they were all homosexual—was that he wanted to be with them. He kept the skulls of the good-looking ones because he did not want to lose them. He told the detectives he felt he could hang on to them if he killed them and kept the skulls. The three heads in the refrigerator and top freezer had the flesh intact and belonged to his last three victims, he said.

After Dahmer detailed many of the deaths without emotion, his initial, four-page confession was completely written out. He read it over and wrote his initials on each page. After he signed the confession, Dahmer was asked if there was anything he would like to do or if he was hungry. "He stated that he was not hungry and probably will not be hungry for a long time," Kennedy wrote in his report. Dahmer said he wanted just to sit and talk about the murders a little bit more.

Later on Tuesday, Dahmer asked for Kennedy and Murphy to come back to the jail so he could give them additional information on what he had done. "I've told you everything already.

I have nothing to hide, so I might as well tell you about these ones [murders] I forgot," Dahmer said to the detectives.

When his words were exhausted, he was escorted to a jail cell in the Police Administration Building.

In the hours following his confession, Dahmer quickly became a curiosity to Kennedy's fellow officers.

Considered highly suicidal, Dahmer had an around-the-clock police guard monitoring him at the city jail, and was dressed in a gray paper jumpsuit so he could not use his clothing to hang himself. The officers guarding him told me later how eerie it was to be so close to a confessed serial killer. They felt uncomfortable being isolated with him. I found it disquieting just to be near him in a courtroom full of armed deputies.

The nightly parade of felons through the jail took a back seat to the famous prisoner. Most of the jail cells are on the fifth floor of the Police Administration Building, but Dahmer was kept separately in a cell at the end of a long hallway on the sixth floor. These cells are generally used when the fifth-floor cells are filled, but on this night, the whole floor was reserved for Dahmer.

Officers in the jail observed that when Dahmer was given the customary jail fare of a bologna sandwich for dinner, he ate the meat but not the bread. Some of the officers tried to make conversation with him but were told by Dahmer, "I've got a lot on my mind."

During one officer's eight-hour shift, Dahmer did not sleep at all and complained that the food was bad. Cops' curiosity being what it is, several stopped up to peer through the metal bars at the city's most notorious prisoner. Another officer related what happened when Dahmer was escorted down to the fifth floor to have a full set of fingerprints and handprints taken. The usual boisterous rancor exchanged by surly felons and their arresting officers was absent as they all fell silent and pressed their bodies up against the concrete wall of the hallway as he passed.

"They were in awe of him. They parted to let him through and stared at him like he was some kind of celebrity or something," one cop observed. "The jail on a hot summer night is a pretty noisy place. This guy comes past and you could hear a pin drop."

Dahmer walked with his head down, almost embarrassed that people recognized him, one officer said. "Just by the way people were reacting to him, I think the scope of what he had done was starting to sink in for him."

His jailers remembered Dahmer's second day in jail as especially difficult for him because he was not allowed to smoke in his cell. Detectives offered him cigarettes to coax him through his statements, but he became terribly antsy when he had to endure the days and nights without nicotine. Officials later decided to let him smoke so he would be more cooperative in giving police his statements, sparking debate over whether or not Jeffrey Dahmer was receiving special treatment while incarcerated.

Several days after his arrest, Dahmer was visibly perturbed by the inevitable "Dahmer jokes" echoing through the halls. As the prisoners in the cells around him at the city jail and later at the Milwaukee County jail were released, they spun stories of his nasty retorts to those who taunted him for the local media.

Published reports alleged that Dahmer got special meals, was allowed to smoke when others were not, and had so many visitors that the traffic interfered with visits to other prisoners. Jail records showed that Dahmer was allowed to see only police investigators; his attorney, Gerald Boyle, and his staff; and family members approved by Boyle.

One former inmate told the *Milwaukee Sentinel* that the guard outside Dahmer's cell "reads him the paper, and talks to him about what he did to people and things."

Jail administration officials consistently denied that Dahmer received any special treatment.

New prisoners asked where the "chop-chop man" was, according to the *Sentinel*. Every facet of Dahmer's life was under scrutiny. One *Sentinel* headline read: "CHOP-CHOP MAN:" INMATE DETAILS DAHMER'S JAIL LIFE. It was right out of the tabloids. It was also reported that prisoners often taunted Dahmer, frequently with homosexual insults, when they walked by his cell. A former inmate told *Sentinel* reporter James B. Nelson that Dahmer replied to the taunts by saying "I wish it was you I had." The inmate told Nelson he feared Dahmer but spoke to him once, briefly: "I asked him why he did it, and he said, 'That's my business.' "

Most cops I spoke with later remembered Dahmer as being remarkably calm as he sat quietly in his cell, and they were amazed that he had the ability to do what he did. We sat around for days and months afterward trying to theorize about why he did it. Someone commented that he looked like a normal guy. I answered that most killers I had seen rarely foamed at the mouth.

How many times had I interviewed a neighbor who, when told the man next door had just shot his wife and kids, said "Oh, he was a quiet man." But then later, I always found out that there was something in his past, some latent hate the perpetrator could not get beyond, that stuck in his gut and manifested itself in the deaths of innocent people.

All of us close to the case were certain that somewhere in Jeffrey Dahmer's childhood a dark fantasy had begun.

4

Boys Will Be Boys

May 21, 1960–August 1978

In my early days on the police beat, I once remarked to a cop at a murder scene that the man who had just shot his wife in front of the couple's two children did not possess a single redeeming quality, that he represented the dregs of society. I couldn't think of enough names to call him.

The officer looked at me and, with a half-smile, said, "He was somebody's baby once."

They all were. Once.

Jeffrey Dahmer was born to Lionel Dahmer, a chemist, and Joyce Dahmer in Milwaukee on May 21, 1960, but he grew up in the posh suburb of Bath, Ohio, just outside Akron. Its lush landscapes, decorated with riding stables and tennis courts, were a far cry from the seedy Milwaukee neighborhood where Dahmer's apartment was found.

Ever since the discovery of Dahmer's heinous crimes, journalists had been digging to ferret out any childhood indications that he was a budding serial killer. Ever since that first night in his apartment, I wanted to know why. I found myself getting carried away with Dahmer's past because I felt there just had to be an explanation. After talking to countless psychiatric professionals and experts on serial killers, I discovered sometimes there just isn't.

"I remember how he came thundering through the house when his grandparents came to visit," Lionel Dahmer remembered, with a glint of happiness, as he spoke with a reporter.

It was important to include quotes like that in our stories, quotes that could come from any of our parents. They helped us understand that Jeffrey Dahmer was not always a criminal, and they helped convey to the readers how a father could not easily disown a son, no matter what he did.

There were some oddities in Jeffrey Dahmer's childhood, but the most consistent information portrayed a boy who felt alone, rejected by a world he later decided he did not want to fit into anyway. In 1966, for example, six-year-old Jeffrey was in first grade at Hazel Harvey Elementary School in Barberton, Ohio. Just after his baby brother David was born on December 18, his teacher wrote on his report card that little Jeffrey seemed to feel neglected.

The media has widely reported that he was sexually abused as early as age eight. Dahmer's probation file referred to a statement by Lionel Dahmer that his son had been abused by a neighbor, followed by a notation by the parole officer saying that "may be reason why subject [Dahmer] has problems with sexuality issues." But none of the allegations accusing the neighbor as well as Lionel Dahmer himself had been substantiated. Lionel Dahmer has denied that such a conversation with the parole officer ever took place, and Jeffrey Dahmer told police he had no recollection of such abuse. Nonetheless, the story of possible abuse made page one of both Milwaukee newspapers.

So many of us wanted to believe that something had traumatized little Jeffrey Dahmer, otherwise we must believe that some people simply give birth to monsters.

In 1968 the family moved to Bath, where Jeffrey attended Bath Elementary School. The house in Bath was a large, rambling ranch-style wood home on 1.7 wooded acres, complete with a spring-fed pond, and seemed to typify the idyllic place to raise a family. Neighbors said the family was not involved in any church, but during his confession, Dahmer told Kennedy he was raised as a Protestant. Somewhere along the line, he confessed, he started to consider himself an atheist.

While Jeffrey was in elementary school, Lionel Dahmer gave him an introductory chemistry set. Jeffrey developed a keen interest, experimenting with the chemicals, quickly learning what they could do to insects and small animals. Neighbors recalled Jeffrey's fascination with dead animals, at first merely a child's collection of insects preserved in jars with some type of chemical, but later a stash of dead animals retrieved after they had been run over or hit on the neighboring roadsides—animal heads impaled on sticks in the woods behind the Dahmer home and dried-out animal skins. He even fashioned a little animal cemetery in his back yard. Years later, not far from the burial ground he created as a child, he would scatter the human bones of his first murder victim.

Boyhood pals recalled his being interested in the insides of animals, how things worked underneath the skin he so carefully removed and dissolved in chemicals. One day while fishing with some neighborhood youngsters, he chopped his catch into little pieces so he could see the inner workings. Even stranger, Dahmer fancied listening to his chums' heartbeats and liked pressing his head to their chests so he could hear.

The Jeffrey Dahmer that Sue Lehr, a Bath neighbor of the Dahmers' knew, died, she said. She remembered feeding Jeff cookies and wanting desperately to hug him "to ease his pain." She had difficulty connecting the monster in the bright orange prison-issued jumpsuit on television with the eight-year-old boy she knew many years ago—the boy who went sledding in her back yard or played ball with her son Steve. Lehr remembered Jeff as a child who wanted very much to please adults, a child who anticipated what she expected of him and would try to do the right thing.

"I think that his wanting to please adults was a sign of a problem," Sue Lehr said. "Not everyone saw Jeffrey skinning animals and collecting bones."

Sue's son Steve was Jeffrey's playmate and entrusted him with his newspaper route when Steve was on vacation. The two liked a game they called Ghosts in the Graveyard, a game played at night. "Everybody has a kid in their class that's a little different, a little bit strange. You just kind of brush it off because he's going to outgrow it or he's just going through a stage," Steve Lehr said.

Psychiatric professionals agree that cruelty to animals, craving attention, and vivid fantasies are childhood characteristics of sadistic criminals. But no one noticed that young Jeffrey Dahmer needed to see someone who could address his problems.

In 1974 Dahmer went to Revere High School, where he played clarinet in the high school band his freshman year, played intramural tennis his sophomore through senior years, and worked on the school newspaper, the *Lantern*, his junior year. But for all the appearances of normal school activities and average grades, classmates remembered Jeffrey Dahmer as a loner with an odd fascination for dead animals and a kid who just didn't fit in. In the days after the murders had been discovered in Milwaukee, the newspapers and television stations were rife with his classmates' recollections. One who asked his name not to be used remembered Dahmer tracing bodies on the floor with chalk while another recalled a full-blown alcoholic. Martha Schmidt, a sociologist who had attended high school with Dahmer, described him as tortured and lost at a very early age.

A number of Dahmer's former classmates said they felt something tragic was going to happen to Jeff; they expected to hear that he had killed himself. Schmidt recalled their sophomore year, when Jeff sat next to her during first period at eight A.M. with a Styrofoam cup filled with scotch. "I sort of smelled his cup and thought, That's interesting. And then he just sat there in class and drank scotch," she said.

Schmidt believed what happened to seventeen young men might have been prevented had someone intervened in those early days. "Somebody could have taken that sixteen-year-old kid and asked him, 'Why are you drinking scotch?' "

Dahmer's prom date, Bridget Geiger, remembered an escort who did not dance with her or peck her on the cheek good night, but who ran out to get himself a hamburger from a fast-food joint in the middle of the dance and then returned, leaving food wrappers strewn about the floor of his car. Terrified he would stick his date as he fumblingly attempted to pin on the corsage, he surrendered the flowers to Bridget's mother. Bridget recalled becoming Dahmer's date at the urging of her friends, despite having heard stories about his heavy drinking.

The last time Bridget saw Dahmer was when he invited her to his parents' home for a séance. Someone suggested to Jeff that they call Lucifer and, feeling uneasy, Bridget bolted for the door. "I felt uncomfortable around him because he was so weird and so emotionless," she said later.

It was all just an unpleasant memory until July 22, 1991. After the story broke, Geiger saw that private experience billed in one tabloid as HIGH SCHOOL BEAUTY'S CHILLING PROM DATE WITH THE DEVIL.

Dahmer was a class clown who was amused only by the bizarre, according to one classmate, but his high school guidance counselor said Dahmer was not a discipline problem. His intramural tennis coach recalled, "He was a kid who minded his own business."

Tangible evidence of Dahmer as a prankster, but not necessarily as a budding serial killer, appeared on page ninety-eight of the 1978 Revere High School yearbook, in which Dahmer showed up for the National Honor Society photo even though he was not a member. His face was blacked out before the books went to press.

Being blacked out of the picture was exactly what was happening in eighteen-year-old Jeffrey's home life during his senior year of high school. His parents were in the throes of a bitter divorce and fought over custody of Jeff's little brother David, then twelve. First, Lionel sued for divorce, charging Joyce with "gross neglect of duty and extreme cruelty," then

Joyce countersued with the same charges. She was eventually awarded custody of David. Lionel had argued against placing David with Joyce because of what he alleged in court documents to be her "extreme mental illness."

Jeffrey, then eighteen, was not an issue in the custody battle. He was busy with other things.

On or about June 18, 1978, eighteen-year-old Jeffrey Dahmer had already committed his first murder.

The divorce was granted on July 24, 1978. According to court documents, Lionel stopped by the house on August 26, a date set by the court for his visitation with David, only to be greeted at the door by Jeff, who told his father that Joyce had fled with David to Chippewa Falls, Wisconsin, a few days before, abandoning Jeff. Before she left, Joyce Dahmer instructed Jeff not to tell his father where the two had gone, court documents said. When Lionel arrived, the house was in shambles, there was no food in the refrigerator (which wasn't working anyway), and Jeff had no money. In a trip back to court when he discovered Joyce had left the state, Lionel was awarded custody of David.

Once she had settled in Chippewa Falls, a town near where she had been born, police records indicate that Joyce was called to the police department after David was involved in criminal damage to railroad property during which some switching mechanisms were destroyed. It is unclear how long Joyce stayed in Chippewa Falls, but voter registration records at city hall show that she voted in 1988. While in Chippewa Falls, she put herself through school, graduating with honors in 1982 from the University of Wisconsin—Eau Claire, with a bachelor of arts degree in speech.

Likely the biggest news story ever to hit Chippewa Falls was chronicled in the July 25, 1991, *Chippewa Herald Telegram*, with a front-page headline: MOTHER OF ACCUSED MASS MURDERER LIVED HERE.

Joyce Flint—she has reclaimed her maiden name—is today a case manager for the Central Valley AIDS Team in Fresno, California, which offers help to AIDS patients. She has refused all interviews. As the mother of an accused serial killer, she may fear condemnation by a society that believes parents have some control over what becomes of their offspring.

Lionel Dahmer, also not given to chatting with the press, says that he feels a great responsibility for what happened. "In retrospect, I wish I had done more in terms of keeping track of what he was doing. I feel guilty and I feel a great sense of shame," he told the television tabloid program "Inside Edition."

"He [Jeffrey] was always secretive. He would never open up to me, but then, sometimes he would. I would not say it was a good relationship. I tried my damnedest to instill interest in trying to become interested in something in life, education. I tried to get him to accept Christ," Lionel Dahmer told the *Milwaukee Journal*. Lionel was a member of the fundamentalist Church of Christ; when Jeff moved to his own apartment, Lionel sent him audio and visual tapes about Christ.

Something inside Jeffrey Dahmer seemed to crumble just when his parent's marriage did. Puffing vigorously on cigarette after cigarette following his arrest, Dahmer unfolded the details of his first murder for Detective Kennedy.

He was eighteen, had just graduated from high school, and his home life was in turmoil. Eighteen-year-old Steven Hicks of Coventry Township, Ohio, was hitchhiking from a rock concert in Chippewa Lake Park, Ohio, and was last seen by his family June 18, 1978, when he left for the concert.

Dahmer offered Hicks a ride and an invitation to his parents' home on ritzy Bath Road for a few beers. Dahmer could not remember what they talked about, only that they later got drunk and had sex. But when it looked like Jeffrey Dahmer was again going to be abandoned, cast aside by someone else in his life, things got ugly.

When Hicks tried to leave, Dahmer said, they got into a physical fight, trading fisticuffs until Dahmer reached for a barbell and struck Hicks in the head, killing him. "The guy wanted to leave and I didn't want him to leave," Dahmer told Ohio police.

Left with Hicks's 160-pound body, Dahmer, possibly remembering his childish deeds with animals, dragged the corpse to a crawl space underneath the house, dismembered it with a kitchen knife, and placed the parts in plastic bags. He first kept the bags in the car but then decided it would be more efficient to bury them in a wooded area behind the house. He left them to decompose for about two years while he was in the army.

He returned from the army and dug up the bags, pummeled the decomposing body with a sledgehammer to break the bones, and scattered the pieces about the woods. He told police he burned Hicks's wallet and cut up a necklace Hicks was wearing. He tossed the knife he used off a bridge into the Cuyahoga River.

Thirteen years later, in 1991, Dahmer could draw a map showing Ohio investigators precisely where the remains of Steven Hicks had been discarded on the former Dahmer family property in Bath Township. During his confession, however, Dahmer could remember his first victim only as a hitchhiker named Steve, a "white guy about nineteen years old."

The Hicks family never gave up hope. Most of Dahmer's victims' families told me the same thing. The ones who didn't even get their loved ones' remains back, because they were told there were none, still cling to a thread of hope.

Hicks's family was used to Steven's staying out, but finally, on June 24, 1978, Martha Hicks reported her son missing to the Summit County Sheriff's Department. Summit began the kind of investigation the Milwaukee victims' families wished they had gotten into the disappearance of their loved ones. Summit police retraced the route Hicks might have taken from the rock concert and interviewed countless friends and relatives. The family offered a twenty-five-hundred-dollar reward for information leading to his return. Steven's name was entered into a national computer network set up to help locate missing people.

Several days after the discoveries in Dahmer's apartment, two Ohio law enforcement officials, Bath Police Lt. Richard Munsey and Summit County Sheriff's Department Detective John Karabatsos, arrived in Milwaukee to question Dahmer in connection with Hicks's disappearance. Milwaukee police had contacted Ohio police to determine whether there was a missing-person report on a hitchhiker during 1978, the year in which Dahmer told Milwaukee police he had killed a hitchhiker.

Dahmer identified Hicks with the same vacant look he wore when he identified the next sixteen victims. "Yeah, that's him," Ohio police quoted Dahmer as saying when they showed him a photograph of the missing man.

On September 17, 1991, Jeffrey Dahmer was finally charged with aggravated murder in the case of Steven Hicks.

Although the revelation of what had happened in their tasteful neighborhood shook Bath, Ohio, residents, a number of law enforcement officials from the suburbs have told me, "You'd be surprised what happens out in the quiet neighborhoods." Crime does not run rampant through suburban streets, but it is conducted in secret.

After the wealthy suburb of Bath, Ohio, Jeffrey Dahmer's next extended stop would be another quiet spot: West Allis, Wisconsin. Amid the modest homes and tidy yards where people moved to escape the rising crime rate of Milwaukee, he would kill and dismember four young men.

5

Life at Grandma's House

August 1978–September 1988

After his parents' 1978 divorce and the ensuing ugly custody battle for his brother David, Jeffrey Dahmer's entering Ohio State University as a business major might have seemed a positive step.

But college proved another failure, marked by Dahmer's mounting alcohol abuse. Those acquainted with him—no one really *knew* Jeffrey Dahmer—remembered a room brimming with liquor bottles. Many freshmen spent their first semesters drinking to excess because most were out on their own for the first time, but Dahmer brought liquor bottles to class and often returned to his dorm room drunk and, on occasion, would pass out on the street.

In the fall of 1978, campus police questioned Dahmer in connection with the theft of a watch, radio, and $120 from the dorm, but no charges were ever filed. He quit school soon after.

On December 24, 1978, Lionel Dahmer married Shari Jordan, who told her college friend Pat Snyder that she was less than enthralled with her two stepsons and described them as her "nemesis."

"I wouldn't call them a family," said Snyder, who had known Shari for twenty years, since the two had attended Kent State University in Ohio. "Shari never mentioned the children when she was out with girlfriends shopping—other than to say she despised David and Jeff was no damn good. She was very upset that Lionel had to pay child support." Later, Pat Snyder appeared on national television and characterized Shari as "the epitome of the wicked stepmother." Snyder was one of a number of people who came forward with recollections about the Dahmer family.

Five days after his father's remarriage, Dahmer enlisted in the U.S. Army. On January 12, 1979, he reported for duty at Fort McClellan in Anniston, Alabama, hoping to become a military policeman. Shortly thereafter he was reassigned to Fort Sam Houston in San Antonio, Texas, as a medical specialist. On July 13, 1979, he was off to Baumholder, West Germany, to serve as a combat medic (with duties similar to a nurse's aide's) at a medical aid station.

His bunk mates recalled the strange suitcase Dahmer fashioned into a bar, complete with a martini shaker, stirrer, and all the fixings. His chief weekend activity was to concoct drinks and shut out the world as he listened to Black Sabbath tapes on his headphones until he passed out. Sometimes he would disappear for the entire weekend without a word to anyone. Often, he returned hours late and, as time went on, he would come back from a weekend days late.

It was hardly a Kodak moment, but his bunk mates snapped a photo of him as he lay passed out on the bed after a drinking binge. Years later that photo would make international news and become a hot item for the tabloids.

Private First Class Jeffrey Dahmer never spoke of his family, nor did he hear from them. He didn't bother anyone; he just kept to himself, except for his belligerent outbursts when he drank. A number of those outbursts consisted of racist epithets, such as *nigger*, directed at black soldiers. Ironically, as it turned out, he did not fare well as a medical specialist because, as he told one commanding officer, he did not have the stomach to do much more than take a patient's blood pressure. He could not stand to prick anyone to draw blood.

At first, I thought we of the media were just trying too hard to find a trail of bodies from Dahmer's adult years. The police looked on his capture and confession as a chance to clear their books. The discovery of a serial killer enabled police departments to clear their respective missing-persons cases.

But we could not ignore the call to the *Journal* newsroom shortly after the case broke from a German tabloid, asking us if Dahmer had confessed to any of five unsolved mutilation murders occurring when Dahmer was stationed at Baumholder. After that the newsroom was abuzz with speculation: How many bodies could be out there? Where else did he visit and who's missing there?

For example, police in Germany continue to be baffled by the case of Erika Handtshuh, a twenty-two-year-old hitchhiker found stabbed and strangled on November 30, 1980, a few days after she left Heidelberg. Her frozen body, her hands bound with cord, was discovered in the snow about fifty miles from Baumholder.

Both Milwaukee and German police eventually theorized there was no connection between Dahmer and the murders. As far as we knew, all Dahmer's victims were homosexual males.

On March 24, 1981, just nine months before the end of his three-year enlistment, Dahmer was discharged under an army regulation concerning alcohol and drug abuse. He joked to his bunk mates as he prepared to leave for the States, "Someday you'll hear about me again."

David G. Goss, Dahmer's squad leader, recounted for reporters his conversation with Dahmer as the two drove to the
airport to ship him home. "There was something bugging him
in Germany. I knew he had a troubled past, and I knew he had
something that was gnawing at him. He'd say there was something he could not talk about," Goss recalled.

After his exit from the army, Dahmer went to Miami and
stayed for a year. He worked in a sandwich shop and told Kennedy, "Nothing of this nature [murder]" happened during his
stay in Florida.

But despite Jeffrey Dahmer's repeated assertions that he had
committed no murders outside the state of Wisconsin, except
for killing Steven Hicks in Ohio, the investigations into his past
did reveal a bizarre coincidence.

Adam Walsh, a six-year-old boy, was abducted from a shopping mall in Hollywood, Florida, on July 27, 1981; two weeks
later, his head was discovered in a canal in Vero Beach, about
120 miles away. Police in Hollywood tried to establish but have
since ruled out any connection with Dahmer's presence in Florida at the same time, and the disappearance of Adam Walsh
remains a mystery.

It seemed Dahmer's stay in Florida proved uneventful, and
he returned to Ohio about six months later and moved in with
his father and stepmother.

On October 7, 1981, Dahmer was arrested at the Ramada
Inn in his hometown of Bath, Ohio, and charged with disorderly conduct—having an open container of alcohol (a bottle
of vodka) and resisting arrest after Bath police asked him to
leave the motel bar, Maxwell's Lounge.

Lionel Dahmer told reporters that, at that time, he was getting very worried. "He roamed around the bars and repeatedly
stayed until closing time, and then he would demand more
drinks," Lionel said. "They'd usher him out. Sometimes there'd
be fights. He'd get hurt badly. He was attacked several times
and had stitches over his eye and broken ribs."

Later, after the Milwaukee murders, Lionel Dahmer thought
he had found the solution. "This was probably a very wrong
thing to do," he said, "but I didn't have the wisdom to do anything differently, so we sent him to his grandmother's [Lionel

Dahmer's mother, Catherine] to live. A new scene. They loved each other, and he'd help her with the chores," he told reporters.

Several months after his arrest in Ohio, in early 1982, Jeffrey Dahmer moved to West Allis, Wisconsin. A new start. In the next seven years that he lived with his elderly grandmother, he would be arrested for public drunkenness, masturbate in front of two boys at a riverbank, and would kill four times in her home.

Catherine Dahmer lived in a modest, two-story frame house in West Allis, a neighborhood of mostly blue-collar workers and numerous corner taverns. Her home was tidy and had a side door that led to the basement, so her grandson enjoyed some privacy. He got a job at the Milwaukee Blood Plasma Center, drawing blood from donors, a strange choice given his distaste for pricking people that he had acknowledged to a superior when he was in the army.

Jeffrey Dahmer's life was uneventful through the summer of 1982, when he was arrested at the Wisconsin State Fair on August 8. He was charged with drunk and disorderly conduct and, according to the police report, "did lower his pants in the presence of approximately 25 people, including women and children." He was fined fifty dollars.

Four years went by and on the surface, all seemed calm in Jeffrey Dahmer's world. He and his grandmother shared a caring relationship, and her neighbors recalled seeing him at work in the yard and helping her with errands. Since January 1985, Dahmer had worked as a mixer at the Ambrosia Chocolate Co., earning about nine dollars an hour. But something was churning inside him, an anger that had been building since his teens, when he realized he was gay. Dahmer became a fixture on Milwaukee's gay bar scene and was remembered by regulars and club owners as a loner who just sat at the bar and drank.

On September 8, 1986, Dahmer was arrested for lewd and lascivious behavior after masturbating in front of two twelve-year-old boys on the banks of the Kinnickinnic River in Milwaukee. One of the boys was interviewed on national television after Dahmer was charged with fifteen of the murders. He recalled asking Dahmer if he was having a good time. "Yeah, I'm having a great time," the boy remembered Dahmer answering. He and his friend laughed at him and ran to tell the police. At his arrest, Dahmer confessed to police that he had masturbated in public about five times in the preceding months. "He doesn't know what changed him to make him suddenly start doing this, and that he knows he has a problem and he wants to get help," the report read. The charge was reduced to disorderly conduct, and Dahmer was sentenced to one year's probation and some therapy.

The gratification of masturbating in public decreased, and Dahmer began to experiment on humans, in a chilling prelude to his later deeds. He frequented the Club Baths in Milwaukee, a gay bathhouse later closed, in 1988, by health authorities. Patrons typically walked around clad in towels to choose a partner, and the two would end up in a private room. A former employee said that in the summer of 1987, "We had to kick Dahmer out because he was drugging people in his private room. One person from Madison was unconscious and we couldn't revive him. We called the paramedics and they took him to the hospital. He was in the hospital for a week to ten days." Police came to interview bathhouse employees and eventually questioned Dahmer. None of the victims wanted to press charges, however, so the matter was dropped.

Dahmer had laid the groundwork for murder in Milwaukee, but his targets kept getting away. He would have to perfect his methods.

In April 1988, Ronald Flowers, from Zion, Illinois, told West Allis police from the hospital that Dahmer had invited him to his grandmother's house and given him, he believed, a drugged drink. Dahmer also stole his money and jewelry, Flowers said.

Dahmer's story differed. He admitted the two had got drunk and passed out. But when they awoke, Dahmer said, he walked Flowers to the bus stop and gave him money for the fare.

The police could find no traces of any sort of drug in Flowers's system at the hospital. Besides, Dahmer's grandmother told police she saw Jeffrey walking a man to the bus stop. Lacking enough evidence, West Allis police dropped the investigation.

Jeffrey Dahmer had slipped through the cracks again.

As I uncovered more and more information about those early offenses, I realized the system could not be blamed, not yet. The police could not force a man who didn't want anyone to know he was a patron at a gay bathhouse to press charges.

In late 1987, Dahmer began to kill young men in Milwaukee. According to his confession, Dahmer's first Wisconsin victim was Steven W. Toumi, twenty-four years old.

Police believe Catherine Dahmer hadn't the vaguest idea of what was happening in her basement. In a newspaper interview, Shari Dahmer said Catherine Dahmer descended the basement stairs one night when her grandson was engaged in some sort of activity with another man, and neither was dressed. "Don't come down here. You don't want to come down here," he called out to his grandmother, according to Shari Dahmer. Jeffrey did not want to be interrupted.

According to Dahmer, in November of 1987, while living with his grandmother, he picked up a white male, approximately twenty-five years old, at Club 219, one of the more popular gay bars in Milwaukee. The two took a room at the Ambassador Hotel, a seedy rooming house-type hotel smack in the middle of the high prostitution area of the city. They became drunk and passed out.

When Dahmer awoke, he said, Toumi was dead and blood was coming from his mouth. He then bought a large suitcase from the nearby Grand Avenue Mall and put the corpse inside. Calling a cab, he returned to his grandmother's, where, after having sex with the corpse and masturbating on it near a floor drain in the basement, he sliced the flesh off the corpse. Finally, he dismembered the remains, placed the parts in plastic bags, and threw them in the trash.

Regulars at the gay bar C'est La Vie noticed that "the blond guy named Steve" had stopped coming around and speculated as to whether something had happened to him or if he had moved. Toumi was last seen alive on September 15, 1987, when he left his Milwaukee apartment.

Toumi grew up in Ontonagon, a mill town in Michigan's Upper Peninsula along Lake Superior. His parents reported him missing to Milwaukee police in December 1987. His father, Walter Toumi, scoured the city for clues to his son's whereabouts, questioning friends and passing out posters with Toumi's photograph. Walter Toumi said Milwaukee police originally told him they could do nothing about his son's disappearance because there was no sign of foul play.

Experts on the case do not know why Dahmer refused to discuss how Toumi died. He confessed to seventeen murders with details graphic enough to make veteran investigators cringe as they read the reports. He identified Toumi from a photograph sent to Milwaukee police by the man's family, but he has held fast to his explanation that when he woke up, in the hotel, Toumi was dead. Dahmer also told Kennedy that many times when he had sex with men, no violence was involved.

"It's entirely possible that he does not remember," said Professor James Alan Fox, dean of the College of Criminal Justice at Northeastern University in Boston and an expert on serial killers. "If he was drinking heavily, he could have blacked out. Or maybe his victim said something to him that made him block out what happened. Even to a serial killer, some things may be too traumatic to remember."

Dahmer was not charged with Toumi's death because police were unable to link Dahmer positively to his murder, and Toumi's remains have never been found. Officials close to the investigation said that Dahmer could possibly at least be charged with failure to report a death.

Two months after Toumi died, Dahmer met James (Jamie) Doxtator, a fourteen-year-old he picked up at a bus stop outside Club 219 around one in the morning. Young men who couldn't get into the gay clubs because they were underage often cruised or hung out in front of buildings frequented by gay men who might be more interested in a young boy than in the drinks and dancing inside.

Jamie was known to local police as a car thief and a hustler. He had been arrested for loitering or prowling in front of the gay bars on September 22, 1987.

Dahmer told Kennedy he thought Jamie was Hispanic and about eighteen when he met him in January 1988. At fourteen,

Jamie was nearly six feet tall. He was not Hispanic but Native American, half Stockbridge Indian and part Oneida Indian.

Dahmer invited Jamie to earn some money by posing nude, watching some videos and having a drink at his grandmother's. They went back to his grandmother's place and had sex. Dahmer gave him a drink with sleeping pills dissolved in it, and when Jamie fell asleep, Dahmer strangled him with his hands. He dismembered the body with a knife by the basement floor drain and broke up the bones with a sledgehammer. Then he put the bones in plastic bags and threw them in the trash. He told police he did not keep any part of the boy.

Dahmer could not identify Jamie from a photo taken when the boy was arrested in September 1987, but he did remember two scars close to each of the boy's nipples that were approximately the circumference of a cigarette.

West Allis police said Jamie's mother, Debra Vega, was living in a Florida motel when they contacted her about her son's death. She had last seen Jamie on January 16, 1988, reported him missing, and then left Milwaukee in 1990. Vega described her son as a teenager who liked to play pool and ride his bike. He had a reading problem and did not get good grades in school.

When she had first heard about Dahmer, she thought Jamie might have been a victim, but she discounted it soon after. "When I heard that the victims were black, Hispanic, and Laotian, I thought I didn't have to worry," Vega told reporters. She added that he had two small scars in the area of his nipples that looked like cigarette burns.

Interviewing the families of Jeffrey Dahmer's victims was gut-wrenching. They were overwrought with grief and anger that Dahmer had slipped through the system so often, and most readily allowed reporters into their homes for interviews. They wanted to tell the world that the whole business was wrong; most said the police just didn't do enough to locate a missing person who belonged to a minority group.

My story-of-a-lifetime was evolving into a very human tale. The family of Richard Guerrero, Dahmer's fourth victim, took me in and taught me more about journalism than I ever learned in school. I sat with them through the preliminary hearings and the countless questions from other reporters. I was embarrassed when reporters pounced on their home and rang their phone off the hook. I was the only *Journal* reporter who was bilingual in Spanish and English, so Richard's parents felt comfortable telling me their most intimate feelings.

In March 1988, just two months after murdering Jamie Doxtator, Dahmer met Richard Guerrero, a handsome twenty-five-year-old of Mexican descent, whose family knew nothing of his secret life until his death. Even then, they refused to acknowledge that he was gay. Guerrero, the youngest of six children, was last seen by his family on March 24, 1988.

Dahmer said he met him in March in the Phoenix Bar, a gay place near the Club 219 in the gay-bar area of Milwaukee. He asked Guerrero to come to his home to take photographs, watch videos, and have sex with him. At the house they had oral sex, and then Dahmer drugged him with sleeping pills in his drink. While Guerrero was asleep, Dahmer said, he strangled him, had sex with him, and masturbated on the body before he dismembered it, and disposed of it as he had done before. He kept none of Guerrero's body parts.

After his arrest, Dahmer told police Guerrero's picture was in a missing-person ad placed in the *Journal's* classified section by Guerrero's family. When police located the ad, Dahmer verified that Guerrero was his fourth victim.

"We've been going through this for the past three-and-a-half years, you know, wondering what happened to him, said Janie Hagen, Richard Guerrero's sister. When Richard was first missing, Janie immediately assumed he was dead. "I couldn't believe he would just get up and go and not let anybody know that everything is fine. If he wanted it to be like that, he would have at least called my mom and let her know everything was okay instead of leaving us in the dark like that with my mother praying to God every day that the good Lord will send her son home."

Hagen dogged the police about finding her brother and became the family spokesperson when Richard Guerrero was discovered to be one of Dahmer's victims. Janie complained that the police simply did not care to look for people like her brother. Once, she said, she saw the police folder with Richard's missing report inside it stamped CASE CLOSED.

"They took everything as a joke," she said. "My brothers were not liked. They were known to the police for minor things like disorderly conduct, and they would go in cars and rip off the radios and stuff. You know, petty things. Nothing big ever. They would get stopped for nothing."

Richard Guerrero had a criminal record dating back to age ten, when he was arrested for burglarizing a house. The pattern continued for fifteen years, including numerous arrests for thefts from autos, robbery, armed burglaries, and two arrests for prostitution.

Nonetheless, his family refused to believe he had a secret life. He couldn't be gay, they said. Not Richard.

"I don't believe he had a secret life," his sister still insists. "When he wasn't with his family, he was working at a pizzeria downtown, hung out with friends. They're trying to make me believe he lived another life. I said there's no way in the world you're going to have me and my family believe he had another life.

"He was always broke. He never had any money. He had three girlfriends. He spent time with Mom and helped her clean the house and ran errands for her. Where in the world could he do this secret stuff? Maybe he went in that bar because it was cold and he wanted to wait for the bus. You can't make me believe he was gay. The only way I think Dahmer could have got him was by luring him with money or a party," Hagen insisted.

Richard left his mother's at eleven-thirty on Saturday night, March 24. He often crashed on his sister's sofa, and had stayed with Janie the night before because he had been out with friends.

"The first thing he always did when he got in the door was call Mom," Janie remembered. "He didn't want her to worry."

Richard had spent most of Saturday at a family gathering at his aunt's home across the street from Janie's, drinking all day with his uncles, watching videos, and eating. That evening Janie went out with her husband, and Richard was babysitting and watching movies with Janie's two-year-old daughter, Raquel, on his lap at his mother's.

Janie called to check on them. "It was raining that night. I was at a pay phone and I was cold, and I was trying to cut Richard off because I was cold," Janie recalled. "He said, 'Well, take care.' And those were his last words to me."

At eleven-thirty P.M., he dressed and told his mother he had to leave the house. Janie assumed he had something planned for that night.

"It was as if he knew he wasn't going to return. He said, 'Everything that's upstairs is yours, Mom.' He kissed her on the cheek, as he did every time. It's a Mexican tradition. The parents say God bless you in Spanish, *Que Dios te bendiga.*"

His mother, Irene Guerrero, remembered looking out the window and seeing her son walk down the alley toward a friend's house. His friend was heavy into drug dealing and told police he never saw Richard that night. "Maybe he dropped him off somewhere. He seems like he's covering," Janie said.

Just two weeks before he died, Richard and one of his girl-friends accidentally overdosed on some pills and were rushed to the Milwaukee County Medical Complex, where they stayed for two days. According to medical records, Richard was assigned to a hospital psychiatrist and had an appointment to see him on March 30, two days after his disappearance. Janie Hagen, looking for answers, wanted to know if he showed up, but when she and her family went to see the doctor, he refused to talk to them. Police did not check it out.

Only after a reporter from the Spanish-language Univision network interviewed the family, once the Dahmer case broke, did anyone get information on the hospital stay. Richard never kept his appointment.

Janie Hagen's eleven-year-old daughter, Maria, has followed her mother's every step looking for Richard. She doesn't care about what her favorite uncle did when he wasn't with her. She did not want to be sent out of the room when I asked her mother if maybe we shouldn't talk about the case in front of her. She still wakes up in the middle of the night with nightmares about what Jeffrey Dahmer did to Richard, and she cries for him.

"I know what's going on," she said. "It makes me feel bad to see all the people talking about my uncle now. When he was missing before, no one cared. Now that a famous man killed him, now all of a sudden, people care."

Sixteen other families felt the same way.

Her uncle's death is also teaching her about prejudice. As Maria listened, her mother explained that if Richard hadn't been Hispanic, someone would have acted sooner. Janie Hagen cited a young white girl from southern Wisconsin, Berit Beck, abducted on her way to a computer seminar in 1990. Every night news stories covered her disappearance, and her picture was on semi-trucks and fliers statewide. Her bludgeoned body was finally discovered after an intensive search.

Frustrated when the police turned up nothing, the Guerreros hired an expensive private investigator, who bilked them out of thousands of dollars before they learned he wasn't even working on the case. Janie Hagen declared, "When that white girl was missing they had her picture everywhere. We could have done that too. But we went with what the private investigator said. He said maybe my brother was involved in a drug deal that went bad. If he is, we don't want to give him that exposure, he told us. We didn't know anything. No reports, he just came over and talked with the family. He was always on vacation."

Richard's father, Pablo, was the only one in the family with a job. He had worked for thirty years as a groundskeeper at a country club golf course in the wealthy suburb of Mequon, driving a little golf cart around the course and picking up stray golf balls. He spent much of his life savings on the private investigator whom they finally decided to dismiss.

Janie wrote to NBC's "Unsolved Mysteries," but they said they couldn't help without a body. "I wouldn't talk to those news programs now. They didn't help me then. Now my brother is a famous victim."

When the family ran Richard's picture with an ad in the *Milwaukee Journal*, what they got were crank calls. Janie did receive one call shortly after the ad ran from a man who talked for over an hour; he described the exact clothing her brother wore the night he disappeared: blue jeans, Dock-Siders, black turtleneck, red sweater-jacket. He gave her his address and phone number, which Janie turned over to the police, but she never heard back from them.

When news of the Jeffrey Dahmer case reached the public, Janie Hagen got the dreaded knock on her door. A Milwaukee police detective asked for the picture of Richard from the 1989 *Journal* ad. He said Dahmer remembered his victim's picture from the classified column of the paper. The police wanted to know what her brother was wearing when he left the house.

"I told them they should have all that information already, but they said they didn't. So I gave them the ad," Hagen said, still exasperated by the experience. "There were all kinds of detectives coming in and out of my house and my mother's house. That went on for the first four days [after the discoveries in Dahmer's apartment]. And then all of a sudden, the fifth day, July 28, they said Dahmer identified Richard through the photo in the paper."

And then it started—the onslaught of media, police, and curiosity seekers. The families complained that the police were unforthcoming and told the press more than they told the victims' relatives.

"The media was scary," Janie said. The cameras swarmed around her home and her mother's. Eager reporters tried to talk to the children and to neighbors. A car pulled in the driveway and reporters surrounded it. The media all wanted to know how the families felt.

Hagen said the rantings of a madman are not enough for her to put her brother to rest. "I'd like to see more proof. I didn't know they could convict a person just from their statement saying they did it. It's almost funny. Now, people are taking it seriously. Before people were just slamming the doors in our faces. I'm really hurt inside. Ever since the murders, I live my days but I just keep thinking about it. You talk to me and I don't hear you."

By the summer of 1988 Dahmer's activities had become too much for his grandmother, so she asked her son Lionel to talk with Jeffrey about finding his own place. As far as Catherine knew, those activities consisted primarily of drinking and carousing with men until all hours.

At his mother's behest, Lionel Dahmer asked Jeffrey about a curious black substance oozing from the garbage can outside. He quickly accepted his son's story about chemically removing the skin from dead animals he had found, just as he had done with the chemistry set Lionel had given him when he was a child.

Catherine Dahmer continued to find her grandson a disquieting presence in her home. Briefly, Jeffrey moved into a seedy apartment building a few blocks from the Oxford Apartments where he would eventually be discovered. However, Catherine's love for him would manifest itself when, despite an arrest for sexual assault later that year, she allowed him to live again in her house.

The discovery in the Oxford Apartments would not occur for several years, not until July 1991. But by September 1988, Dahmer had killed four young men. He would perfect his modus operandi and begin keeping mementos of his victims until thirteen more men were murdered.

Rejected by living human beings, Jeffrey Dahmer turned to the dead.

6

Caught, Not Cured

September 1988–March 1990

On September 25, 1988, Jeffrey Dahmer moved into the shabby brown brick building at 808 North 24th Street where he would live for barely a month.

As if looking for some demented housewarming present for himself when he left his apartment on September 26, he found the perfect target in a thirteen-year-old Laotian boy walking home from school about three-thirty P.M. a block away from Dahmer's building. Dahmer approached him and said he wanted to try out a new camera. He said he had asked a number of others but they had all refused to have their picture taken. Dahmer offered the boy fifty dollars to come to his apartment, about a block away, and pose. The boy went to the apartment, where Dahmer convinced him to partially disrobe. Dahmer shot two Polaroid photos, kissed the youngster on the stomach, and took the boy's penis out of his pants, touching it and telling him to "look sexier for the pose."

In the meantime, the boy drank coffee with Irish Cream liqueur, which, unbeknownst to him, Dahmer had laced with crushed tablets of Halcion, a relative of Valium. Dahmer had the prescription drug because he had told a doctor he was having trouble sleeping.

The boy went home, but his family knew something was amiss because he seemed incoherent and was bumping into furniture. Eventually he passed out. When the family could not arouse him, they took him to the hospital, where doctors discovered he had been drugged. The doctors called the police, and the boy told them where he had gone with the sandy-haired, soft-spoken man.

At two-thirty A.M. the next morning, two officers appeared at Ambrosia Chocolate and hauled Dahmer away from his job at the giant mixer and brought him to the city jail three blocks away.

In a search of Dahmer's apartment, police recovered the coffee cup with traces of the drug and the Irish Cream, a prescription bottle of Halcion, and a Polaroid camera.

Dahmer told Milwaukee Police Detective Scott Schaefer, who interviewed him the night he was arrested for assaulting the boy, that he had no idea how old the victim was because "it's so hard to tell," according to Schaefer's report. Dahmer could not remember if the youngster had told him he was a freshman in school, as the boy had claimed. He also denied ever touching the victim's penis or kissing his stomach.

Dahmer explained that the drugging was inadvertent: he always drank coffee from this cup, from which he also drank his own prescribed medication. He did not wash the coffee cup because he was generally the only person to use it. He added that if the boy had drugs in his system, they must have been from some residue left in the cup. He then asked Detective Schaefer how the victim could give so coherent a statement when he was supposedly drugged.

Dahmer said the boy was fine when he left the apartment with the fifty dollars.

Dahmer was arrested for sexual exploitation of a child and second-degree sexual assault. His bail was set at ten thousand dollars, which his father paid, and Jeffrey Dahmer returned to live with his grandmother.

At his preliminary hearing on September 30, 1988, Dahmer pleaded not guilty and was freed on twenty-five-hundred-dollars cash bail. Assistant District Attorney Gale Shelton was the prosecutor, and Lionel Dahmer hired a well-known defense attorney, Gerald Boyle, to represent Jeffrey.

On January 30, 1989, Dahmer pleaded guilty to second-degree sexual assault and enticing a child for immoral purposes. He awaited his sentencing, scheduled for May 23, at his grandmother's home.

Just two months after pleading guilty in court, Jeffrey Dahmer's depression, loneliness, and possibly fear for his fate, led him back to the gay bars for solace. He told Kennedy that a year after killing Richard Guerrero (he did not mention him by name), he met a black man, about twenty, at La Cage Aux Folles, a popular gay bar in the same area as his other hunting grounds, Club 219 and the Phoenix.

Anthony Sears, twenty-four, of Milwaukee, was last seen by a friend who left him and Dahmer near Dahmer's grandmother's home after the three had left La Cage Aux Folles together on March 25, 1989. Sears, who managed a restaurant in a rough area of Milwaukee, aspired to be a model. He had a few brushes with the law, including several arrests for shoplifting and one for fraudulent use of a credit card. Dahmer identified him from a photograph.

"Tony was a photo fanatic. He loved to have his photos taken. That's the only way I can figure it," said Sears's mother, Marilyn. He was apt to run off with his friends for days at a time, so it wasn't until her son had been missing for four weeks that Marilyn Sears began to worry.

Dahmer told Sears he had come from Chicago to visit his grandmother. He offered Sears money to be photographed. He and Sears had sex at his grandmother's home, after which he gave Sears a drink with sleeping pills in it. Dahmer confessed he strangled Sears, had sex with his corpse, and dismembered the body.

This time, however, he kept the head and boiled it to remove the skin, later painting it gray, so that in case of discovery, the skull would look like a plastic model used by medical students. Dahmer saved the trophy for two years, until it was recovered from apartment 213 on July 23, 1991. Later he explained that he masturbated in front of the skulls for gratification and wanted to keep them with him.

Anthony Sears seemed to be a sort of last hurrah for Dahmer before his sentencing on May 23.

Still on bail when he killed Sears, Dahmer was being monitored by a Department of Probation and Parole psychologist. In a letter to Judge William Gardner, who would preside over Dahmer's sentencing, a bail monitor wrote that since Dahmer had been meeting with the psychologist, "he has begun to come out of his shell and is more verbal, amiable, and relaxed. He has become less lethargic and more willing to interact in community events instead of staying home constantly." All the while, Anthony Sears's painted skull was tucked away among Jeffrey Dahmer's belongings at his grandmother's house.

Judge William Gardner sat on the bench May 23 as Assistant District Attorney Gale Shelton and defense attorney Gerald Boyle made their arguments for sentencing. The statements by Boyle, Shelton, and even Lionel Dahmer proved prophetic, even eerie, given the later developments in the case.

Gale Shelton had worked for eleven years for Milwaukee County District Attorney E. Michael McCann and spent the last six years in the sensitive-crimes unit. She was short—barely five feet, two inches tall—with straight, shoulder-length brown hair. Shelton was always gracious, but a spitfire all the same, when I would bother her at home or on a weekend with a question on a story. "Just get it right," she barked at me once when I telephoned her home on a Saturday night. I knew she was probably smiling when she said it.

Based on a pre-sentence investigation, a report of findings about Jeffrey Dahmer's past, Shelton argued for a prison sentence of five to six years. She described what she felt was a "deeply disturbing picture" of Jeffrey Dahmer's life.

"In my judgment it is absolutely crystal clear that the prognosis for treatment of Mr. Dahmer within the community is extremely bleak, and the reality is that treatment within the community is just plain not going to work," Shelton pleaded. "His track record exhibits that he is very likely to re-offend.

"Mr. Dahmer's perception that what he did wrong here was choosing too young a victim, and that that's all he did wrong, is part of the problem," she said.

Shelton pointed out that the thirteen-year-old boy did not look like an adult and said she felt Dahmer preyed on him because he looked like a soft-spoken young man who could be easily victimized. The boy told her Dahmer had asked him what grade he was in, and he answered, "A freshman." "So," she continued, "Mr. Dahmer knew full well he was not dealing with a consenting adult. He instead was tricking a person who he knew was a child."

The Assistant District Attorney refuted the "inadvertent" drugging of the boy with evidence of the physical/physiological impact the drugs had on his system. The boy said he remembered Dahmer pouring a white powder into the mug and Dahmer's repeated entreaties to keep drinking.

"I have seldom seen such a bleak portrait of the prospects for treatment within the community," she said. "It is clear that Mr. Dahmer has no insight into his problems."

Shelton noted that Dahmer's previous offense for lewd and lascivious behavior (masturbating by the river) also involved children. She was disturbed that he subjected children to his sexual acting out. He claimed he did nothing wrong, that he was just urinating.

She pointed out that when Dahmer was in therapy for the lewd-and-lascivious-behavior conviction, he appeared to be cooperative and receptive. Then she added, "But anything that goes below the surface indicates that deep-seated anger and deep-seated psychological problems that he has, that he's apparently completely unwilling or incapable of dealing with."

One court-appointed psychologist who analyzed Dahmer after his arrest for sexually assaulting the boy reported that Dahmer could not have been less cooperative, that he did not delve into his problems at all. Dahmer felt that it was a wasted expense to continue alcohol or sex offender treatments, that he would not benefit. Two other psychologists concurred.

The three professionals further agreed that Dahmer displayed a strong preponderance of anger, resistance, and evasiveness. He alone could be very manipulative. One doctor referred to him as a schizoid personality and recommended intensive treatment, even hospitalization. Another remarked Dahmer had many problems involving his sexuality.

Those observations were made in 1989, two years and twelve murders before he was caught. They were made by people who were merely looking at Dahmer as a possible pedophile, hardly a serial killer.

Shelton concluded, "Given his unwillingness to cooperate and the extreme emotional instability and serious disturbance which all of the doctors who have talked to Mr. Dahmer state in very strong terms, and I think his lack of motivation to do anything to change will lead to only one reality, and [we need to be concerned with] the protection of the community. The only hope for treatment for Mr. Dahmer has to occur within a prison setting."

Boyle, a pudgy Irishman with a full head of silver hair and wire-rimmed glasses, spoke next. He pleaded vehemently for a stayed prison sentence.

"I understand that certain people have to go to prison, but I don't think that they should be considered people for prison because when they were under some kind of court-ordered doctor's care on a disorderly-conduct charge and felt they hadn't done anything wrong, that that's indicative that forever more they are going to be a danger to society."

Boyle said that since his arrest in September 1988, Dahmer had been functioning in society without any intensive psychological or alcohol-abuse help and had done nothing similar to the assault on the Sinthasomphone youngster again.

The attorney argued, "We have a sick man here who hopefully, with the right kind of treatment, with the right kind of structure and the right kind of treatment, that he be given an opportunity of trying it outside the prison walls. The kind of things that Jeff Dahmer needs are more available through the probation department with a very strong prison sentence withheld and a very long period of probation . . . so we don't have another incident of this nature."

Boyle described Dahmer as "very alone in the world" and as having a "monastic and Spartan" lifestyle. He characterized Dahmer as "very semi-sick. I say 'semi' because he hasn't manifested the sickness."

And Boyle praised Dahmer's good work ethic, which he said, was very important for him to maintain.

"We don't have a multiple offender here. I believe that he was caught before it got to the point where it would have gotten worse, which means that that's a blessing in disguise; and I submit to you as an officer of the court as best as I can, having had a lot of contact with this man since I was hired to represent him, that there has been no recurrence of this type of conduct."

Boyle was doing his job, no matter how distasteful, vigorously defending his client as the legal canons of ethics dictated he must. Boyle had also defended numerous police officers and was known as their fierce advocate.

Twenty-four years earlier, in 1968, Boyle as a Deputy District Attorney, had prosecuted the first serial murder case in the history of Milwaukee County. Boyle got a life prison term for Michael Lee Herrington, the son of a Kansas City police officer, who was convicted in the stabbing deaths of a ten-year-old girl and an eighteen-year-old woman, both from Milwaukee, as well as the attempted murder of another young girl who escaped his attacks.

Now, ironically, he was defending a serial killer.

Gerald Boyle was always media-friendly. No matter how quickly he was rushing out of the courtroom, he would always stop to give me a quote, even during Dahmer's first hearings on the murders in late 1991. We reporters tried to con, charm, and wheedle information out of him about his most famous client, but he always caught on. It is a testament to the cunning and manipulativeness of Jeffrey Dahmer that he was able to con people like Gerry Boyle.

Whether Dahmer fooled his father may never be clear. Lionel Dahmer did know that his son was not well, but he offered his support for Jeffrey when he spoke at his sentencing in 1989:

"I've been through this ordeal with Jeff all the way. From my involvement, everything that Jeff has done it seems it's been in connection with alcohol. I want to leave you with the impression that I'm behind Jeff in whatever happens and intend to follow as I have been very closely and support him as much as I can."

And then Jeffrey Dahmer spoke in his own defense.

"I don't know how much weight you put on what I have to say. I am an alcoholic. Not the sort that has to have a drink every single day. But when I do drink, I go overboard; and I imagine that labels me as being an alcoholic."

Judge Gardner spoke to Dahmer about his drinking.

"You may be [an alcoholic]. You may not be. My experience is that drinking lessens one's control. It lowers some of the inhibitions that we might have, the pressure we have [to behave] in socially responsible ways. Those things get lessened when you drink. It doesn't make you an alcoholic, but it may make you a criminal, which is where you're at."

Jeffrey Dahmer's comments at his sentencing provide the closest look we get into how he could manipulate people using words. We would later learn those words were those of another inmate.

"I've been a fairly regular drinker ever since I was in the army for three years to serve in Germany. The prosecution has raised very serious charges against me, and I can understand why. What I've done is very serious. I never meant to give anyone the impression that I thought otherwise. I've never been in this position before. Nothing this awful. This is a nightmare come true for me. If anything would shock me out of my past behavior patterns, it's this.

"The one thing I have in my mind that is stable and that gives me some source of pride is my job. I've come very close to losing it because of my actions, which I take full responsibility for. I'm the one to blame for all of this. What I've done has cut both ways. It's hurt the victim, and it's hurt me. It's a no-win situation.

"All I can do is beg you, please spare my job. Please give me a chance to show that I can, that I can tread the straight and narrow and not get involved in any situation like this ever again. I would not only ask, I beg you, please don't destroy my life. I know I deserve a great deal of punishment.

"I'm not trying to elicit your sympathy, but I would ask you please don't wipe me out completely."

At the time he made his plea, Jeffrey Dahmer had, unbeknownst to anyone else, wiped out five men's lives completely.

In his statements to the court, Dahmer also admitted he had a sexual problem, namely, that he was homosexual. When Gardner asked if he had relationships with adult males, Dahmer answered:

"I have had in the past, not recently. This enticing a child was the climax of my idiocy. It's just, it's going to destroy me, I'm afraid, this one incident. I don't know what in the world I was thinking when I did it. I know I was under the influence.

"I do want help. I want to turn my life around despite what the prosecution has told you. She doesn't know me like I know myself. This one incident has jolted me like nothing else."

But it hadn't. What jolted Jeffrey Dahmer was that he had been caught, and he had to figure out how he was going to maintain his freedom.

Gail Shelton's insight into the psyche of Jeffrey Dahmer proved accurate, but Judge Gardner was more convinced by Dahmer's penitent statements and Boyle's arguments against a lengthy prison sentence. Gardner admitted that the sentencing was difficult. He said, "I'm really concerned that unless there's some type of substantial change in yourself, that you are going to repeat, because it's a drive. It's almost a biological urge that you have. You've got to learn to control. It may never go away, but your conduct has to change."

Dahmer responded, "I can't stress it enough that I desperately want to change my conduct for the rest of my life. I imagine you may think I'm saying that just because I'm sitting here facing prison. I mean that sincerely that I do want to change."

And when it was all over that day, Judge Gardner believed him and opted to send Dahmer into the community. The prison system offered no alcohol program at the time; Gardner told Dahmer if he sent him to prison without the treatment, "You'd probably come out worse than you are right now."

On the second-degree sexual assault charge, he stayed a sentence of five years and put Dahmer on probation for five years instead. He ordered Dahmer to spend one year in the Milwaukee County House of Correction under work release so he could continue his employment. Instead of the prison, complete with barbed wire and barred cell doors, he would go to a correctional center which was more like a dormitory.

On the charge of enticing a child for immoral purposes, Gardner stayed a prison sentence of three years and scheduled probation to run concurrently with the five-year term.

In the end, Dahmer would serve ten months in jail with work-release privileges and would be on five years' probation, during which time he had to report monthly to a probation officer. He was to have no contact with anyone under the age of eighteen. He was also told to get psychological counseling and some type of inpatient or outpatient alcohol treatment.

That was it.

The sentence could have been ten years in prison.

No member of the Sinthasomphone family was in court to argue for a stiffer sentence. The family later claimed they had not been notified.

After Dahmer had been arrested for the murders of seventeen people and we discovered he was on probation, some of the local media ran editorials decrying Gardner's actions; others said he could not be held responsible because he had no way of knowing what would become of Jeffrey Dahmer. Most agreed that due to the severity of the charges against him, Dahmer should have been watched more closely.

At a news conference just after Dahmer's July 1991 arrest, Boyle said the sentence was appropriate at the time: "He had no bad marks, he was doing everything his probation officer and everyone else told him to do. I don't think anybody in the world would have thought this young man was capable of doing what he is accused of doing."

Starting May 23, Jeffrey Dahmer had a new home at the Community Correctional Center two blocks north of the Police Administration Building and five blocks west of Ambrosia Chocolate. In November, Dahmer was granted a Thanksgiving pass for twelve hours. He was supposed to be back at 10 P.M.

but did not return until 4:55 A.M. He was intoxicated and bragged to other inmates that he had drunk a quart of Jack Daniels that day. He never made it to his grandmother's house where his family had gathered for the holiday and where, ostensibly, he had wanted to go. He lost two days of good time, or credit toward a reduction in his sentence.

About two weeks after Thanksgiving, Dahmer handwrote a note to Judge Gardner, asking for early release:

"Sir, I have always believed that a man should be willing to assume responsibility for the mistakes that he makes in life. The world has enough misery in it without my adding more to it. Sir, I assure you that it will never happen again. This is why, Judge Gardner, I am requesting from you a sentence modification. So that I may be allowed to continue my life as a productive member of our society."

Someone else was also writing to Judge Gardner. Lionel Dahmer, frustrated at not being able to get his son into some kind of treatment program, wrote to Judge Gardner, asking him not to grant Jeffrey early release:

"I have tremendous reservations regarding Jeff's chances when he hits the streets. Every incident, including the most recent conviction for sex offense, has been associated with and initiated by alcohol in Jeff's case. I sincerely hope that you might intervene in some way to help my son whom I love very much and for whom I want a better life. I think it best to ensure my relationship with Jeff that no one tell him of my efforts towards effective treatment. I do feel as though that this may be our last chance to institute something lasting and that you can hold the key."

There has been considerable speculation as to what happened to Dahmer in prison. His stepmother, Shari Dahmer, told reporters, "He had no light in his eyes. Jeff lost his soul in there. He said he'd never go back to prison. Something happened to him in prison that he would never talk about." It is common knowledge that there is a code of justice among convicts, according to which rapists and child molesters are often raped by other prisoners. Some have also speculated that Dahmer developed a hatred for blacks in prison, but while in the

Army, long before he entered prison, he was known to make derogatory remarks about blacks.

After serving not quite ten months of his sentence, Judge Gardner granted Dahmer early release from the center on March 2, 1990. Once again, Catherine Dahmer gave her grandson a home, but on the condition that he quickly find himself a place of his own.

Dahmer's probation officer, Donna Chester, was required to meet twice a month with her clients and make regular home visits. But in Dahmer's case, she asked to be excused from the home visits because of the large caseload—121 clients—she was required to manage and because he lived in a bad neighborhood. Her supervisors agreed to waive the requirement. When I read the logs Chester kept of her conversations with her new client, it was apparent that Jeffrey Dahmer was hopeless as a productive member of society, which he had promised Gardner he would become. He was constantly depressed and did not want to solve his own problems.

Chester's case objective was for Dahmer to be drug-and-alcohol-free and to identify sexual feelings and issues. She asked him to start thinking about who he was and what he believed would make him happy in life. She gave him the number of an alcohol treatment program to call.

In early April 1990, Chester wrote that Dahmer was receptive to discussing sexual feelings. He brought his laptop computer to the session but admitted he was using it as a crutch to keep himself busy and to not think about what happened.

Dahmer told Chester he had no friends and had isolated himself from society. He said he drank alone, and that was when problems arose. Chester advised Dahmer to work on alcohol issues and "then we will begin to discuss sexual tendencies," she wrote. Dahmer "felt more comfortable now he knew he was not being judged for his sexual purpose. Subject stated would be more comfortable talking about his feelings now."

On April 27, 1990, Lionel Dahmer told Chester that his son said he was attending an alcoholic treatment program once a week. According to her notes in the probation log, he also told her that Jeffrey had been abused by a neighbor boy at age eight.

Chester wrote, "Maybe reason why subject has problems with sexuality issues."

That same day, Chester wrote that Dahmer seemed depressed and was having problems finding a place to live within his budget, even though his paychecks averaged three hundred dollars a week. He said he had no furniture and had problems managing money. "Does not want to solve own problems. Looks for others to help him," she jotted in the log.

On May 14, 1990, Jeffrey Dahmer found an apartment at 924 North 25th Street, apartment 213.

He now had a home of his own. It was to become his personal slaughterhouse.

7

His Own Abattoir

May 1990–May 1991

As the night of his confession wore on and Jeffrey Dahmer detailed his activities for Detective Kennedy, a pattern to his murders began to emerge.

Most often he lured his victims to his apartment by offering them money to pose for pictures or view male homosexual videos. Dahmer told police that all his victims knew that homosexual activity, and possibly posing for photos, was the idea.

Once in his apartment, Dahmer typically put crushed sedatives in a mixed drink for his guest. Once his victims were knocked out by the drug, Dahmer usually strangled them, using his hands or a leather strap he had bought specifically for that purpose. He tried an assortment of chemicals to drug the men, even experimenting for a time with ether.

He also experimented with chemicals to dispose of the body

parts. Dahmer eventually settled on hydrochloric acid, so that after a few days, the body parts would turn sludgy and could easily be flushed down the toilet. He preserved genitals and other parts in formaldehyde as trophies of his deeds. Before he dismembered his victims, Dahmer often cut them open so he could photograph them with his Polaroid, or he waited for rigor mortis to set in so the corpse could appear to be standing in the picture. He saved a number of those photos in an album. He told police he was aroused by the heat emanating from a body he had just cut open.

Sometimes he boiled the victim's heads to keep as trophies, using a household cleaner called Soilex to boil a head clean. He estimated it took a couple hours to strip the flesh completely off the bone. Dahmer purchased gray spray paint from a downtown Milwaukee art shop to color the boiled skulls and make them appear artificial. He said he began this procedure of keeping the skulls after killing Anthony Sears at his grandmother's home. He cut up all the victim's identification and jewelry and threw it in the garbage, but police nevertheless found the identification of two victims in the apartment.

Dahmer chose to live in an area of the city into which he could melt and operate unnoticed. The four square blocks around his apartment housed low-income residents who kept police busy twenty-four hours a day.

The area was 69 percent black, and housing was overwhelmingly—89 percent—renter-occupied. There were few single-family homes; 84 percent of the dwellings were in buildings with three or more units; and rents averaged $280, compared with $363 in Milwaukee County. The median home value there was $33,000, compared with $65,273 for the county.

Dahmer hoped to blend in with the 2,378 people in the blocks in which he lived. His probation officer, Donna Chester, would not visit his new neighborhood because, she told her superiors, it was too dangerous. She did not know that the greatest danger lurked in her client's apartment.

Chester met Dahmer on May 15, the day after he moved to his new home. She wrote in her log that Dahmer said his job was going well and that he was interested in real estate and might look into courses at the Milwaukee Area Technical College. Dahmer missed his appointment the following week, on May 22, as he did several times, but he always had an excuse. Most often, he claimed he overslept or was sick.

On May 29, Chester noted that Dahmer looked bad. Usually neat, he appeared unkempt and unshaven. He told Chester he was "ripped off" at his apartment by someone who took his watch, three hundred dollars, and all his clothes. No police records indicate that Dahmer called to report what had happened. Chester told him he needed to move out of that area, but Dahmer said there was nothing he could do except learn from his mistake and try to find a better place to live.

When Dahmer saw Chester on June 11, he seemed very depressed and, she noted, had a problem with sexual identity. He told her he was not getting enough sleep, and then went on to say he knew he preferred male partners but he felt guilty about it. He said he was not involved in any sexual activity at that time and planned to remain celibate. Chester cautioned Dahmer that problems could arise if he were not careful about his sexual preferences, and told him to contact a gay rights organization if he needed to talk about his feelings.

It was the way he explored his feelings that got him into trouble.

A little over a month after Dahmer moved into his new home, he met Eddie Smith, a twenty-eight-year-old black man, at the Phoenix Bar in mid-June, and offered him money for sex and to pose for pictures. The two men took a cab to Dahmer's apartment, where they had oral sex. Smith passed out from a drugged drink, and Dahmer strangled and dismembered him.

Dahmer said he took four or five photographs of Smith during the dismemberment process. This time, he disposed of Smith's body completely by placing it in garbage bags and throwing the bags in the trash in back of the building. Dahmer also got rid of the photos he had taken.

Smith's remains have not been found, but Dahmer identified his victim by saying he wore a headband like an Arab. Smith's sister, Carolyn, said her brother was called "the Sheikh" because he frequently wore a turbanlike wrap around his head. He aspired to be a professional model but he ran into trouble with the law.

Carolyn Smith last saw her brother on June 14, 1990, shortly before the annual Milwaukee Gay Pride parade; he had been dancing at the gay bars. She reported her brother missing June 23. Nearly a year later, in March 1991, she received a telephone call from a white man who said not to bother looking for Eddie because the caller had killed him. "It was late and I picked up the phone, and the man said, 'You don't have to bother looking for your brother.' I asked him, 'Why not?' and he said, 'Because he's dead.' I asked him how he knew that, and he told me, 'Because I killed him,'" Carolyn Smith told reporters as she wiped away tears with the back of her hand.

Dahmer told police he made the phone call, and members of several other families reported receiving similar calls.

Carolyn Smith recalled the hours waiting for news of her missing brother after the family heard about Jeffrey Dahmer. "They said on television that Saturday that all the eleven bodies they found in his apartment had been accounted for," Carolyn Smith said. "And I thought, 'We're in the clear.'" Then the police called, telling them that Dahmer had identified Eddie Smith as one of his victims. Carolyn Smith then went to Dahmer's apartment building, where I met her for the first time.

I had been knocking on apartment doors and interviewing Dahmer's neighbors when I spied Carolyn Smith staring at the wooden door to apartment 213. I asked if a relative of hers was one of the victims, and when she said yes, I asked why she had come. It all seemed so gruesome. "I just wanted to see if those were the last steps Eddie took," she said, breaking into sobs.

Carolyn Smith is a large black woman, with long hair pulled severely back from her face and cascading down her back. Always colorfully and fashionably dressed, she became a fixture at all the gatherings and press conferences involving the Jeffrey Dahmer case. She did television talk shows and always had time to answer one more reporter's question in hopes that someone would understand how she felt. She turned her anger into a crusade to find out how the murders had happened and whether they could have been prevented.

In the two years before the discoveries, while families agonized over what had become of their loved ones, Donna Chester was still reporting on Dahmer's behavior in her monthly log. "Subject [Dahmer] has been attending treatment program. Subject appears depressed all the time. May be an act. Agent will monitor subject more closely." When the two met on June 25, Dahmer denied any sexual involvement and said he had no desires because he had been so busy working double shifts at Ambrosia due to the summer vacations of other employees. Chester noted that she "reminded him of the consequences that will happen if there is any acting out." She briefly mentioned the possibility of a home visit but discounted it because he lived in a "very bad area."

A short time after he had killed Smith, Dahmer met Ricky Lee Beeks, a thirty-three-year-old black man of Milwaukee— who used the alias Raymond Lamont Smith—at the Club 219 in July 1990. Dahmer offered him money to be photographed, have a drink, and watch videos. Beeks went home with Dahmer, passed out from a drugged drink, and Dahmer strangled him. He then removed Beeks's clothing and had oral sex with him after his death. He dismembered the body, keeping the skull and painting it. Dahmer identified Beeks through a photograph.

It was not unusual for Beeks to be gone for long periods without contacting his family. They last saw him May 29, 1990. Beeks had been living with his half-sister, Donita Grace, and he had a ten-year-old daughter who lived in Rockford, Illinois.

Beeks had just gotten out of prison and came to Milwaukee to live with her, Grace told reporters. Beeks was known to police as James Green, Mark Brown, and Raymond Lamont Smith, and he had a criminal history that included convictions for first-degree sexual assault (rape), disorderly conduct, criminal damage to property, theft, and criminal trespass to a dwelling. Grace was surprised to learn he was Jeffrey Dahmer's seventh victim because she had heard that he had been shot.

Dahmer told Kennedy that by the time he killed his seventh victim, he had become more adept at cutting up the bodies.

Dahmer was on a roll. He had a method and tools, and he could keep the men he took home with him forever. His probation agent observed he was depressed and his appearance was poor, but she still refused to conduct a home visit. Even if she had, however, there might not have been anything obviously amiss except for the odor, which he was always able to explain away.

As I combed the gay bars and talked to numerous people in the homosexual community, I was put in touch with a fifteen-year-old Hispanic boy who, I was informed, had an incredible story to tell. He was another young man who got away.

The fifteen-year-old was assaulted by Dahmer on July 8, 1990, but was unable to give police enough information to identify his assailant at that time.

I went to the boy's home and discovered that his foster mother did not speak English and was very upset to think her son might have ended up in the murderous clutches of Jeffrey Dahmer. She was also distraught at discovering the boy was gay, but she said that despite the stigma in the Hispanic community, she loved him and would try to understand.

The boy said he was standing outside the Phoenix Bar that July day, when Dahmer promised him two hundred dollars if he would pose nude for some photographs at his apartment. The boy went to the apartment, but when Dahmer insisted he drink from a glass Dahmer gave him, the boy refused. The bedroom VCR was playing *The Exorcist* while the boy was lying on the bed, face down, posing for pictures. Suddenly Dahmer hit him on the back of the head with a rubber mallet and tried to strangle him.

He managed to convince Dahmer that he would not call the police if Dahmer let him go, and he fled when Dahmer called a taxi for him. When the boy arrived home, he told his foster mother that he had been assaulted but gave her few details because she did not know he was gay. The next day he was treated at a local hospital for bruises.

The boy and his foster mother told the story to their social worker, who promised to contact police. The police made one visit to the house, and the family never heard from them or the social worker again. The boy could remember only the name Jeffrey.

And so Dahmer slipped away again.

"I was filled with terror at the thought he was a victim," the boy's foster mother told me in Spanish. She explained that the boy, who was known to disappear for short periods, had not been seen by anyone when the Dahmer case was being played out in the local papers. When the police came to her door wanting to question him about what happened when he was with Dahmer, the boy's foster mother thought her boy was one of the victims.

The day after the incident with the fifteen-year-old Hispanic boy, Dahmer met with Chester. He was an hour late for his appointment and told her he had woken up late and fallen down the stairs and injured himself.

When Dahmer finally showed up at one-forty-five P.M., Chester wrote he "looks rough." He brought his camera to the session and tried to sell it to one of the probation agents, saying he had severe financial problems. Dahmer claimed he had a lot of hospital bills when Chester asked what he was doing with all his money, since he was averaging three hundred dollars a week at Ambrosia. Further, according to Dahmer's financial records, he had only one outstanding hospital bill for $323.94. Chester gave Dahmer information on food pantries and free meal sites.

She wrote in her log, "Agent believes subject is blowing money, but not sure on what. Subject appears defensive if questioned where his money goes. Asked subject if he is involved with someone or is picking up guys. States no. Subject's falling down stairs may have been another assault on him."

Not knowing he had failed at murder the night before, Chester added, "Subject's appearance has gone way down since [he] moved on [his] own. Subject depressed, talked about suicide."

Dahmer told Chester the only solution to his financial problems was to "jump from a tall building." Even though he refused to look at anything in his life positively, Chester believed Dahmer's problems were primarily monetary, and she wrote that he had too many other problems to have much of a sexual drive.

In September, two months after the incident involving the fifteen-year-old Hispanic boy, Dahmer met Ernest Miller, a twenty-four-year-old black man, in front of an adult bookstore on one of the main streets in Milwaukee's gritty central city.

Whenever I walked down that street on a story, I always kept one eye peering over my shoulder at whoever was walking behind me. The sound of any footsteps always made me suspicious.

Miller, an accomplished dancer, had left his aunt's house and walked to the adult bookstore, where he met a sandy-haired, personable man.

It was routine by then.

Dahmer offered Miller money to come to his apartment. He recalled taking several pictures of Miller in various sexual poses, and then the two had sex.

Miller passed out from a coffee-and-rum drink laced with sleeping pills; Dahmer cut his throat with a large hunting knife, put the body in the bathtub, and used the knife to dismember him. He told Kennedy that he filleted the skin from Miller's body, put the flesh in trash bags, and threw it out. He kept Miller's skull, painted it, and kept it with the others. He also bleached the skeleton, photographed it hanging in the shower, and kept it. He put Miller's biceps in the freezer.

The question was inevitable. During the confession, Kennedy asked about cannibalism. Dahmer said the only body parts he ever consumed were Ernest Miller's. He ate Miller's biceps because they were big and he wanted to try cannibalism. Then, somewhat irritably, Dahmer said he did not want to talk about that anymore.

"It's hard for us," said Ernest Miller's uncle, Stanley. "When we last saw Ernest, he was full of life, a very caring and loving person. And when we went to the coroner's office, there was nothing but a skeleton."

Whenever Stanley Miller came to court for one of Dahmer's hearings, he wore a photograph of his nephew pinned to his lapel. Jeffrey Dahmer had identified Ernest Miller from the same photograph.

The skeleton photographed hanging from the shower spigot was no longer merely gruesome. It was once a person who had had a name and a life and people who loved him. Finding out about the people made what I had seen more difficult to think about as the identification process wore on. My wanting the big story was eclipsed by the sadness I felt when yet another family

told me about the life Dahmer had snuffed out so systemati-
cally.

The murder scenarios Dahmer described were similar, but
sometimes there was a twist. When he met twenty-two-year-old
David Thomas, of Milwaukee, in September 1990 near the C'est
La Vie gay bar, he offered the young black man money to come
back to his apartment. The two sat and talked as they drank
but did not have sex. Dahmer gave Thomas a drugged drink,
killed him, and dismembered him. He said he killed him even
though Dahmer did not want to have sex with him because he
thought the man would wake up and be angry with him.

Since Thomas wasn't his type, Dahmer told Detective Kennedy, he kept none of the body parts. However, he did photograph Thomas while he dismembered him. Leslie Thomas,
David's sister, identified her brother from the facial portion of
a photograph Dahmer had taken.

Thomas's girlfriend, Chandra Beanland, twenty-four, reported him missing on September 24, 1990. The two had a
three-year-old daughter, Courtia. Beanland, like many of the
other victims' relatives, said it was not unusual for David to be
gone for weeks at a time: "Usually, he'd be gone for two or
three weeks, and then he'd call and come home."

Thomas had a lengthy criminal history with the Milwaukee
police, including a rap sheet listing thirteen aliases. He had
been arrested five times for battery, sixteen times for retail
theft/shoplifting, and numerous times for resisting or obstruct-
ing a police officer. He was picked up for attempted armed
robbery and for beating a victim with his fists. He served a total
of almost six months in jail and, once released, violated his
probation. He was arrested for shoplifting just five months before he met Jeffrey Dahmer.

Police records indicate that Dahmer was the victim of an
armed robbery the same day David Thomas was reported missing, September 24. Dahmer told the police he had been approached by two black males near North 27th Street and West
Wisconsin Avenue, close to where he had picked up Ernest
Miller earlier that summer. The man who accosted him, at
about eight-twenty P.M., asked him for money and then threatened to shoot when Dahmer refused to give him any. The sus-

pects took ten dollars and a bus pass from Dahmer's wallet, returned the wallet, and fled. It was the third time Dahmer had been robbed since being on probation. His luck just didn't seem to be going well.

Things were quiet for Jeffrey Dahmer between September 1990 and February 1991. In this period, Dahmer was chronically depressed. He attended alcohol and mental health treatment programs, but it seemed as though no progress was being made. He was diagnosed at one treatment facility as manic-depressive. Chester's October reports noted that Dahmer's appearance had improved, but his attitude remained very negative. She described him as a chronic complainer and a materialistic spendthrift. "Subject [Dahmer] also gets angry at people who make a lot of money, saying, 'Why are they so lucky?' and he 'hates' them for having so much," she wrote.

In November, Catherine Dahmer phoned Ambrosia to see how her grandson was doing. Dahmer said the call made him feel as though someone cared about him. He had been giving Chester the impression that he preferred being alone and that he did not like to go places and meet people.

In hindsight we know he liked meeting people, it was the rejection he couldn't handle. Doing things his way, people never left him.

Dahmer was worried about seeing his father and brother at his grandmother's house for Thanksgiving in 1990 because, he said, he was ashamed of his behavior and did not want to hurt his family. He talked to Chester about his mother, Joyce, in December, and said he had not spoken or written to her in five years. At Chester's suggestion, he decided to send his mother a Christmas card.

When the subject of Christmas came up, Dahmer was uneasy about seeing his father and brother again. He said he was uncomfortable around his family because "his father is controlling, and he has nothing in common with his brother who attends college, and he [Dahmer] is embarrassed about his offense," Chester entered in the log. He added that his family was supportive of him.

Dahmer continued to fool Chester. In January, he said the only reason he got involved with the Laotion boy was because he'd been drinking, and it would never happen again because jail was a deterrent, he just could not go back to prison. He admitted to himself that he was gay and said, "That's the way I am, so fuck it." He denied any involvement with others.

In February 1991, Dahmer struck again. Eight more young men would lose their lives before he was caught. The first of these was Curtis Straughter, an eighteen-year-old black youth of Milwaukee, waiting for a bus near the Marquette University campus a few blocks from Dahmer's apartment. It was the same with Straughter as with the nine others before him. Dahmer offered him money to go to his apartment and had oral sex with his victim after he passed out from the drugged drink. Dahmer strangled him with the strap he had bought for that purpose and dismembered Straughter's body while taking pictures. He kept his skull but did not paint it.

Curtis Straughter—identified through dental records and from a photograph shown to Dahmer—had lived with his grandmother, Catherine Straughter, who last saw her grandson February 18, 1991. He was a high-school dropout who joined Gay Youth Milwaukee, a group for young gay men, when he was fifteen. He aspired to be a model and he wrote songs, but he earned his living as a nursing assistant, a job he had lost shortly before he disappeared. Two aliases were listed in his police file, Demetra and Curta. He was arrested in 1987, when he was just fourteen years old, for two counts of second-degree sexual assault.

He told friends he planned to get his high-school equivalency certificate and attend modeling school. Those same friends were puzzled when they heard he was one of Jeffrey Dahmer's victims because of Straughter's open hostility toward white men.

Dahmer had taken some vacation days around the time Straughter was murdered. He told Chester he was using the time to rest and work on straightening out his finances, but two weeks later, he said he was broke and would walk sixteen blocks to work. Toward the end of February, Chester commented that Dahmer was again beginning to look disheveled and unshaven. She also noted that Dahmer had severe problems with his sexuality and that if he did not work them out he was in danger of "reoffending."

In March, Joyce Flint Dahmer telephoned her son, their first contact in five years. Dahmer told Chester his mother knew he was gay and had no problems accepting it. They promised to keep in touch.

Errol Lindsey, a nineteen-year-old black man, was devoted to his mother, Mildred, who last saw the youngest of her six children on April 7, 1991, when he went out to have a key made.

Lindsey met Dahmer near a key shop on the corner of North 27th Street and West Kilbourn Avenue, just two blocks from Dahmer's apartment, and accepted Dahmer's offer of money to return to his apartment. After Lindsey consumed a drink laced with drugs and passed out, Dahmer strangled him and then had oral sex with the corpse. Dahmer dismembered the body and saved the skull without painting it. Lindsey was identified with dental records and from a photograph in which Dahmer recognized his victim.

Mildred Lindsey had trouble understanding how her son came to be killed not merely by a murderer, but a monster. "I can't understand how it happened, how he [Dahmer] met Errol," she told reporters. "Errol wasn't the type to talk to just anybody. He went to work and then he came home. He was a mama's boy. He wouldn't even go out with his friends without calling me to see what I was doing."

I met Mildred Lindsey the day after the discoveries in Dahmer's apartment. She huddled in the back of the building with residents and curious onlookers and hoped for some clue to her son's disappearance. "I think he's dead," she told me softly.

Although Errol Lindsey had had his brushes with the law—an arrest for injury by conduct regardless of life, one for being party to an arson of a building, and an arrest for aggravated battery with a knife—Lindsey left behind a legacy of art and hope. His eighth-grade art teacher, Dorothy Klein, had saved her favorite student Errol's watercolor of a house with two trees in front of it and has since shared it with her other students.

"I can't get past being mad at the system first," Keely Favors

Watkins, Lindsey's cousin told reporters. "Jeffrey Dahmer was not allowed to do anything that the police and the judicial system did not allow him to do."

Jeffrey Dahmer continued to plod through the judicial system, meeting dutifully with his probation agent twice a month. When he met with Donna Chester at the end of April, he remained morbid about his problems and did not try or want to work to change his life. In mid-May, finances still posed a serious problem for Dahmer, and Chester characterized him as a compulsive buyer who could not manage money.

Police detectives pounded at Dahmer's door on May 4, 1991, after twenty-six-year-old Dean Vaughn, a black man who lived upstairs from Dahmer, was found strangled in his apartment. Dahmer told them he did not see or hear anything. Vaughn's murder remains unsolved, although many have speculated on a link to Jeffrey Dahmer.

When I returned to Dahmer's apartment later that Tuesday, the day after the discoveries were made, I met Barbara Hughes-Holt, whose brother, Tony Hughes, had been missing since May 24, 1991.

Tony Hughes, thirty-one, had been a deaf-mute since contracting pneumonia as an infant, but he communicated through sign language, writing notes, and lip-reading. Tony, a black man, had moved to Madison after a neighbor of his was killed in Milwaukee, but he returned the night of May 24 to visit his sister Barbara.

About ten-thirty P.M. Hughes decided to go to Club 219, where he could feel the music's reverberations and make friends. He was known in the gay bars as very gregarious and friendly.

When Jeffrey saw Hughes at Club 219—the two had met there in 1989—he passed him a note offering him fifty dollars to come to his apartment to pose for some pictures and watch videos. Hughes nodded yes.

At the apartment, it was business as usual for Jeffrey Dahmer: first, the drugged drink for his victim, then death and dismemberment. Dahmer kept Hughes's unpainted skull with the rest. He identified him through a photograph.

When Hughes did not return to his sister's home, the family was panicked. They talked to patrons at Club 219 and eventually papered the city with flyers with Hughes's picture on it. The *Milwaukee Journal* and the *Milwaukee Sentinel* published stories on the missing man.

Shirley Hughes, Tony's mother, is a deeply religious woman who taught a Bible class at Garden Homes Evangelical Lutheran Church in Milwaukee. She could teach classes in coping. I talked with her at one of Dahmer's early courtroom appearances. "I'm not angry," she said. "It's not anger at work here, with the help of the Lord. I feel hurt because of the way he died. I'm here for my son. I don't want revenge, I just wanted to see the man."

When I interviewed families like the Hugheses, they always asked me, as if I would have the answer, why wasn't Dahmer caught sooner? Victims' families also asked me about the infamous stench and how could people just do nothing.

Even Dahmer was aware of the odors wrought by his human refuse. He told police the body parts gave off an awful smell in the trash, but no one ever did anything so he just kept following his usual routine.

People asked me, "Where were the police?"

As it turned out, they had been there.

8

Deloused and
Unemployed

May 27, 1991, 2 A.M.

John Balcerzak, Joe Gabrish, and Rick Porubcan were decorated Milwaukee police officers whose actions on May 27,
1991, were subsequently portrayed as tantamount to murder.

Of all the wild rumors that filtered in and out of the newsroom during the first days of the case, one of the most explo-
sive, potentially, alleged that Dahmer and his fourteen-year-old
victim, Konerak Sinthasomphone, had had contact with police
the night Dahmer killed the boy. (In what Dahmer had repeatedly told police was a bizarre coincidence, Sinthasomphone's brother was the victim of the sexual assault in 1988,

for which Dahmer received ten months in prison and for which he was on probation at the time of his arrest in July 1991.)

I discovered from a detective that police had questioned Dahmer about his relationship with Konerak and then handed the youngster back to Dahmer. The detective undoubtedly considered it merely an interesting coincidence and did not realize the incident would enrage the community. In our conversation, it wasn't even the first subject he brought up.

I immediately told the editors about the story, but I knew it would be tough to pin down. Acting on orders from Police Chief Philip Arreola's office, clerks quickly purged from the police computers any reports involving contact with Jeffrey Dahmer, so any documents backing up what I learned were going to be hard to come by. We could not go with a story that serious without some confirmation.

I talked to police lieutenants and captains and I quizzed Dahmer's neighbors. Finally someone gave me the name Glenda Cleveland, and I went to her house early Thursday afternoon.

Cleveland, thirty-six, lived in a brown brick building next door to the Oxford Apartments where Jeffrey Dahmer made his home. She invited me into her apartment and confirmed that the identification of Konerak Sinthasomphone's body was not the police's first contact with the boy or with Dahmer.

By the time I tracked down Glenda Cleveland, she had already phoned a local television station, wanting to tell her story on camera. Getting beat on a story is not a happy experience when the editors get hold of the reporter. Either because the paper was scooped by TV or most likely because no one realized the magnitude of what I had learned, the story I wrote was edited down to a few paragraphs, and the tiny article was buried inside the paper.

It took weeks for the events of May 27, 1991, to unfold. Through police testimony, as well as statements from Cleveland, her niece Nicole Childress, and her daughter Sandra Smith, the night in question was eventually re-created.

On May 26, 1991, Dahmer met Konerak Sinthasomphone at the Grand Avenue Mall in downtown Milwaukee, where Dahmer offered the boy money to pose for pictures. Police said the fourteen-year-old already had a history of prostitution in his juvenile record. Dahmer's neighbors also told me, after the May 27 incident was made public, that they remembered seeing an Asian boy in the building with Dahmer before.

Konerak accepted Dahmer's offer, and the two went to Dahmer's apartment, where Konerak posed for two photographs in black bikini briefs and both watched videos. Konerak drank a drugged beverage and passed out, at which time Dahmer had oral sex with him.

Dahmer had run out of beer, so he left Konerak to go to a bar for more. Apparently, while Dahmer was away, Konerak revived and fled.

"The boy was obviously disoriented and tried to flee from this crazy man," Cleveland told me, shaking her head. "It was obvious to me. I can't believe that the police couldn't see something was very wrong. Anytime you see anyone running down the street buck naked, well, you wouldn't want to be patted on the back and sent home."

Cleveland's eighteen-year-old daughter, Sandra Smith, called the 911 emergency police line at two A.M. to report that something was amiss when she saw the boy running naked, before Dahmer returned.

"O.K., hi . . . I'm on 25th and State and there's this young man, he is butt naked, he has been beaten up, he is very bruised up, he can't stand . . . he has, he is buck naked, he has no clothes on, he is really hurt. And I, you know, I ain't got no quarter on him [she did not know who he was], I just seened him. He needs some help . . . ," Smith told the police operator. She did not give her name.

At 2:06 A.M., Police Officers Joe Gabrish and John Balcerzak, of Squad 36, had just finished investigating a man with a gun when the radio dispatcher sent them to the location Smith described.

"Squad 36, you got a man down. Caller states it's a man badly beaten and he's wearing no clothes, lying in the street at two-five and State. Anonymous female caller. Ambulance sent."

A few minutes later, the officers arrived at the alley where fire department paramedics had been on the scene since 2:07 A.M. They had already wrapped Konerak in a blanket. They said the boy was not bleeding from the buttocks, as it was later widely reported, but instead had a scuffed knee, most likely from falling as he ran up the alley. Dahmer, who had returned from the store to all the commotion, was standing near the boy.

As the officers tried to evaluate what was going on, the women who called 911 were shouting at them. One of the officers told the two women he would talk with them in a minute, but the yelling continued. Cleveland told me that her daughter and her niece, Nicole Childress, eighteen, tried to intervene when the police arrived, but the cops ignored them. Cleveland did not come downstairs. The police say that the yelling women became hostile and profane and would not wait until they spoke with the boy and Dahmer.

Another squad car also arrived on the scene, with Officers Rick Porubcan and Pete Mozejewski. Mozejewski waited in the car while Porubcan got out to see if he could assist Balcerzak and Gabrish. The paramedics determined that their services were not needed and left.

Two other women were also there that night, but they did not come forward until two weeks after all the accusations against the officers had been reported extensively in the media. The women, a mother and her daughter, were what cops call "wannabes," or people who listen to police scanners and follow cops on their assignments.

The two wannabes followed Gabrish and Balcerzak to the assignment and witnessed the entire scene from about a half-block away. They felt the officers did nothing inappropriate and corroborated the cops' stories that the women who had called 911 in the first place acted belligerently toward the officers.

Dahmer told police the boy was his houseguest and that he had had a little too much to drink and was apparently acting crazy, as Dahmer said he always did when he drank. Konerak, propped up against the squad car, remained incoherent, unable to give police a statement. Dahmer produced his own picture identification, and the officers were satisfied that this was a "domestic situation" that probably did not require police intervention.

Dahmer explained that the two men were friends and that Konerak, whom he identified as John Hmung, was nineteen.

In later photographs, as well as the photo of Konerak posing in his bikini briefs, he appeared to be at least nineteen years old. Police were later angry when the media continued to run Konerak's eighth-grade graduation photo, showing a boy with a wide, cherubic smile. When more recent photos were released, the boy appeared to be much older than fourteen.

Just to be sure the intoxicated man was indeed a houseguest of Dahmer's, the three officers—Gabrish, Balcerzak, and Porubcan—escorted Dahmer and Konerak to Dahmer's apartment. Police on the scene did not run a check on Dahmer's record because they had no reason to believe he was giving them a false name or that a crime had been committed. There was no other indication that anything was amiss.

Once inside the apartment, the officers saw that Konerak's clothing was neatly draped over the arm of the sofa and that the place appeared well-kept. Konerak sat on the sofa by himself as the officers continued to talk to Dahmer. The boy gave no indication that he wished to leave; he did not try to run away when the three police officers were there and able to assist him or when the officers were leaving. Police later speculated that the boy did not want his family to know how he earned money and was afraid of the police. Dahmer also showed the officers the photos of Konerak in the black bikini briefs to prove they knew each other. There was no evidence of any child pornography.

Hidden from view in the bedroom was the body of Dahmer's latest victim, Tony Hughes, whose three-day-old, decomposing corpse was laid out on the bed.

One cop told me later there was a stench, but it did not smell like a dead body. "It smelled like somebody took a dump in there," he said. Defecating in one's apartment is not a crime, nor is it sufficient basis for a search warrant.

Dahmer later confessed that when police left the apartment, he strangled Konerak and then had sex with the boy's corpse. He took more photographs, dismembered the body, and kept his unpainted skull. The boy was identified through dental records.

After leaving the apartment, Balcerzak and Gabrish went downstairs to their car and saw that all the witnesses were gone.

"The [original 911] call was anonymous, so there was no place to go to follow up," Gabrish said. "We didn't seek witnesses door-to-door because we didn't feel there had been a crime."

In the squad car, Balcerzak got on the police radio at 2:22 A.M. and told the dispatcher, "The intoxicated Asian naked male [laughter heard in the background] was returned to sober boyfriend [more laughter] and we're ten-eight." The term *ten-eight* is a radio code used by the Milwaukee police to let the dispatcher know they are available to take another assignment.

A few minutes later, the dispatcher sent Balcerzak and Gabrish to a battery complaint. Balcerzak got on the air and said, "Ten-four. It'll be a minute, my partner's gonna get deloused at the station [laughter in the background]."

It was only one word, but that word would be examined and reexamined in the months to come: *deloused*. Police rules forbid inappropriate transmissions on the radio, but I shudder to think what people would hear if someone tape recorded an office or newsroom over the course of an eight-hour day.

The literal meaning of *delouse*, according to Webster, is "to get rid of lice." For cops, delousing meant going back to the police station, washing up, and applying a disinfectant spray after riding around in the squad car for a while and dealing with people inside fetid homes and on dirty streets. There have been times when squad cars have been sent to be exterminated of cockroaches or even fleas.

One of the first ride-alongs I did with the police, a cop told me never to stand still in the rundown inner-city houses because if I was stationary, it was easy for little critters like cockroaches and lice to crawl up the insides of my pants legs. Because cops routinely came in close contact with unsanitary conditions, it was not unusual for them to disinfect, or delouse, themselves several times a night. Glove compartments in all squad cars were equipped with a liquid bactericide to splash on their hands. It was all in a day's work to arrest intravenous drug users and prostitutes known to bite cops or to sit with a lost child who was infested with head lice. Being a cop emblematized the old cliché, "It's a dirty job, but somebody's got to do it."

With only two hours clocked in that night, Balcerzak and Gabrish had responded to eight calls, including domestic violence complaints, men with guns, and reports of gunshots fired in the street. They handled a total of fourteen assignments during their shift.

When they returned to the station about an hour later, Gabrish went to the restroom to wash up while Balcerzak was called to the phone. Glenda Cleveland wanted to know what had happened when the police were on 25th Street.

When the transcripts of Cleveland's calls were published, their contents would bury the officers. Her pleas for Balcerzak to listen to her that Konerak was just a boy turned public sentiment away from the police as fast as the Watergate tapes turned it from Richard Nixon.

CLEVELAND: Yeah, uh, what happened? I mean, my daughter and my niece, ah, witnessed what was going on. Was anything done about the situation? Do you need their names or . . .

BALCERZAK: No, I don't need that . . .

CLEVELAND: You don't?

BALCERZAK: Nope. It's an intoxicated boyfriend of another boyfriend.

CLEVELAND: We, how old was this child?

BALCERZAK: It wasn't a child. It was an adult.

CLEVELAND: Are you sure?

BALCERZAK: Yep.

Legally, as Cleveland was not one of the parties involved in the incident, Balcerzak did not even have to speak to her. He tried to assure her that the officers' decision was correct.

BALCERZAK: Ma'am, I can't make it any more clear. It's all taken care of. He's with his boyfriend and in his boyfriend's apartment, where he's got his belongings also . . . And that's where it's released . . . I'm going to explain to you it's all taken care of. It's as positive as I can be . . . I can't do anything about somebody's sexual preferences in life.

Cleveland continued to plead for several more minutes that Konerak appeared to her to be a child, but Balcerzak assured her that all the information the police were able to gather at the scene indicated that Konerak was an adult.

To compound an already bad situation for the police, Cleveland told me she called them back two days after the incident, after reading a newspaper article about the Sinthasomphone family's distress over their son's disappearance. She told the police she believed he was the same boy she saw with Dahmer two nights earlier. She pleaded with them to come to her apartment and take the three women's statements.

"They told me they were investigating a murder and didn't have anyone to send," Glenda Cleveland told me. "They said they would send somebody when they had a chance." They never did.

Cleveland tried another tack. On June 3, she called the local Federal Bureau of Investigation office. She read the news article over the phone and explained that Konerak was still missing after being in police custody and that the Milwaukee police would not listen to her. The FBI assured her they would investigate the matter, but in the seven weeks until Jeffrey Dahmer was arrested, Glenda Cleveland never heard back from the FBI. Local FBI officials said they checked to see if they had jurisdiction in the case—if there was reason to believe Konerak was taken across state lines. "A full investigation was not instituted," FBI officials told reporters.

On Tuesday, July 23, Glenda Cleveland read the Jeffrey Dahmer story in the paper and discovered that the man with whom she had seen the boy two months earlier might have murdered several people in his apartment. Cleveland again called the police.

"I said to them, 'Now, are you going to come here and take our statements?' "

When the story broke, the already racially polarized city was up in arms and tension grew. I could walk down the streets and feel it. In just a few days the public would hear the tapes of the officers conversing with the dispatcher, complete with background laughter, as well as the recording of Balcerzak's telephone conversation with Cleveland. Cleveland's pleading on behalf of Konerak touched everyone who heard it.

A number of veteran officers admitted to me reluctantly that, while cops try not to second-guess each other's decisions on the street, Cleveland's pleading might have prodded them to go back just to be sure. Others told me they would not have left any incoherent person but would have sent them for detoxification at the county hospital.

The black community groups alleged that had Dahmer not been white, he would have been run through the police computer for a record check and then promptly arrested.

A Laotian community spokesman said that had Konerak been a disoriented white boy, the police would have protected him better and sought to get him help that night.

And gay community activists said that police did not want to deal with homosexuals, period. They alleged that homophobia was rampant in the Milwaukee Police Department and that kept homosexuals—who are tax-paying, law-abiding citizens—from receiving the police service to which they were entitled.

With growing community pressure on him, Milwaukee police chief Philip Arreola, in an unprecedented move, suspended the three officers on July 26, 1991, before an investigation into their actions. The officers were relieved of their guns and badges and suspended with pay. Usually in grave situations, such as when an officer shot a suspect or was involved in an incident encompassing great bodily harm, the cop was given three days' mandatory administrative leave. When he returned to work, he might be placed on limited duty, meaning he would be taken off the street and assigned to a station answering phones or shuffling papers. For Balcerzak, Gabrish, and Porubcan, suspension before an internal investigation was tantamount to branding the three guilty.

On August 2, 1991, Milwaukee County District Attorney E. Michael McCann requested that Wisconsin Attorney General James E. Doyle review the conduct of the officers to determine whether he should bring criminal charges against them. In a report issued on August 28, less than a month later, Doyle found no charges were warranted.

"In each of the many situations that the officers were assigned to handle, they repeatedly exercised discretion and judgment," Doyle said. "While in hindsight, we wish that the officers had handled the encounter with Dahmer differently, we are firm in our belief that they cannot be criminally prosecuted for their actions."

They could not be charged with failure to report child abuse because they did not know Konerak was only fourteen. Numerous witnesses told investigators from the Attorney General's office that the boy appeared to be anywhere from sixteen to twenty years old.

By state statute, when a police officer is called upon to exercise discretion or judgment, he cannot be prosecuted for the manner in which he does so.

Nor could the officers be charged with misconduct in public office, because there was no evidence of any intent to obtain a dishonest advantage for themselves or anyone else during the May 27 incident. There was also no evidence that they had falsified the memo books in which they jotted information from the scene or the reports they wrote on the events of that night.

The state Attorney General also decided that the officers' failure to discover Hughes's body in the next room did not constitute misconduct in public office. Dahmer permitted the officers to enter the living room but did not offer them a tour of the entire apartment. If the officers did not suspect that any criminal activity had occurred, there was no need to ask for Dahmer's consent to view the entire apartment.

The Attorney General also found there was no basis for a criminal charge against the officers because they failed to do a record check on Dahmer that would have revealed his previous conviction for sexual assault. No law imposed a duty on an officer to make a criminal record check in every situation. It was a discretionary matter.

The situation did not fall under the classification of "domestic abuse," because Dahmer and Konerak were not residing together, and it could not be proven beyond a reasonable doubt that the officers had reasonable grounds to believe that Dahmer had committed a crime against Konerak.

As for failing to render aid to an injured person, there was conflicting evidence as to Konerak's physical appearance during the incident. Accounts differed on whether the boy was bleeding, specifically from the buttocks, as some claimed. Dahmer later told police he had not had anal intercourse with the boy before he killed him. Most witnesses interviewed said they noticed the boy's scraped knee. There was no evidence that the officers were confronted with a medical emergency.

Attorney General Doyle did question the manner in which the officers conducted their on-the-street investigation and said had they interviewed the civilian eyewitnesses, they might have scrutinized Dahmer's story more closely. He decided their handling of the case might have been questionable, but it was not criminal.

The officers were afforded private face-to-face meetings with Chief Arreola, but Balcerzak and Gabrish felt the Chief already had his mind made up before they met. "Every time I attempted to answer questions, I was cut short or interrupted by him," Gabrish said.

After hearing that the Attorney General believed the officers had not acted criminally, many of us in the media thought Chief Arreola would at least discipline them with some time off without pay. We were therefore shocked when the Chief of Police went on live television September 6, 1991, and announced that he had fired Balcerzak and Gabrish. Porubcan's firing was held in abeyance for one year, pending satisfactory monthly reports from his commanding officer.

When he announced his decision, Arreola said there were no names of witnesses in the officers' memo books or any information pertaining to the assignment; they failed to help an incapacitated person; they did not call for a supervisor; and they ignored Glenda Cleveland's impassioned pleas.

Their careers were over.

As a police reporter, I have covered police funerals and encouraged their spouses to confide in me. I was on a first-name basis with most of the department, including the command staff. I had always been professional, yet friendly, with the officers I dealt with because I was so eager to find out what made them tick and how they coped with their jobs. I have always wanted to know a lot about cops because to me, they were a most fascinating breed.

It should surprise no one that I chose a cop to spend my life with. A friend once asked me why I didn't find myself a doctor or a lawyer; I answered that in my line of work, I was bound to fall in love with a cop or a criminal. I am pleased it was the former.

I know a lot of good cops. And I know some bad ones. They are extremely cliquish, and they not only stick together on the job but in their private lives as well. Because of a residency requirement mandating that Milwaukee police officers and firefighters live within the city limits, most lived in an area on the southwest side of Milwaukee nicknamed "Municipal Meadows," where the crime rate was the lowest. They tended to socialize with one another, and I would venture to say that most wives or girlfriends became bored when their spouses or dates got together and rehashed the previous night's assignments. I usually hung around the cops when I heard them talking about their jobs, excited rather than bored with their stories.

But I have often disagreed with them. I am still troubled that a person who was uncommunicative and shaky physically was not tended to, sent for detoxification, or taken to a hospital.

As I learned about the family of victim Richard Guerrero, I also came to know John and Paula Balcerzak. John Balcerzak, thirty-four, was a six-year veteran cop whose work drew special notice, including nineteen merit arrests. He won attention in 1989 when he guided eight people out of a burning building. He was in the middle of arresting a shooting suspect when a fire erupted at a nearby house, so he handcuffed the suspect to a tree, then helped the evacuees. He had dark hair and brown eyes that glowed beneath thick black eyebrows. He also sported what I call the "requisite police mustache," the growth that, by department regulations, could not extend beyond the corners of the mouth. I don't know why, but almost all of them wear mustaches.

Balcerzak's next-door neighbor said of him, "He's extremely

conscientious people, and he's a great family man. He loved his job, and his whole family is going through hell because of the way they prejudged him."

Balcerzak and his wife Paula tried desperately to insulate their two small daughters—one still in diapers, the other in elementary school—from the furor erupting outside their home. Reporters swarmed the house and rang their phone off the hook. At the same time protesters carried signs condemning them in front of the Third District police station where Balcerzak had worked.

The officers were not identified in the media until the *Milwaukee Journal* came forward with their names and records. At the time, one editor said that the three cops had been cardboard characters long enough and that the community should know them as people. It was then that Balcerzak told me he canceled his subscription and Gabrish stopped reading the paper.

Throughout the entire process, the two maintained that they acted correctly on the night of May 27.

"I believe I was as good a cop as I have ever been on that night," Balcerzak said. "Dahmer was a straightforward, calm, convincing person who voluntarily came forward with information with no hint of any stress and no hint that he didn't want us to continue with our investigation."

Gabrish resented the characterizations of himself and his partner as racists. "We've been made out to be some sort of uncaring twosome, some sort of monsters," he said. "We chose to work in the inner city because we wanted to help where we thought it was needed most."

Gabrish, twenty-eight, was single and had been an officer for six years. He was tall and handsome with sandy brown hair that he parted down the middle and feathered back from his face. Before joining the department he had worked for a year as a police aide, someone who performs clerical duties. He also had nineteen merit arrests.

The third officer, Rick Porubcan, was twenty-five and married at the time of the incident. He had been an officer since February 1990 and had just finished his probationary period when he ran into Jeffrey Dahmer. He was a computer whiz who helped set up a software program for the Gold and Silver

Unit, which checked pawnshops for stolen items. Porubcan declined all interviews and never publicly discussed what happened that night.

None of the officers involved spoke easily about the death of Konerak Sinthasomphone, and none had taken it lightly.

I had seen John Balcerzak in early July 1991 at the annual police department summer picnic. He was settled into a lawn chair, bouncing his little daughter on his lap, surrounded by his friends, laughing and full of life. When I saw him next, I tried to interview him about being fired from the department. The only constant from the picnic scene was his friends, the cops who always stuck together. I believe that intense sympathy was mustered among the officers for Balcerzak and Gabrish because every cop realized that he could have been the one who made the wrong decision and ended up on the chopping block.

After his firing, Balcerzak lost at least twenty pounds, and his face was thin and pale with sunken cheeks. When I saw him at his home, he was slouched in his favorite brown recliner and brightened only when his little girls bounced into the living room or when he paused to take a phone call from Gabrish. Although reporters are supposed to hold objectivity in the highest regard, I know few who remain impartial all the time. It tore at my heart to watch the pain on Balcerzak's face as he talked about what had happened.

Balcerzak gave one interview to a Milwaukee television station, on the recommendation of his attorney, and looked as uncomfortable, as he later confided, as he felt. A principled man, Balcerzak refused to accept any deal to return to the department that included an admission of guilt. He wondered out loud where all the people he had helped over the last six years had gone. He was incredulous that people called him and his partner racists.

Balcerzak was in Arizona on July 26 when he learned he had been suspended. Paula's father was ill with cancer, and John was pumping gas into the family car at a filling station when he heard the news of the suspensions on the car radio. Balcerzak said later, "It was a very difficult time to be isolated and have no conversation with anyone from the department and without any way to respond to the things that were being said."

In the months to come, I would see Paula Balcerzak at every community rally held in support of the police. She usually sported a custom-made T-shirt that read SUPPORT THE POLICE along with a little blue ribbon that became a requisite accoutrement for police wives. Paula transferred her personal anguish at her husband's plight into an angry but productive fight to get the public to support the police and understand why they should.

Paula not only coped with her father's terminal illness but also supported her husband emotionally and kept her family together. I thought she could give me her secret. Paula just smiled and squeezed my arm: "I have no idea, Annie. I just don't know any other way except to deal with it one day at a time."

Joe Gabrish may have had a more difficult time because, as a single man, he did not have the constant support of a live-in family and children to fill his thoughts. He took his suspension and subsequent firing very hard, but at least a parade of friends frequently appeared at his home.

Early Tuesday, July 23, 1991, when he learned Dahmer had been arrested, Gabrish had gone immediately to his supervisor to tell him that he and other officers had had contact with Dahmer back in May.

Gabrish was watching the television game show "Jeopardy!" when the local newscaster interrupted and announced his suspension. He commented later, "It was upsetting and scary to be sitting in my living room and find out that you're suspended, especially after I had come forward to a commander with information that we'd been there."

Laurie Eggert, the Milwaukee Police Association's attorney, represented both Gabrish and Balcerzak. Porubcan retained his own counsel. Eggert described the way the officers relived the event every day:

"There's always second-guessing. Nobody could go through what these officers went through without rethinking it and wondering if there was something they could've done to save this boy's life," she said. "What you vest in a police officer is the authority to make decisions, and he has to live with the decisions he makes."

Chief Arreola saw things differently. "Since police officers are public servants entrusted with great powers and responsibilities, they must be held to the highest standards of accountability," he said.

Arreola was the first cop from outside the Milwaukee Police Department to become its Chief, something that most of the rank and file resented from the start. The cops believe that their Chief should be someone who had worked his way through the ranks in Milwaukee. They feel that the Chief must be aware, from firsthand experience, what the problems in the department are and how they can best be solved.

Arreola is tall, olive-skinned, and very athletic, as evidenced by his Class A racquetball rating at a local health club. In the two years I had covered Philip Arreola since his arrival in Milwaukee, I never saw the smile leave his face. Some said his mouth was just shaped that way, kind of like the Joker's in *Batman*. Arreola always seemed to be smiling inappropriately; he even smiled when announcing some dire news. That, too, made him ripe for attack. But no one could argue that he was dead serious when he made his decisions.

No love was lost between the press and Arreola, who broke precedent with his policies of not releasing information to the media. We had enjoyed a rather liberal information policy with the former police chief, Robert Ziarnik. Arreola was also very distant when spoken to; his manner was extremely stiff during interviews, although, in all fairness, one commander who thought quite highly of the Chief said, "He has to warm up to you." Somehow, I couldn't see the day when I would have a warm conversation with Philip Arreola. True, cops and reporters were natural enemies, but this adversarial relationship the Milwaukee media had with Arreola severely hampered our news-gathering efforts.

As a result of the Jeffrey Dahmer case, Arreola's name was constantly in the headlines, on national television, and on some pretty uncomplimentary T-shirts and buttons that read DUMP

ARREOLA, complete with the Chief's picture encircled in red with a slash across his face, like the international "No" symbol.

Additional fallout from the case came when the Milwaukee Police Association, the police officers' union, released survey results showing that as of August 6, 1991, a month before Balcerzak and Gabrish were fired, an overwhelming 93 percent of the police officers questioned had "no confidence" in their Chief.

Philip Arreola was police union president Bradley DeBraska's favorite target. DeBraska was a favorite with the press because he always had a comment and he could be counted on for controversy. And we could call him at home at all hours.

"When something goes wrong, this Chief immediately suggests that the officers are guilty and you must prove your innocence," DeBraska said. "It's a complete reversal of due process."

Balcerzak agreed that his treatment throughout the incident gave him cause to wonder. "I would like to be a police officer," he said. "That's what I chose for my career. Whether I would be able to be an effective officer after what I've gone through during this entire ordeal, that's a question that I would have to answer if I was given that opportunity."

The families of the victims, probation officer Donna Chester, Judge William Gardner, all wished they or their loved ones hadn't believed Jeffrey Dahmer. John Balcerzak and Joe Gabrish were no different.

People, especially we in the media, forget cops are human beings with families and souls and very strong feelings about their jobs. The burden of what they do weighs heavily on them, just as we feel the impact of our stories.

But they are not allowed to make mistakes.

9

Out of Control

June 30–July 22, 1991

Jeffrey Dahmer had eluded the authorities again. He would quickly push aside the May encounter with police and go on about the business of murder.

Probation officer Donna Chester's log notes hinted at problems with her client but did not necessarily suggest a killer. On June 10, she wrote that Dahmer continued to deny any sexual involvement or drinking. He had been attending an AODA—Alcohol and Other Drug Abuse Assessments—treatment program, but it appeared he went merely to fulfill his obligation to the court.

Dahmer visited Chicago on June 30, the day of that city's Gay Pride parade. Dahmer frequently traveled the ninety miles south to Chicago because it offered new, young faces.

Several large nightclubs on Halsted Street cater to thousands of gays. Jeffrey McCourt, editor of the *Windy City Times*, a gay weekly newspaper, said the size of Chicago's gay population would allow a person to move through gay bars without being recognized. "We have seventy-six gay bars down here versus your eight in Milwaukee," McCourt said. "Dahmer had access and anonymity in Chicago that he wouldn't have had in Milwaukee."

Matt Turner, a twenty-year-old black man, also known as Donald Montrell, was a Chicagoan. He met Dahmer after the parade at a Chicago bus station. Turner accepted Dahmer's offer of money to pose nude and watch videos at Dahmer's Milwaukee apartment. The two went to Milwaukee on a Greyhound bus and then went to Dahmer's apartment, where Turner sipped a drugged drink. Dahmer used the leather strap to strangle Turner and then dismembered him, saving his head in the freezer in a plastic bag and putting the body in the big blue barrel in his bedroom. Dahmer identified Turner from a photograph supplied by the Chicago Police Department.

Turner, a runaway, had most recently left his home in Flint, Michigan, and fled to Chicago, where he ended up in the Teen Living Program, a halfway house for runaway young men. People there described Turner as troubled but promising, because he was bright and articulate. Like some of Dahmer's other victims, Turner was interested in being a model, which made an offer of being photographed even more attractive. Matt Turner's stepfather, who watched Turner head off to the parade, was the last person to see him alive.

Rosa Fletcher, Turner's natural mother, was shocked when she heard about the death of her only child. "You always thought about something happening to other people's kids, but you never think about it until it happens to your own child," she told reporters.

The Turner family filed a $4.5 million lawsuit against the Milwaukee Police Department, claiming that Turner would still be alive if the officers had acted correctly on May 27, 1991. Turner's stepfather, Wadell Fletcher, said he was "all for it" if the lawsuit could be some sort of atonement for his stepson.

Less than a week after he had killed Turner, Dahmer returned to Chicago, this time to Carol's Speakeasy, a gay dance club. Jeremiah Weinberger, a twenty-three-year-old native of Puerto Rico, was a regular at the club. He was last seen there on July 5, 1991. According to Dahmer's confession, Weinberger's death deviated a bit from the others because he spent the night with Dahmer and was the only one to wake up the next morning.

At Carol's Speakeasy, Dahmer offered Weinberger money to come with him to Milwaukee to pose and watch videos. After riding a Greyhound bus to Milwaukee, the two arrived at Dahmer's apartment, where Weinberger stayed for two days before Dahmer killed him. The first day, Dahmer confessed, they had oral sex, and on the second day Weinberger unknowingly set off old feelings of abandonment when he told Dahmer he wanted to leave. Dahmer felt forced to return to his ritual.

Dahmer gave him a drink with medication in it and strangled Weinberger with his bare hands after the man passed out. Dahmer took photos while he dismembered his victim and put Weinberger's head in the freezer and his body in the blue barrel. Dahmer identified him from a photograph; dental records confirmed it was Weinberger.

One of Weinberger's friends was with him the night he disappeared with his new acquaintance. When Weinberger asked if he should go with Dahmer to Milwaukee, the friend told Weinberger that Dahmer "seemed all right." Later he said, "Who's to say what a serial killer looks like?"

After Weinberger's disappearance, friends distributed posters with pictures of him in the bars, asking for any information on Weinberger's whereabouts. One was even posted in Milwaukee's Club 219. But Jeremiah Weinberger was not the only one missing, and word began to spread in the bars that people were disappearing.

While Chicago's gay community buzzed, Dahmer continued to talk with his probation officer, Donna Chester, about how dismal his life was. On July 8, 1991, Dahmer told her he was coming close to being fired from his job due to being late and absent. He said losing his employment would be a good reason to commit suicide. Chester also indicated he was getting bored with discussion of his sexual problems. She warned him that problems could occur if he did not pay attention to those issues.

Dahmer had a much bigger problem. He was completely out of control.

Tired of the bars, or maybe just because the opportunity presented itself, Dahmer went to the streets near his home to find his next victim. On July 12, he met Oliver Lacy, twenty-three, on 27th Street, just around the corner from his apartment, and invited this black man to his house to pose for photos. Lacy told Dahmer he was on his way to his cousin's home.

Dahmer told police that once in his apartment, the two disrobed and gave each other body rubs. When Lacy fell asleep from a drugged drink, Dahmer strangled him and then had anal sex with the corpse. Dahmer dismembered the body, placing Lacy's head in the refrigerator in a box and keeping his heart in the freezer, "to eat later." Lacy's head would be discovered ten days later when Officer Rolf Mueller opened the refrigerator.

Oliver Lacy, the youngest of Catherine Lacy's three sons, had moved to Milwaukee from Chicago about four months earlier. Lacy was engaged to Rose Colon, the mother of his two-year-old son, Emmanuel Lacy. Colon was hospitalized with medical problems after hearing of Lacy's death.

His family became concerned on July 12, when he failed to return from his job at a janitorial and cleaning service. His mother alerted police July 13.

Catherine Lacy had gone to the apartment building along with the other curiosity seekers for some kind of clue concerning the whereabouts of her son. She had been reading the stories about Jeffrey Dahmer's crimes, and had a dull ache in her gut. "I felt something was wrong, because my son would call me," she said.

Her answer came from a police detective who came to her home.

I was embarrassed to be a reporter at Catherine Lacy's Milwaukee home on July 24, one among scores of television cameras and reporters camped out in front of her home. "The first victim to be identified" story was a big one, and we were all there to get our piece of it. We weren't alone, though, because as the news began to spread, cars crept by to look at the house where "a Dahmer victim" lived. Minutes before we arrived, Catherine Lacy had returned from identifying a photo of her son's severed head at the Medical Examiner's office.

Catherine Lacy was a soft-spoken woman who told us she understood why we were all there. She invited about a dozen of us into her home. I watched television cameramen jockey for position around the easy chair in which she sat with her granddaughter on her lap, shoving microphones and tape recorders toward her face. In their zeal to be the closest, the throng tumbled framed photographs to the floor, nicked wooden furniture, and left dirty smudges on her glass-topped coffee table. One photographer stood atop a wood table, leaving a muddy residue when he dismounted.

A proud mother, Catherine Lacy displayed a number of photographs of her son as she was blinded by the flash of strobe lights from still cameras and the bright television lights. She told us, "I don't know how the person lured my son. Unless it was a person he knew. Or it had to be more than one person, because Oliver is not the type you can put your hands on."

Because she talked with reporters from all the media at the same time, the race was on when she finished. The television people ran to get the story on the air, and print reporters like myself dashed for phones, hastily composing our stories in our heads to make our deadlines.

Later I discussed the day's events with Tom Held, the police reporter at the *Milwaukee Sentinel*, and we agreed the whole affair was shameless. But we also agreed that no one there could or wanted to return to the newsroom without the "Dahmer's first victim identified" story. Compassion for the Lacy family would not be considered an acceptable excuse.

Jeffrey Dahmer's world was crumbling. After spending the day and much of the evening with his grandmother, who had been hospitalized, Dahmer reported to work late on July 14, 1991, and was fired from Ambrosia Chocolate for chronic lateness and absenteeism. He told Chester that he had been drinking beer since being fired. She wrote in her log that she ordered him into the office on July 16 "to discuss his relapse." Chester noted that she would try to contact the factory's union representative to see if they could help Dahmer get his job back. Dahmer told Chester he was reluctant to see her because he had not bathed or shaved for the past three days (ever since he had killed Oliver Lacy).

Dahmer called Chester on July 17 and said he had fallen asleep and was unable to come in the previous day, his usual excuse for missing one of their appointments. He showed up on July 18 unshaven, wearing dirty clothes, and continually yawning during his meeting with Chester. He was distraught over his pending eviction from the Oxford Apartments for non-payment of rent. She gave him the name of emergency housing set up by the Salvation Army in case he was evicted. Chester also emphasized that he had to get a job, and she told him things were not as bad as they appeared.

Dahmer knew better.

It was the last time Donna Chester saw Jeffrey Dahmer until she picked up a newspaper four days later. He left her office and committed his last murder the next day.

On July 19, while riding a city bus, Dahmer spied Joseph Bradehoft, a twenty-five-year-old white man, of Milwaukee, waiting for a bus on Wisconsin Avenue near the Marquette University campus. Dahmer saw a six-pack of beer under Bradehoft's arm, got off the bus, and approached him, using a tried-and-true offer of money to pose for photographs and to watch videos.

Bradehoft returned to the apartment with Dahmer, where the two had oral sex. After Bradehoft drank a drugged drink, Dahmer strangled him while he slept and dismembered the corpse. He put his head in the freezer, with the heads of Turner and Weinberger, and stuffed his body in the same blue fifty-seven-gallon barrel in which the bodies of Lacy, Weinberger, and Turner were decomposing. Bradehoft was identified through his driver's license, which Dahmer kept.

Bradehoft was married and had three children, ages two, three, and seven. He was from Minnesota but was visiting his brother Donald, in Milwaukee, to look for a job. Donald was the last person to see his brother alive, when Joseph left the apartment for a job interview on July 19.

Joseph Bradehoft had a history of violence, including an arrest for domestic assault when he struck his girlfriend (whom he eventually married) in 1987. According to the police report, Bradehoft came home drunk, threatened and punched her, grabbed a butcher knife, and left the house threatening to slash the tires of her car.

In less than three weeks, Dahmer had killed four men. He would try one more time.

On July 22, 1991, Jeffrey Dahmer met thirty-two-year-old Tracy Edwards near the Grand Avenue Mall and made him the same offer he made the others: money in exchange for photographs at his apartment. According to Dahmer, Edwards accepted, and the two were off to Dahmer's apartment for a photo session.

Edwards told a different story. Edwards said he was with friends at the mall when Dahmer approached and invited them to a party at his apartment. Dahmer even said his girlfriend would be there. Edwards had seen Dahmer walking in the neighborhood, so he felt Dahmer wasn't a total stranger. He claimed there was no mention of homosexual activity. "He seemed like a regular guy," Edwards remembered.

Edwards said his friends never showed up at the apartment because Dahmer had given them a different address. When the two were in the bedroom, where the movie *The Exorcist* was running on the VCR, Dahmer slapped a handcuff on Edwards and pulled a knife from under the bed, pressing it to Edwards's chest. Edwards added that Dahmer pulled a skull out of a file cabinet and began rubbing it, telling Edwards how he would stay with him, too. Luckily, Edwards punched Dahmer and kicked him in the chest and was able to flee. Tracy Edwards spent five hours in hell and lived to tell about it when seventeen others had died.

When he spoke with reporters the next day, Edwards effusively praised the officers who arrested Dahmer. But soon afterward, he appeared on the TV talk show "Geraldo" with his attorney to announce that he was suing the City of Milwaukee because, he claimed, the officers taunted him and made him go back up to the apartment alone. He said he "always tries to obey the laws," so he went back up to the apartment as the police told him to, but when he saw Dahmer again he just couldn't stay. Edwards claimed he eventually convinced the officers to accompany him to the apartment. Watching the show, I was amazed that Edwards would return to the apartment where he knew he had so narrowly escaped death.

Mueller and Rauth were upset and surprised by Edwards's allegations. Cops who saw Edwards, still wearing the handcuff on his wrist, at the police station shortly after Dahmer's arrest heard Edwards loudly thank the police for being there and for "rescuing" him.

I can't say whether I believed Tracy Edwards's story of what happened in the apartment, but I can say that when I met him a few days after Dahmer's arrest, he was soft-spoken and appeared genuinely frightened. I'm sure he has spent a lot of time since then thanking God and reevaluating his life. But I had been in that apartment, too, in fact, just an hour or so after Edwards left it, and what I saw there differed from what he told the nation in the weeks following Dahmer's arrest. What really happened in the apartment only Edwards and Dahmer know. I did not see alarms on the windows and doors, nor did I observe the dozen locks on the door that Edwards described.

Tracy Edwards appeared on national talk shows and told his story to supermarket tabloids around the world for as much as a thousand dollars a story. Many people read those stories and watched Tracy Edwards tell his tale, including a couple of law enforcement officials from Tupelo, Mississippi.

According to Tupelo Deputy Police Chief Jerry Crocker, Edwards's publicity blitz caught the eye of some Tupelo detectives. "Hey," they said to each other, "we took this guy to the grand jury in November. What's he doing in Milwaukee?" He had been indicted by a Tupelo grand jury in November 1990 for sexual battery in the alleged rape of a fourteen-year-old girl (he had originally been charged with capital rape, which carries the death penalty in Mississippi). He left Mississippi in the fall of 1990, while free on bond, and moved to Milwaukee in June 1991.

On August 8, 1991, about two weeks after his escape from Jeffrey Dahmer, Tracy Edwards was charged in Milwaukee County Circuit Court with being a fugitive from justice in Mississippi. Today he is in Mississippi awaiting trial on the rape charges.

The killing was over. All told, Jeffrey Dahmer had killed ten blacks, three white men, a Laotian boy, a Native American, and two Hispanics. The remains of eleven victims were found in his Milwaukee apartment.

Four families whose loved ones were killed after the May 27 incident, including the Sinthasomphones, filed multimillion-dollar lawsuits against the City of Milwaukee and the three police officers who had contact with Konerak on May 27.

While the community mourned those killed by Jeffrey Dahmer, one Milwaukee police lieutenant observed that while some murder victims were innocent, others were not. Lt. Kenneth Meuler was a veteran homicide investigator. His observations might seem callous, but Meuler believed that in many cases of criminal homicide, the victim is often a major contributor to the criminal act.

"This idea of victim involvement is contrary to the public's popular impression that criminals are distinct from their innocent victims," Meuler wrote in his master's thesis, entitled "The Characteristics and Behavior of Homicide Victims: A Case Study of Milwaukee, Wisconsin." He wrote the thesis in August 1990, a year before the Jeffrey Dahmer case broke, but his insight had direct applications.

Meuler identified four types of victims:

Innocent non-participating victims: People who did what they could, within reason, to avoid being victims. Other than possibly being in the wrong place at the wrong time, these victims did nothing to attract their assailants or contribute to the offense. Neither their life-style nor their actions immediately preceding their death attracted the killer or provoked the killer's actions.

Innocent facilitating victims: Law-abiding people who made it

easier for the killer because of their general carelessness, negligence, or unnecessary risk-taking. This type of victim provided some opportunity or incentive for the offender to act.

Criminal facilitating victims: People whose death was the direct
result of being involved in some criminal activity.

Criminal precipitating victims: People who were the first aggressor, so that the offender was physically threatened or
harmed in some way.

All of Jeffrey Dahmer's victims facilitated him in some way,
which is not to say that they deserved to die, but rather that
their life-styles and unnecessary risk-taking contributed to their
deaths. That many of Dahmer's victims had arrest records was
also a characteristic of a victim who was instrumental in his own
demise.

This book is the first to publish any of the victims' criminal
records (see Appendix B). After all seventeen victims had been
identified, I went to my editors at the *Journal* to inform them
I had tracked down all of their arrest records. No one else had
this information, and I argued that the records went directly to
the commonality of the people Dahmer chose and the kinds of
people likely to have been attracted to him. These data would
help us answer the questions of how he went unnoticed and
what his victims had in common.

The editors refused. Subsequently they discussed the issue
on the editorial page and explained their decision not to write
on the subject: "the families have suffered enough." Besides,
the editor in chief wrote, most of the arrests were of a petty
nature.

Some of the victims of those crimes would disagree. Many of
Dahmer's victims had put people in the hospital; they had stolen, rifled through other people's homes, and some had even
raped. Despite our zeal to get every angle on the story, I was
troubled that this information was glossed over.

Our concern for the victims' families did not keep editors
from sending reporters to camp on those families' doorsteps
until someone came out and talked, hoping to placate us
enough so we would go away. Nor did it keep editors from
running banner headlines such as BODY PARTS LITTER

APARTMENT in the same size type they used for Scud missile attacks in Iraq.

Many of Dahmer's victims went to a stranger's apartment because they wanted to make a few bucks by taking off their clothes and posing nude. The youths who left gay bars with men they didn't know were leading lives full of risks and, in the end, were killed as a result of their own negligence and recklessness. They were looking for nameless, faceless sex.

"This case is not indicative of gays any more than Ted Bundy is indicative of straights," said Terry Boughner, publisher of the *Wisconsin Light*, a biweekly newspaper for the gay community. Promiscuity is not indigenous to the gay community; plenty of heterosexuals cruise the straight bars and leave with a different partner every night.

Meuler used an analogy of crime prevention to explain his reasoning about victims whose behavior made it more likely that they would become a victim of a crime. "We tell people if you use better security in your home, you stand a better chance of not being victimized. If you don't get involved with drugs or with people who are criminals, then you are less likely to get into trouble."

In November 1991, WISN-TV, a local Milwaukee television station, ran a week-long series entitled "Flirting With Danger," an examination of Milwaukee's gay community and how many gay promiscuous practices had *not* been curtailed since the Jeffrey Dahmer case. Boughner commented that while it was easy for the straight community to condemn gay bars and what happened there, there was nowhere else in Milwaukee for young, gay males to meet others like them. The bars were where Jeffrey Dahmer chose most of his victims. Young men sat or leaned up against the bar while others walked past and stared at them—cruising. Returning a look can be consent, averting the head, a rebuttal.

Boughner declared, "If we had a community center and the mechanisms to run it, it wouldn't end the bar scene or prevent a Jeffrey Dahmer from striking, but it would help. The black, Irish, Jewish communities have had institutions and methods to take care of their members. The gay and lesbian community does not."

Boughner suggested that I spend some nights at the bars where Dahmer hung out, to watch and learn. I talked with bartenders and club owners about their most notorious patron. I learned that wherever he went, Dahmer sat at the bar and drank many screwdrivers, but he never spoke to the bartenders, nor did he tip them. He was always the aggressor with the men he met, usually very pretty men, almost boyish, willowy, and effeminate; "stereotypically gay," one bartender told me. Dahmer was a loner who spoke to no one until he spotted someone he wanted, and he tended to shun anyone who tried to cruise him or pick him up. It had to be his decision.

Boughner explained that young men still experimenting with their homosexuality and not known to family and friends as homosexuals were the perfect prey for Jeffrey Dahmer. Their life-styles—nights spent cruising the bars—contributed to their downfall.

"That is a dark side of our lives," he continued. "Many young people get themselves involved in terrible things in those places. But where are they going to learn how to date? Where are they supposed to learn to socialize? They were lonely, they'd been thrown out, scared and pitiful in many ways. They're made-to-order to be preyed upon by someone like Dahmer."

Milwaukee, because it is so close to Chicago, often attracts transients to the gay community. Boughner believes that is one reason Jeffrey Dahmer operated unnoticed for so long.

"Just because you see somebody for a while and then you don't doesn't mean that some horror has happened to them," he said. "There is always a social focus in any community, and for the gay community in Milwaukee, you either go to the bars or there's no social focus."

Jeffrey Dahmer had hungered for affection, and looked for it in the bars, but he never had any idea how to get it so it would last. Relationships in the bars were transitory, and he couldn't bear to be left.

For a while after the Dahmer story broke, numerous patrons at the gay hot spots told me people just weren't going home with anybody. "If the moralists wanted abstinence, they got it," Boughner said.

But when the furor quieted down, gay life returned to the way it was, with young smooth-skinned boys prowling the bus stops outside the gay night spots and men inside looking for love and acceptance, but just for a night. They still stand out there at those bus stops, and some find what they're looking for. It's too late for the ones who found Jeffrey Dahmer.

10

A Human Jigsaw Puzzle

July 23–August 16, 1991

The physical remains of eleven lives were transported to the Milwaukee County Medical Examiner's office. After the atrocities were revealed, one of the most pressing questions was: Who were the victims?

Milwaukee County Medical Examiner Jeffrey Jentzen called in a team of experts to assist in the identifications: three pathologists who worked for Jentzen, a forensic dentist, and a forensic anthropologist. Early on, when Jeffrey Dahmer's attorney Gerald Boyle said his client was cooperating fully with the police, people had the impression that Dahmer was giving the police the names of his victims. In fact, he couldn't, because in most cases, he never asked them who they were or he simply could not recall.

He did remember precisely where he had scattered the bones

Jeffrey Dahmer's senior picture from Revere High School in Ohio.
Shortly after he graduated in June 1978, he killed his first
victim, Steven Hicks, a hitchhiker Dahmer picked up near his Bath, Ohio,
home. Dahmer confessed he did not kill again until 1987.
(Photo courtesy of WISN-TV, Milwaukee)

In early 1982, Jeffrey moved into his grandmother's West Allis home.
Catherine Dahmer allowed her grandson his own private entrance on
the left side of the house. The door led to the basement, where he
made his home and where he killed four males. The house is now for sale.
(Photo courtesy of Robert Enters)

When he moved to Milwaukee, Dahmer discovered the area where the
gay bars were located and used this street as his hunting ground.
The Phoenix Bar, in the foreground, the C'est La Vie behind it, and
Club 219 just beyond the C'est La Vie, were his favorites.
(Photo courtesy of Robert Enters)

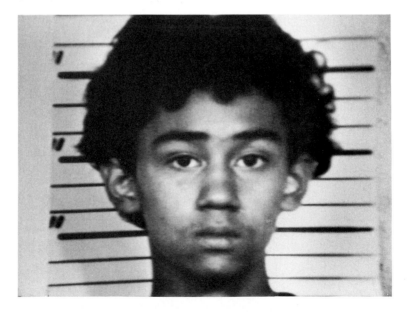

The bus stop in front of the Phoenix is where Dahmer met fourteen-year-old
Jamie Doxtator (bottom), whom he killed in January 1988. Young men
often hung out at the bus stop so they could pick up bar patrons on their way out.
(Photo courtesy of WISN-TV, Milwaukee)

The front and back views of the Oxford Apartments in Milwaukee, where Dahmer killed twelve males. Neighbors said he always brought his guests in through the back door.
(Photos courtesy of Robert Enters)

Glenda Cleveland, the woman whose empassioned pleas to police to convince them Konerak Sinthasomphone was a minor were ignored.
(Photo courtesy of WISN-TV, Milwaukee)

Konerak Sinthasomphone, the fourteen-year-old victim who was with Jeffrey Dahmer on May 27, 1991, when police were called to the apartment building to investigate a report of a naked man running down the alley.
(Photo courtesy of WISN-TV, Milwaukee)

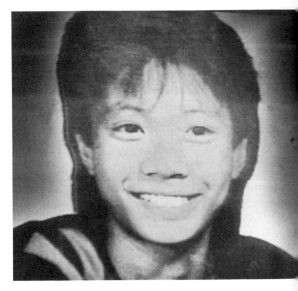

Oliver Lacy, the first victim to be identified, disappeared July 15, 1991. Police Officer Rolf Mueller opened Dahmer's refrigerator and discovered Lacy's head inside.
(Photo courtesy of WISN-TV, Milwaukee)

Police sealed the door to Dahmer's apartment, but people still came just to touch the door or to stare at it. Family members of victims walked up to it, saying that they wanted to retrace their loved ones' last steps.

(Photo courtesy of WISN-TV, Milwaukee)

A hazardous waste removal worker hauls the blue barrel that contained several torsos in a chemical bath. Dahmer kept the barrel in a corner of his bedroom.

Fury over the Dahmer case was not limited to officials, as he became a target for graffiti artists. This one was done by members of the Vice Lords gang. (Photo courtesy of Robert Enters)

Left to right: Milwaukee County District Attorney E. Michael McCann, County Medical Examiner Jeffrey Jentzen, and Police Chief Philip Arreola gave several press conferences as victims were identified.

Left to right: Wisconsin Attorney General Jim Doyle, Mayor John O. Noquist and State Representative Gwen Moore answered the public's questions during a press conference in front of a local church.
(Photos courtesy of WISN-TV, Milwaukee)

Left to right: Robert Kleismet, president, International Union of
Police Associations, AFL-CIO; Bradley DeBraska, president,
Milwaukee Police Association; Ken Murray, attorney for the
Milwaukee Police Association. DeBraska announced the
Association's overwhelming vote of "no confidence" in Arreola
at a press conference. (Photo courtesy of WISN-TV, Milwaukee)

(Photo courtesy of WISN-TV, Milwaukee)

lice Chief Philip Arreola
nounces his decision to
spend Officers
hn Balcerzak, Joe Gabrish,
d Richard Porubcan for returning
nerak Sinthasomphone to Dahmer
. May 27, 1991.

Jeffrey Dahmer during his three co[u]
appearances: (left) His initial
one on August 6, 1991.

(right, middle) At his preliminary hearing
on August 22, 1991, with his attorney
Gerald Boyle.

(right, bottom) At his
arraignment on September 10,
1991, when he pleaded not guilty
by reason of mental disease or defect.
The average-looking man attracted
scores of people who wanted to get
an up-close look at a serial killer.
(Photos courtesy of WISN-TV, Milwaukee)

of Steven Hicks, his first victim, and many of the exact dates when he killed seventeen people, along with details about each murder. But it took old-fashioned police work to identify them.

In the CIB—Criminal Investigation Bureau—investigators were overwhelmed by the case. Never in its history had the Milwaukee Police Department investigated a serial murder. Milwaukee's top cops were challenged and quite proud of themselves when other jurisdictions commended them on their work. Just because Jeffrey Dahmer had confessed did not mean the police had nothing to do.

In the days following the discovery, thirty to forty detectives were investigating the case, running down leads and trying to reconstruct the sixteen local murders.

Coincidences began to emerge when police received inquiries from different states where mutilation murders remained unsolved. In several cases, Jeffrey Dahmer had been in the state at the time of the murder.

A Fresno, California, man, Patrick L. VanZant, failed to return home on May 4, 1990, two months after Dahmer was released from the House of Correction and at about the same time Dahmer was reported to have been visiting his mother in Fresno. A human foot believed to be VanZant's was discovered about four months before Dahmer was arrested.

Florida police tried to link Dahmer to little Adam Walsh, who was murdered while Dahmer was living there; they have since ruled him out as a suspect. And police remain baffled by the mutilation murders of several women during the time Dahmer was stationed in Germany; his bunk mates told inquiring reporters that Dahmer would disappear for entire weekends and be secretive about where he had gone.

As leads came in from all over the country, mounting concern in the CIB over leaks to the press prompted the creation of what the cops called "the Dahmer Room." Only personnel directly involved in the investigation of the Dahmer murders were allowed access to the room, which contained all pertinent information on the case.

A giant chalkboard listed the names of the sixteen Milwaukee victims. Police were trying to create a visual method to track identification of the victims when they had a brainstorm.

Every time a body part was scientifically named by the medical examiner, investigators became frustrated trying to identify the victim. While consulting the encyclopedia one day for the location of a particular part, they were inspired to make eleven photocopies of the book's anatomical chart, one for each skull recovered from the apartment. They tacked the eleven charts on the walls of the Dahmer Room, circled the parts on each picture that had been found and identified as that particular victim, and then attached the police photograph of that body part.

At the same time, cops in the CIB fielded hundreds of phone calls from across the country from people who had heard about Jeffrey Dahmer and wanted to give them information in hopes of finding a missing relative. Because of increasing speculation that Jeffrey Dahmer had possibly traversed the country and committed mutilation murders everywhere he went, Dahmer issued a statement through his attorney, Gerald Boyle.

"I have told the police everything I have done relative to these homicides," Dahmer said. "I have not committed any such crimes anywhere in the world other than this state, except I have admitted an incident in Ohio. I have been totally cooperative, and I would have admitted other crimes if I did them. I did not. Hopefully this will put rumors to rest."

For the reporters, it did not. We called cities where Dahmer had traveled, lived, and been stationed in with the Army, asking them for their more notable missing-persons cases. The newsroom was ensnared in chaos as we took calls from concerned relatives of people who had disappeared from California to Germany, and we pursued famous missing-persons cases, looking for a link to Jeffrey Dahmer.

The job of identification proved less chaotic for the forensic professionals assigned to the case than it was for the police. The process was less difficult than it could have been because the bones from the apartment were whole, not shattered or broken up. Of the eleven skulls, three were boiled and painted, four were boiled and unpainted, and four had most of the flesh and hair on them because they had been kept in the refrigerator or the freezer. There were also four skeletons in the fifty-seven-gallon blue barrel in Dahmer's bedroom, and another skeleton, which had been bleached, was hung in the closet.

The pathologists in Jentzen's office began by examining the body parts, taking X-rays, and preparing for the dental examinations. Pathologists dealt with the soft-tissue and toxicology screens from the remains. Later, other forensic professionals examined the teeth and bones.

A number of techniques were used in the identification process. Generally, fingerprinting is the most reliable form of identification, but after a certain amount of time, the skin of the fingers decomposes, along with the rest of the body. As a result, dental records were used to identify the majority of the remains found at the apartment.

The forensic dentist, Dr. L. Thomas Johnson, a Marquette University School of Dentistry professor, had been involved in forensic dentistry for thirty years. He made X-rays and compared them to dental records of missing people whose families supplied them to police. Johnson also examined and compared gum tissue, but teeth are more useful because they resist destruction by fire and the elements. Teeth are so useful in the process that the National Crime Information Center maintains a national bank of dental records to help identify missing people.

Because all but two (Jamie Doxtator and Konerak Sinthasomphone) of Jeffrey Dahmer's seventeen victims were adults, tracking down their identities was difficult. Because police are reluctant to take information about a missing adult, no missing-persons reports existed for many of them. Without evidence of foul play, the police can do little in such cases. Because of a manpower shortage, the department did not have enough officers to follow up on all the cases. When an adult decides to live elsewhere, he (or she) can do what he wants.

Oliver Lacy and Joseph Bradehoft were named first because their identification papers were found in the apartment. Their next of kin were contacted, and their families confirmed the two men's identities from photographs.

Jentzen had brought in Dr. Kenneth Bennett, a professor of biological anthropology at the University of Wisconsin. Bennett was a forensic anthropologist who provided information based on bone characteristics. In his thirty-year career, he has dealt with about a hundred dismemberment cases.

"Forensic anthropologists get the stuff nobody else can do anything with," Bennett told me. He tried not to hear much about the Dahmer case after he began working on the identifications, which was difficult, so as not to prejudice himself into finding certain particulars.

When Bennett walked up to the autopsy table, he first tried to determine the victim's ethnic affiliation: white, black, or Asian. He had seen several thousand skulls in his career and could determine the race by the architecture of the head. Next, he took measurements of the skeletons to determine how tall the person was and measured the bones. He could determine the stature within an accuracy of one to two inches. Determining the sex of the victims was aided when there was a full pelvis. Without one, measurements of the leg and wrist bones or certain characteristics of the head were taken; Bennett said he could be 85- to 90-percent confident in determining the sex.

The collection of whole bones proved easier for Bennett to deal with than fragments. Bones were not blueprints like fingerprints, but pieces could be matched to the body based on size as well as matching several pieces with each other. Sometimes there were markings on the bones from a past wound or surgical procedure; sometimes one end of a bone was discovered to fit in the socket of another.

For Bennett, the Dahmer case was unusual only in that so many people were involved, although he also admitted that it was strange that the skulls were painted and had holes in the tops, the latter, it was later discovered, evidence of Dahmer's crude efforts at lobotomy. To him, the work at hand was limited to the single bone or set of bones on his autopsy table. "My work on the Dahmer case pretty much confirmed what the forensic dentist found," Bennett said.

Because Bennett was expected to testify at Dahmer's trial, he rarely tried to learn how each man was murdered. "Most of the time, I don't have any idea about how it all turns out," he said. "I rarely ever follow up. I supply whatever data I can, and the police take it from there."

For eleven of the families of Dahmer's victims, the identification of their loved one's remains meant that his death was real. There could be no more doubt. They still had to endure the media and the trial, but at least eleven people's families got a body back.

But for the families of Jamie Doxtator, Richard Guerrero, Eddie Smith, Steven Toumi, and David Thomas, the crime was worse than murder because they may never truly know their loved one's fate. None of their remains was recovered; Dahmer confessed that he kept nothing of them. He identified four sufficiently for the District Attorney to charge him with their murders. They could not prove he killed Toumi. Dahmer remembered a peculiar scar on Doxtator's chest, Guerrero's picture in the paper, the turbanlike wrap that Smith wore on his head. Thomas was identified by his family through a photograph Dahmer took of him during dismemberment. Dahmer also gave police dates of death for each of his victims that corresponded to the time when each was reported missing.

Mark Jelacic, who runs the Jelacic Funeral Home in Milwaukee, said that the families who could not see the remains would have a difficult time with the grieving process. "Seeing is believing," he told me. "Before a person can experience grief, there has to be a loss. They have to see a loss. If you have to confront the fact that someone has been lost but you cannot see the remains, there will always be questions in a person's mind."

Jelacic has dealt with a number of dismemberment cases, usually from auto accidents. He said as morbid as it may seem, it is important that people see something, even if only a bone or a fragment, especially in cases when the loss is unexpected, like murder.

"When the loss is unexpected," Jelacic said, "people are always holding out hope. They may have those feelings for years. When they finally see some part of the person, that's when people really start to leave the denial phase of death behind them."

He remembered the case of a Milwaukee woman who had lost her husband in the Korean War but received no remains until many years later. Jelacic took the bones and arranged them with the man's clothing. The widow was grateful for the display. After years of hearing from the government that her husband had been killed in action, she could finally lay him to rest in her mind. "Now, I know where he is," she told Jelacic when she thanked him.

As for the families in the Dahmer case who received no remains, Jelacic said they might have been comforted because they could share their grief with others. "It's an old cliché, but grief shared is grief resolved," he said.

For the family of Steven Hicks, Dahmer's first victim thirteen years earlier, his identification would be a painstaking process. Several days after the discovery in Milwaukee, two dozen technicians and police swarmed over Dahmer's boyhood home in Bath, Ohio, following a map Dahmer had drawn that pinpointed where he had shattered Hicks's remains. In addition to police personnel, Bath officials called in several anthropologists from nearby Kent State University and one from the Smithsonian Institution in Washington, D.C.

Investigators cordoned off the 1.7-acre lot and used a grid system to divide the property for a detailed search. They also used metal detectors to look for any discarded teeth that might have had fillings. Authorities searched a dirt-floor crawl space under the house where Dahmer used to play and hide as a youngster, and where as an adult, Dahmer told police, he had buried Hicks's body for a time. They cleared away brush and sifted dirt through screens to detect any bone fragments.

Because what they recovered was thirteen years old, investigators performed DNA tests and tried to match it with a swatch of Hicks's hair which his parents, Martha and Richard Hicks, had saved in a photo album of him as a child. When he disappeared, they set the hair aside, hoping it could help in a genetic test someday to identify their son. Hicks's parents also gave blood samples to help enable DNA testing identify some of the bone fragments.

Then, using a process known as genetic fingerprinting, scientists sandblasted the bone pieces to remove the surface bone and also to minimize the risk of contamination from other sources of DNA. The bone was then pulverized, divided into two samples, and the DNA extracted.

In their search, investigators also used Luminol, a chemical that could illuminate traces of blood, even thirteen-year-old blood, and found hundreds of bone fragments, dried blood on the crawl space dirt floor, and a bloody handprint on the cinderblock wall of the crawl space. They pulled out clumps of rags to test for bloodstains. Police also discovered scars and chips from sledgehammer blows on a slab of rock behind the home. Dahmer had confessed that he had pummeled Hicks's bones with a sledgehammer before scattering them in the woods.

A funeral for Steven Hicks was finally held in October 1991, while two pieces of his skeleton were still at the Smithsonian Institution, where they had been sent for identification.

A statement issued by the Hicks family said, "He had qualities that would make any parent proud. He also had problems not uncommon to youth of the seventies: drinking, smoking, traffic tickets, and the occasional rowdiness of youth. Dahmer's actions have altered our lives forever. As a family, we have spent a great deal of time trying to understand the motivation for such a heinous crime and concluded that some acts are so evil they simply cannot be explained."

Richard Hicks, the boy's father, told the *Akron Beacon Journal*, "Is he [Dahmer] insane? In my opinion, no. He is evil. If I thought killing would bring my son back, I would do it myself." The family finally asked reporters to leave them alone.

At least Martha and Richard Hicks could say good-bye to their son, whose remains were returned to them September 14, 1991.

The family of Steven Toumi, of Ontonagon, Michigan, had no remains to bury. Nor will they see Jeffrey Dahmer prosecuted for their son's murder because Dahmer was unable to identify Toumi sufficiently to be charged in connection with his death. For the Toumi family, there was no justice.

Dahmer told police he wished to assist them in every way possible to positively identify his victims. "If I can restore names to them all," Dahmer said after his arrest, "at least that is something good I can do."

11

"Can I Have Your Autograph?"

We were lured by the lurid.

Not just the media, but everyone—from the cops who investigated Jeffrey Dahmer to the people who purchased anything in print that might hint at some explanation of what had happened.

The Jeffrey Dahmer case left us in the local media reevaluating our policies and prompted many to reevaluate how we do our jobs. It was obvious from the start of the case that the air was ripe for conflict.

Most of the local media honored a police request that Dahmer's police photo be withheld from newscasts and papers on Tuesday, July 23, the morning after his victims were discovered. Officials explained that showing the photo could jeopardize police lineups. One local television station used the photo in a news update early the first day but pulled it later, after receiving a call from the District Attorney's office.

One police investigator, Milwaukee Police Lt. Kenneth Meu-

126

ler, said the use of the photo could prove detrimental. "It could have hurt us. We were trying to hold lineups. The media had no care or regard for our investigation. Their whole thing was to get a story and I thought that was low."

Neither the *Journal* nor the *Sentinel* ran the photo, but both strayed from their policy of withholding a suspect's name until he or she was charged. At three-thirty P.M. the first day, one local television station ran a thirty-minute special on the killings called "Murder Factory." Another station devoted its entire, hour-long newscast to the case, which the news director said they had never done before except for the Persian Gulf war. The murders led "The CBS Evening News" that first day, but ABC and NBC did not mention them at all.

I remember being confused when I discovered the 1988 victim was the brother of Konerak Sinthasomphone, the fourteen-year-old boy police had turned over to Dahmer in May 1991. Could the brother have been a potential victim, too? The coincidence was too incredible to believe. And how many other times had Dahmer had contact with the police?

Reporting on Dahmer's meeting two brothers on separate occasions proved tricky. The paper does not identify the victims of sexual assault, to protect their privacy and because of the stigma stamped on the victim of sex crimes. But by identifying the victim as the brother of the dead Konerak Sinthasomphone, whom the *Journal* had named from the beginning we were essentially identifying the boy who had been assaulted. The newspaper's rules were going to be broken.

Initially, the *Sentinel* identified neither of the boys, citing their wish to protect the brother who was assaulted, but it eventually named Konerak in the paper. Neither paper named the surviving brother. The family eventually held numerous press conferences and did not object to the reporting of the incident.

The media did not build on something that was not there. The public was ravenous for details, and we delivered. At numerous social occasions, I was guided into a corner of the room and asked in whispers to reveal what I did not put in the paper, what the apartment looked like, and was Dahmer really a cannibal. I couldn't get away from the story.

"Oh, my God. How horrible! How awful! Tell me more."
These comments conveyed the mood of the city in the first
couple of weeks.

Reporter Joel McNally wrote a twice-weekly column, "The
Innocent Bystander," in the *Milwaukee Journal*. During the Dahmer case, for only the second time in his thirteen years, the
editors yanked the column before it got into print. (The first
time concerned his satire of a pamphlet explaining that Christian deer hunters need not feel like murderers for enjoying
their sport because they were hunting with the Lord. *Journal*
management told McNally that it would offend too many people.)

McNally's column, an accurate fictional portrayal of the
mood of the city at the time the case broke, follows here, with
his blessing and encouragement:

"The horror! The horror!" the man said. The excitement in his voice was unmistakable.

"Man, you said it," his friend agreed enthusiastically.
"We thought that trial in Racine was horrible. But, that's
just one murder and dismemberment. That's like nothing.
In this case, they say there could be as many as seventeen
bodies."

"I don't even want to talk about it. I don't even want to
hear about it. I don't even want to read every word about
it and watch every minute of it on TV."

"This isn't just 'A Current Affair' or 'Inside Edition'
either. Any trash can get on those shows. We made the
big time with this one. We're talking 'CBS Evening News'
and Larry King.

"Remember how upset the mayor and the police chief
were about *Newsweek* calling us one of the murder capitals
of America. I can hardly wait to see their faces when we're
declared the dismemberment capital."

"Hey," his friend said, as if the idea had just struck him.
"If they keep finding body parts, do you think we could
set the record?"

"Don't get your hopes up. I think they'd have to find a

lot more to catch John Wayne Gacy. The people who keep those stats are pretty strict."

"That doesn't seem fair. There should be special consideration when cannibalism is involved. Who knows how many more disappeared in vats of acid? We should at least get an asterisk in the record books somewhere."

"We're going down in history," the man said. "Don't worry about that. I've heard about Ed Gein all my life. I get tired of all that nostalgia for the good old days. Nothing is ever as good as it was in the old days. Well, they never had anything like this!"

"That's right," his friend said. "Even hardened police officers who've seen all kinds of horrible things say this is absolutely the worst. At first, they thought it was just a domestic dispute among homosexuals. Now, they're calling it homosexual overkill."

"Give me good old normal heterosexuals anytime. They kill people just the right amount."

"You know what really bothered me? It seemed like within minutes all kinds of jokes were floating around. Head jokes. Body part jokes. Refrigerator jokes. That's just so sick."

"Well, you know what that is," the man said. "It's a defense mechanism. The only way some people can bear to think about anything so monstrous is to crack jokes. Something like this is just too horrible for normal human beings to contemplate."

"Man, it sure is." his friend said. "That's what everybody says everywhere I go."

The two were so pumped up they couldn't stop talking about how unspeakable it all was.

McNally was always something of a rebel in his more than two decades in the *Journal* newsroom, and publicly, as well. Active in the newspaper reporters' union, he did not fit the cookie-cutter mold the paper had for its employees, with his long red hair and willingness to criticize management when they deserved it. He took whatever issue the public showed interest in and tried to make people laugh at themselves by satirizing it. He was alternately hated and loved and was universally respected by the local reporters for the way he stuck up for reporters' rights with the management.

"I thought about all the ironies of the Dahmer case and about how people were quite horrified at it all but still wanted to know more," McNally told me. "Management told me that it was too close to the time that all this happened and that we had to be sensitive to the public, yet we ran headlines in huge type on the front page like BODY PARTS LITTER APARTMENT and NIGHTMARE ON 25TH STREET. Much tackier things than my column were in the paper."

McNally was disappointed that the column was pulled, not because he felt it was some violation of the First Amendment, but because he wrote the column in an understated way. Yet it pointed out the ironies, like how disgusting people thought the case was but still wanted to know more of the gory details.

"I think Sig [*Journal* Editor in Chief Sig Gissler] is uncomfortable about satire in general," McNally explained. "They're overly concerned about people complaining about the column and that we're treating the subject too lightly. There was a difference of opinion about what the public would find objectionable."

There was outrage in the newsroom when we heard that McNally's column had been killed. It was an indication that every story would be scrutinized all the way up the editorial ladder. And none of us liked to be censored by newspaper management.

But the guys in the glass offices at the *Journal* were walking on eggshells with this one.

Regarding media sensitivity, others besides McNally cried foul.

The Dahmer story had an immediately obvious racial bent to it because most of the eleven body parts found in the apartment belonged to black men. The media personnel in Milwaukee, as in most cities, were predominantly white, and coverage of Dahmer was initially coordinated by white newsroom managers. Of a reporting staff of about two hundred, only twelve are black.

Eugene Kane, a black columnist and feature writer for the

Milwaukee Journal, felt there was tremendous omission in the early days of the Dahmer coverage with regard to race. Kane wrote about his feelings in an issue of the National Association of Black Journalists newsletter.

Ira J. Hadnot, a black assistant metropolitan editor of the *Journal*, also took issue with the white media's coverage of the case. "Initially, our coverage of the Dahmer murders and the circumstances surrounding the confessed killer missed the perspective of the minority and gay communities," Hadnot said. "I believe this was a substantial oversight. But take a look at the newsroom; it is a microcosm of a community that lacks minority representation in nearly every professional and service area." Kane also faulted television and radio coverage.

"White reporters were so busy covering the discovery of a mass murderer in their midst, any racial issues were an afterthought," Kane said. "But the gay community suffered a particularly offensive slap during the mad rush for scoops and exclusives on the story." Kane was referring to remarks by numerous officials in which they used the term "homosexual overkill" to describe the murders. The black and gay communities vociferously objected to this expression, which linked the separate elements of homosexuality and serial killing, as if one naturally followed the other.

In his article, Kane quoted Mark Rochester, one of the three black reporters assigned to the *Journal*'s metropolitan desk at the time the Dahmer story broke. Rochester noted that two black reporters had pointed out to editors the inappropriateness of the term "homosexual overkill," given no clear indication at that early stage that sexual orientation had anything to do with why those people were murdered.

"I think the black reporters, as a minority group, were much more sensitive than other newsroom staffers to how offensive the term 'homosexual overkill' was to members of the gay community," Rochester said.

Kane told me he hoped the *Journal* newsroom would learn about covering racial issues from the Dahmer case. "In the end, the coverage of Dahmer emphasized why journalism needs to draw from all segments of the community in order to ensure effective coverage of important events," Kane said. "As long as that is not the case, cases like Dahmer will continue to catch the media off-guard."

Terry Boughner, publisher of the *Wisconsin Light*, the newspaper that served the gay community throughout the state, agreed with Kane. "The only person who will ever cover this story and cover it in depth, with the feeling that it needs to be done, is someone who is gay or lesbian, who has spent time in the community, and tries to understand the community," Boughner declared. "There are fine points and nuances of this community and this lifestyle that somebody who has not been a part of it is going to miss completely. That's why the story of how this Jeffrey Dahmer thing has affected the community needs to be told. As far as I'm concerned, it hasn't been told yet."

As I struggled to write more in-depth stories on the case, I contacted Boughner for advice on how to get the story from the gay community. He thought it may very well have been the first time a straight reporter had ever asked him such a question, and he advised me that to cover fully a story that had so profoundly affected the gay community, a simple interview would not do. He told me to go to the gay bars and talk to gays and lesbians about the case. "Act like a writer," Boughner instructed me. He told me to sit at the bar and try to fill myself with what was happening inside; how cruising happened and why. He challenged me to find out what went on in the head of a young man who was alienated from his family and why Jeffrey Dahmer was able to pick up the people he did.

I took Boughner's advice and found an angle to the story that many of my counterparts could not. I was amused to watch the out-of-town media arrive and storm Club 219 to talk to patrons. Boughner leaned over and bet me it was the first time the crew had ever been in a gay bar, and he ventured that a number of the local reporters had met their first gay while pursuing the Jeffrey Dahmer story.

The national media swooped down on Milwaukee as early as the morning my story broke. Even as we searched for new angles, we still watched to see what the national media was doing.

Milwaukee Police Lt. Ken Meuler fielded numerous telephone calls from the press in the first weeks and offered his own analysis of what he saw. "I think the local media were reacting to the national media. If the national media ever come to this city again, I'll act differently," Meuler vowed. "I think when they came charging in here and back-doored us to get information they just burned themselves."

"Back-dooring" is what happens when a reporter can get no information from the person designated to give the details of the case, so the reporter will call a source secretly to get information the official flack will not impart. I have done it, as have most other frustrated reporters. In the Dahmer case, however, cops were so afraid their lines were tapped or that someone would see them even looking in the direction of a reporter, that information was difficult to come by except through official channels. Police department computers had been purged of any information related to Jeffrey Dahmer, and nobody could get at it. You had to know somebody with access to the Dahmer Room to get a jump on anyone else.

"The press could never accept the fact that we would say we're going to have a press conference at ten A.M. and then another one later in the afternoon," Meuler said. "Then the local media would call up and say, 'You know us, can't you give us something ahead of the national media?' I thought that was really unprofessional. Nobody seemed to notice that we were investigating a bunch of murders. If we say we're going to give a press conference at ten A.M., we shouldn't have been deluged with calls between eight A.M. and ten A.M."

I have had many discussions with cops, including Meuler, about my job and why I had to do certain things, but it was always a conversation pursued in vain. When the press conferences occurred at ten A.M., the *Journal* had already put out two editions. Editors ordered us to get whatever was going to be given out at the press conferences ahead of time and told us to explain to the police that since they were going to give it out anyway, why not help out the locals. I believe the concept of newspaper deadlines eternally baffled the police.

Not only was the *Journal* fighting to beat the national media, but we were also engaged in our ongoing battle to scoop the *Milwaukee Sentinel*, the morning paper. One official, who was particularly angry about something the *Journal* had written, vowed to me he would hold his press conferences only on *Sentinel* time, meaning after the *Journal's* deadlines had passed.

The presence of the national media posed some interesting problems for us, because they were celebrities. The idea of accessibility to the *New York Times* was too much to pass up for Stephen Sessions, a twenty-nine-year-old janitor in the building that housed the Milwaukee County District Attorney's office.

Sessions admitted that he photocopied confidential material pertaining to the Dahmer case that he had taken from a desk in the DA's office and arranged to give it to a *New York Times* reporter at a meeting outside a Milwaukee tavern. The *Times* was thus the first news organization with a copy of Dahmer's statements, well before officials were prepared to release the material.

Sessions's attorney, Alvin R. Ugent, said he would argue that his client was talked into it. "This custodian, quite frankly, thought he was performing a public service when he was giving the information to the media," Ugent said. "It was explained to [Sessions] that he had a responsibility to get the information out to the public."

Sessions was fired by the county personnel review board.

The *Journal* ran a statement from D.A. E. Michael McCann saying, "Shame on the *New York Times*. While the extensive media attention given this case is understandable, every professional ought to act responsibly. The public has a right to know, but it also has a right to believe that fair trials will not be thwarted and criminal investigations will not be compromised by overzealous media."

Editors in the newsroom blasted the icon of our profession and decried such action by the *Times*. We reporters laughed as we stood around a colleague's desk discussing the whole matter, and we speculated that the bosses were mad because we hadn't thought of it first.

In addition to the influx of the national media in Milwaukee, the nationally-syndicated talk shows decided to put our city in the limelight. Oprah Winfrey chose as her topic "Are You Raising a Jeffrey Dahmer?," and Phil Donahue assembled a panel of reporters and mothers of murder victims to discuss the case on his show. Geraldo Rivera was not far behind with "Cannibal Killers." *Vanity Fair* magazine stole a ploy from the movie *Silence of the Lambs* and interviewed convicted serial killer Dennis Nilsen, a British civil servant who confessed to killing fifteen men. Nilsen analyzed the Jeffrey Dahmer case and offered his interpretation of why Dahmer did what he did. Hannibal Lecter would have been proud.

The courtroom scenes during Dahmer's appearances were almost laughable. I clawed my way through the crowd like everyone else, pushing to get to the head of the line for the best seat so I could stare at Milwaukee's serial killer for five minutes. Milwaukee County sheriff's deputies learned from Dahmer's initial appearance and ended up with a first-come, first-served policy for his future court dates. I stumbled into the courthouse at five-thirty A.M. for a nine A.M. appearance, but I was not even first in line.

There was also the pool TV and still photographers, a system by which one representative from television and one from the still photographers would be chosen to shoot for everyone. But there was no such pool for print reporters, so it was a free-for-all. We scrunched into hard wooden benches in the courtroom and bumped elbows while furiously taking notes.

Along with the media were the people who attended the proceedings out of curiosity. One woman who came to every appearance had long, greasy brown hair and ripped tennis shoes. We in the press corps nicknamed her "the Ghoul." She buddied up to us, collected our business cards, and tried to find out what sorts of gory particulars had failed to make the papers. It would be insensitive on our part for the families of the victims to see us cracking up over "the Ghoul" while they struggled just to sit in the same room with Jeffrey Dahmer.

I both observed and participated in the sensationalism while attending the Dahmer case. As soon as the story broke about the police having had contact with Dahmer and Konerak Sinthasomphone, *sensitivity* became the buzzword both in the newsroom and at the police stations.

I, along with several other reporters, was amused by the whole idea that we were eagerly decrying the insensitive behavior of police officers who dealt with Dahmer and the fourteen-year-old Laotian boy at the same time that we had insensitivity in our own backyard, or rather, newsroom.

Scores of cops sent me copies of the January 1992 issue of *Milwaukee Magazine*, which reported that a white *Journal* metro reporter, who had covered the Dahmer case, had gone to a Halloween party at another *Journal* reporter's home as Supreme Court Justice Clarence Thomas, complete with blackface. A black editor confronted the reporter in the newsroom and tried to make him understand what blackface represented and how the whole idea made her cry. Black journalists were upset over the insensitivity of a reporter during a period when people's attitudes toward anyone who was not white and heterosexual had become a major issue in Milwaukee.

Cops were livid at accusations of double standards when the piece appeared, and many told me they found it even more difficult to take our allegations of their insensitivity seriously. Newspaper management asked the reporter to write a public mea culpa, a story to appear on the editorial page, rife with tales of enlightenment and apologies for his naïveté.

Funny, that excuse never worked for cops.

And an article in a newsletter for the employees of Journal/ Sentinel, Inc. spoke for itself regarding the sensitivity of the press in the Dahmer case. The story was headlined NEWS OF MASS MURDERS BOOSTS SUMMER SALES, DRAWS ATTENTION TO *JOURNAL* AND *SENTINEL*.

"The Jeffrey Dahmer case, though tragic and sad, was a boon for the Journal/Sentinel, Inc. circulation department. . . . Sales figures soared for the week ending July 28, 1991," the article said.

The media are virtually the only ones who could say that mass murder was good for business.

Until the Dahmer case, the *Journal* was experiencing a steady decline in circulation. The newsletter story touted our sales of thousands of additional papers. And the circulation sales manager for Journal/Sentinel, Inc. boasted in the article, "We sold more total papers that Sunday than we did during the [Persian Gulf] war."

Now there's a statistic we as a city could be proud of.

Not only were we selling papers at a furious rate, but our

local information was in demand worldwide. In the middle of a breaking news story, local reporters were being relied upon to supply other media with information. We did interviews with Irish radio, Canadian television; our quotes appeared in hundreds of newspapers around the world.

We were not the only ones becoming celebrities.

While we chatted with the world press corps, Jeffrey Dahmer was treated to a little celebrity status himself when police approached him for his autograph while pacing in his jail cell.

Officers were assigned to eight-hour shifts as guards for Dahmer. Dahmer would not talk with his guard, saying only, "I've got a lot on my mind." Several officers decided to ask Dahmer to autograph a newpaper with the headlines blaring about death and dismemberment.

"I saw *Silence of the Lambs*, so I knew enough not to give him the whole pen," one officer remembered. "So I took it apart and stuck just the ink cartridge through the bars." When Dahmer asked what he was signing, the officers told him it was just for them. He complied but later told his lawyer.

Most cops keep souvenirs from the job such as pamphlets, certain reports about a bizarre situation, their old uniform shirts—or, maybe, a serial killer's autograph. Officially, however, any unnecessary contact with a prisoner is regarded as inappropriate.

When the newspapers learned about the cops' request for an autograph, they ran cartoons on the subject. The police chief launched an internal investigation and caught two of the guilty officers. Both learned an embarrassing lesson, and the chief mercifully allowed them to keep their jobs. The other officers were never found out.

"It wasn't for financial gain," one officer said. "But my job is more important to me than any souvenir. I'm just thankful I can still do my job after such a stupid mistake."

The whole business about the autograph elicited a chuckle from several reporters, and we secretly admitted to each other that we had thought of doing the same thing: getting Dahmer to scribble his name next to our bylines. But then sanity struck.

There were many moments of insanity during our coverage, especially when we were trying to beat out another reporter for a story. The day I discovered where Tracy Edwards—Dahmer's would-be victim—lived, I sped over to his apartment building. As I pulled my car up to the curb, I spied my police-reporting counterpart from the *Milwaukee Sentinel*, Tom Held, perched on the cement stoop across the street.

We had a good laugh about our both being there when we each thought we had an exclusive. Held later confessed that he had had one of Edwards's neighbors ring him into the locked lobby of the building and, when Edwards did not answer his apartment door, had left, but propped a side door open with a large slab of stone so he could go in and out at will to see if Edwards had returned.

"The pressure on reporters was tremendous," Held said later. "There was internal pressure from myself and the competition that was established among the news media. You're looking at it as the major story of your career."

Finding other reporters to talk to during the coverage was important for my sanity. Held and I talked about burnout from the steady drive to find bits of anything the other guy didn't have. We laughed about his tracking down the cab driver who drove Dahmer home after he had purchased the infamous blue fifty-seven-gallon barrel, and how the taxi driver really had nothing to say.

"I think I'll be a better reporter from all this," Held said. "This reinforced in me that it's very easy to underestimate the impact of something. Even if something doesn't strike you as important at first, there could be a lot of underlying meaning."

Journal reporter Marilyn Marchione, whose reporting from Ohio became the cornerstone for so much of our information in the first days of the case, remembered how she covered the story.

She flew to Ohio on Tuesday, hoping to interview Shari Dahmer, Jeffrey's stepmother. As she pulled into the stepmother's driveway, she saw *Sentinel* reporter Jim Nelson drive up. The two left without a story, however, because no one was home.

The next morning, Marchione read in a Cleveland newspaper that Shari Dahmer had told reporters that the family had found bones and other remains at Catherine Dahmer's West Allis home. Marchione was able to talk with Shari Dahmer by showing her the Cleveland news article. Shari said it was inaccurate. If she wanted to set the record straight, Marchione told her, she should talk to her. Marchione even promised Shari she could listen while she, the reporter, phoned the story in to the paper to make sure it was accurate.

The tactic worked. After forty minutes Marchione won her over, and Shari Dahmer would not talk with any of the other reporters outside the condominium. Marchione spent nearly five hours inside the apartment while Shari alternately talked, cried, and washed her hair in the kitchen sink. At Marchione's request, Shari called her husband Lionel and persuaded him to talk to Marchione over the phone, giving the *Journal* the first interview with Jeffrey Dahmer's father.

"Then came the tough part. I had become a sympathetic ear to someone in a grave crisis," Marchione wrote in a newsroom newsletter account of the interview. "She asked me to throw away my plane ticket and drive with her that night to Milwaukee. I saw it as a chance to cement a relationship with a key member of the Dahmer family. On the other hand, I still had more work to do on the story before leaving Ohio, and the thought occurred to me that the only thing I really knew about her was that she was the stepmother to a likely serial killer.

"I stayed in Ohio. It was a tough decision. I often wonder if I made the right choice."

I'd like to think most of us would try to handle the fragile feelings of everyone involved in the Jeffrey Dahmer case with the same finesse Marilyn Marchione showed with Shari Dahmer. Marchione got the story, but not at the expense of anyone's sensibilities. It was hard not to sound opportunistic when talking with families who were upset over being misquoted somewhere I didn't work, and hard not to try to convince them that if they told me the truth, I could set the record straight.

More often than not, I could not set things right for them. The story was already a runaway train.

Catherine Lacy, mother of Oliver Lacy, the first victim to be identified, probably thought she could somehow help if she spoke with the media. But when she rolled out the red carpet into her living room for the press, reporters and careless cameramen showed their gratitude by stepping on top of her furniture and sending her framed photos shattering to the floor.

Lt. Kenneth Meuler remembered that day and the same scene with each victim subsequently identified. "When the press knew we were on to potential victims, they would camp outside their houses the minute that there was anything close to a confirmation. Boy, they were all over it," Meuler said. "We'd go to the families and tell them their loved one had been identified, and two minutes later it's all over the air, 'Another victim's been identified.' Real cold, if you ask me."

While police were almost at war with the media, we were busy battling each other. About the time the two police officers were fired, I left the *Milwaukee Journal* to report on the Jeffrey Dahmer case for WISN-TV, Channel 12, the ABC affiliate in Milwaukee. I was always under the impression that television reporting would be so much different, but in the Dahmer case, each reporter tried to out-scoop one another.

Television brought Milwaukeeans the Jeffrey Dahmer story live and in color. When a local Baptist minister and his wife went to Dahmer's apartment and performed an exorcism, complete with speaking in tongues and guttural growls as the evil spirits filled them, we watched it all on television. It may have seemed like the ultimate in sensationalism, but it was also a kind of bizarre metaphor of the lengths people went to try and expel the demons of Jeffrey Dahmer.

And, if the truth be told, it was "good TV."

WISN-TV news director Fred D'Ambrosi defended his decision to air the exorcism. "It think it was important to show how far some people were willing to go in this case and how crazy all this stuff was getting. Also, it showed what kinds of emotions were out there in the community."

D'Ambrosi further declared, "I think the media did a good job on the Dahmer case. People who couldn't normally get a voice had a voice because there was so much coverage out there."

Radio even got into the act when Dahmer's neighbors Vernell and Pamela Bass allowed WLS, an all-talk Chicago radio station, to broadcast its morning show from their apartment several days after the murders were discovered across the hall in Dahmer's home.

It seemed everyone wanted to get in on the act, from the two Bath, Ohio, girls who set up a concession stand with coffee, lemonade, and cookies to sell to the throngs of reporters who worked down the road near Dahmer's boyhood house, to some of Dahmer's neighbors who quickly learned they could charge for their interview time.

The job of the local journalists was made especially difficult when the national media showed up and checkbook journalism ran rampant. Television shows like "Inside Edition" and newspapers like the *National Enquirer* had bulging wallets tailor-made for events like this one. I watched as residents were offered rides in limousines; one received five hundred dollars from a supermarket tabloid for his story.

I have always believed that when people are paid for their information, that information should be examined very closely, as should the possibility that their story was tainted by their desire for money. In this case, when money changed hands, some of the residents' stories were considerably embellished from those first interviews they gave me in the back of the building. I believed their comments the first night were the last honest feelings they expressed before all the sensationalism got in the way.

Several days after the story broke, I walked up to a man sitting on the front stoop of the Oxford Apartments whom I had interviewed that first night the discoveries were made. "How are you holding up over here?" I asked, addressing him by his first name. I asked to speak with him again for a piece on how the residents felt about the media onslaught.

"That'll cost you fifty bucks. That's the price now," he said, taking a long drag on a cigarette and squinting at me.

I reminded him that he had talked to me for free the first night, and rather anxiously as we all huddled together watching the horror unfold, so I thought we had a sort of camaraderie going. My face did not appear to be recognizable from the hundreds of reporters he had since spoken with.

He quipped, "That was then. I'm famous now." I can't really

discuss checkbook journalism as a participant because I never worked anywhere with an exceptionally large checkbook.

I decided to try another resident, a woman with whom I had spent a lot of time that first night. I was sure she would remember me. I buzzed her apartment and identified myself through the intercom. She remembered me! She remembered how I tried to comfort her two nights before as she trembled behind her apartment building. I was elated. Surely she would give me a story on how she was coping with the media.

"Oh, hey Annie. I can't talk to no newspapers right now. I'm waitin' for Oprah!"

I surmised she was coping just fine.

There were those who clamored to get into the news. And there were those whose association with the case thrust them unwillingly into the spotlight.

Some of the residents wanted no part of the media, and they gladly took refuge when an anonymous donor treated residents to a night at a hotel so they could escape the unwanted glare of public attention.

"Some people just couldn't take it anymore," said Milwaukee Mayor John O. Norquist. "People deserve a night free of harassment."

When Norquist discovered we knew where the residents were hiding, he pleaded with us not to disclose the location. "The reporter that breaks this story has no soul, because these people need to have some privacy," he said.

The mayor's comments seemed valid to many, especially after some of the stories related to the Dahmer case broke. The thing to remember about the media is that once we give someone a great deal of publicity, that person is fair game for any write-up, no matter how uncomplimentary.

Take Sandra Smith, for example, the eighteen-year-old daughter of Glenda Cleveland, the woman who pleaded with the police to make sure Konerak Sinthasomphone was really an adult. All of the media ran the story of how, in an unrelated incident, Smith had been arrested for beating up a woman the afternoon before seeing Sinthasomphone running from Dahmer. The ticket issued to her said the alleged victim had been accused of making a slur against Cleveland, and the attack apparently was an act of revenge. The victim moved out of the neighborhood because she felt threatened by those involved, said assistant city attorney David Halbrooks. The charges were dismissed because the victim did not appear in court.

Then there was the story of Father Peter Burns, who became a spokesman for the family of Konerak Sinthasomphone. Burns held numerous press conferences and spoke at length about the Sinthasomphone family's tortuous journey to the United States from Laos. He was quoted throughout our coverage beseeching the public for sensitivity toward the boy's family, and Burns talked about how awful it was for tragedy to strike such a young life.

In November 1991, the news broke that Burns was arrested and charged with sexually assaulting two boys at the church rectory. The story led the newscasts and put the Dahmer case back on the front page after nearly three months in the shadows. As of this writing, Burns is awaiting trial.

It took about two weeks after the discovery of body parts in Jeffrey Dahmer's apartment for us to exhaust the nuggets of new material. Fewer and fewer stories on Dahmer appeared in the papers, and he no longer dominated the nightly news.

By the time the furor died down, the media had left countless wounded in their wake while pursuing the story. Unfortunately, at its peak the tidal wave of publicity crested on the frail, eighty-seven-year-old Catherine Dahmer.

On July 24, 1991, the day after the discoveries were made in Jeffrey Dahmer's apartment, Lionel Dahmer tacked up a note on the door of his mother's West Allis home:

"Please do not ring the doorbell or phone. [A Milwaukee reporter] woke us up at 7:30 A.M. after a very hard night of stress and crank calls. Catherine Dahmer cannot endure more harassment. She is 87 years old, just recovering from pneumonia, and had her car damaged in a very recent accident. She really cannot put up with the stress of media people such as yesterday and this morning."

True to form, a reporter called and asked her to comment on the note.

12

Inside a Murdering Mind

An unassuming third-shift worker at the Ambrosia Chocolate Co. in Milwaukee, Jeffrey Dahmer fancied roses, his fish tank, and his laptop computer.

Until July 23, 1991, chances were that no one knew of his very secret desires.

But who would have?

Many people fit the profile of a mass murderer, according to Dr. James Alan Fox, dean of the College of Criminal Justice at Northeastern University in Boston and a nationally recognized expert on mass murder. There are thousands of angry, depressed people out there, and there is no way to tell in that haystack of humanity who is going to be a killer.

Fox, co-author, along with Northeastern University sociologist Jack Levin, of *Mass Murder: America's Growing Menace*, studied serial killers for eleven years. He has testified before Congress on the subject of crime in America. I came to know him while he was working on a new book, *Overkill*, a study of different varieties of serial murder that will include a chapter on Jeffrey Dahmer.

The terms *serial killings*, *mass murder*, and *massacre* are often used interchangeably but in fact refer to distinguishable phenomena. According to Fox, mass murderers typically target people they know and conduct the murders simultaneously. Serial killers kill over a period of time, killing one person at a time and usually using the same method each time. Family massacres are the most common type of mass murder and generally do not attract national publicity. They involve private conflicts in private places, and the victim count usually is modest compared, for example, to the large number of bystanders killed at random in a restaurant shooting.

As I delved into Dahmer's childhood, I believed I would uncover something sinister that would explain how a person could come to commit such acts. For my own peace of mind, I just had to have an explanation. If I discovered that he felt neglected as early as age six, that his mother had abandoned him, and that he was fascinated with dead animals, I could explain why he did it. Fox told me my effort was futile.

"There was nothing we could have done to predict this [tragedy] ahead of time, no matter how bizarre the behavior," Fox explained. "[Dahmer] had an alcohol problem in high school. So do a lot of kids, and they don't all become serial murderers. Most serial murderers do tend to have difficult childhoods, but so do lots of other people. Victims of abuse are just as likely, if not more likely, to grow up and become ruthless businessmen and victimize unsuspecting consumers for pleasure—not just for profit, but because they get pleasure out of other people's pain—as they are to grow up to become serial killers."

Fox believes that some experiences of adolescence and early adulthood are just as critical in determining the fate of someone as their youths, for example, how well he fit in in high school, whether he had lots of friends, what sort of successes he had. It was apparent that Dahmer was devastated when his mother left him and took his little brother with her. But it would take a giant leap to blame Joyce Flint Dahmer or Lionel Dahmer somehow for what happened.

"Ever since Sigmund Freud, we blame everything bad that

kids do on their parents, and that's unfortunate and it doesn't make sense," Fox said. "What we do is scare lots of innocent people who are suffering in their own way for what their kids did. The culprit is Dahmer. Not his father, not his family, not the police."

Fox, who knew many parents of serial murderers, said they go through hell. "In a sense they've lost a child, too, but they don't get lots of sympathy from us," he said. "We should have lots of sympathy for the families of the victims but we obviously have no sympathy for the family of the killer. We think of them as a Dr. Frankenstein who created a monster. We blame them and we hound them."

Hillside Strangler Kenneth Bianchi's mother was hounded out of her Rochester, New York, home by the media, and she still lives in hiding. Yet she never committed the crime; her son did.

"You have psychiatrists who want to theorize that the reason why all these people died is because a child hated his parents and wanted to get back at them indirectly by killing these people," Fox said. "When [Florida killer] Ted Bundy was executed, there was a psychiatrist who said he hated his mother and that's why he killed all the women. We focus too much on the childhood.

"If Dahmer had grown up to become the vice president of a corporation, we would have looked at his background and said that he became a stronger individual because of it."

As I watched the Dahmer case unfold in Milwaukee, I saw our focus shift from the actual killer to a scapegoat for his deeds. As soon as people found out that cops had had contact with Dahmer and his fourteen-year-old victim, we seemed to push aside the fact that Dahmer was the one who committed the murders. Except for the days when Dahmer appeared in court, the papers and newscasts were filled with tales of police insensitivity and community outrage—but not outrage so much toward Dahmer as toward the police.

In Fox's eleven years of studying serial killers, he told me, Jeffrey Dahmer stood out. "He's different than the usual serial killer. He more fits the stereotype of someone who really is out of control and being controlled by his fantasies," Fox said. "The difference is most serial killers stop once the victim dies. Everything is leading up to that. They tie them up; they like to hear them scream and beg for their lives. It makes the killer feel great, superior, powerful, dominant. He rapes her or him while the victim is alive, and when the person is dead, they take the body somewhere and leave it where it won't be found. That's the typical pattern.

"In Dahmer's case, everything was post-mortem. In a certain way, he was merciful, because he drugged his victims. They didn't have the same sort of terror and horror the victims of other serial killers have had. For Dahmer, all of his 'fun' began after the victims died."

Dahmer did not overpower his victims to get them to come to his home; they returned willingly with him to his apartment. He fed them a drugged drink and strangled them when they were unconscious. The victims probably never knew anything terrible was happening to them. Dahmer confessed that he had had sex with some of the victims before he killed them, but for the most part, his efforts were concentrated on them after they were dead. He had oral or anal sex with the corpses and took elaborate measures to pose their lifeless bodies for photographs, using the camera as a means to enhance his fantasy life. He dismembered the victims, preserved some of their body parts, and disposed of the rest.

It would have been a small comfort to share with the families that at least their loved ones did not appear to have suffered before their deaths. But the families were caught in the horror of what happened to them after they were dead.

We know that Dahmer liked to experiment on drying out animal pelts with his chemistry set as a child. Some psychiatrists believe that torturing small animals stands out as a precursor of cruelty to human beings, and that the torture of dogs and cats is more of an indicator of future violent behavior than that of flies, toads, and turtles. When Dahmer performed his experiments on the pelts of squirrels and raccoons, the majority of people I talked to in Ohio did not think he had killed the animals himself but, rather, had collected road kills.

Based on their research, Fox and Levin assembled a composite profile of a mass murderer:

He is typically a white male in his late twenties or early thirties. In the case of simultaneous mass murder, he kills people he knows with a handgun or rifle; in serial crimes, he murders strangers by beating or strangulation. His specific motivation depends on the circumstances leading up to the crime, but it generally deals directly with either money, expediency, jealousy, or lust.

Rarely is the mass murderer a hardened criminal with a long criminal record, although a spotty history of property crime is common. Mass murder often follows a spell of frustration when a particular event triggers sudden rage; yet, in other cases, the killer is coolly pursuing some goal he cannot otherwise attain.

Finally, though the mass killer often may appear cold and show no remorse, even denying responsibility for his crime, serious mental illness or psychosis is rarely present. In background, in personality, and even in appearance, the mass murderer is "extraordinarily ordinary," Fox said. This may be the key to his extraordinary talent for murder. "After all, who would ever suspect him?" Fox added.

Dahmer did have something in common with other serial killers in that he led a rich fantasy life that focused on having complete control over people and was controlled by it.

Fox continued, "That fantasy life, mixed with hatred, perhaps hatred of himself which is being projected into his victims. If he at all feels uncomfortable about his own sexual orientation, it is very easy to see it projected into these victims and punishing them indirectly to punish himself."

"He hated anyone who was more gay than he. This was his method of punishment. He could be attracted to these people and then feel extremely horrible about it, and he lashes out at them as opposed to himself. So it's a combination of his hatred for these victims, mixed in with some racial hatred, combined with fantasies that do involve this idea of cutting up people."

While most of Dahmer's victims were black—and a great deal was made of that fact by Milwaukee's black community—it was not clear whether he hated blacks enough to target them deliberately. Our only indication of an animosity toward blacks was the various racial slurs that former prisoners at the Milwaukee

County House of Correction and his Army bunk mates remember him uttering.

"Murders instigated by racial hatred are surprisingly rare in a country that has experienced so much racial conflict and violence," Fox said. Interestingly enough, while blacks commit half the homicides in this country (in Milwaukee, 75 percent of the city's 1991 homicides were committed by blacks, who are 40 percent of the population), only one in five mass killers is black, according to Fox.

Fox characterized the serial killer as a "skillful practitioner" because he murders repeatedly without getting caught. In most cases, police do not realize that a number of homicides were the work of one person until the killer is apprehended.

In a bizarre sort of way, Jeffrey Dahmer's crimes seemed very matter-of-fact when discussed clinically with someone like James Fox. But sociology aside, there will always be those who like to bring the explanation down to basics: "He was crazy."

At the January 1992 trial, Dahmer's attorney, Gerald Boyle, used the insanity defense in an unsuccessful effort to keep Dahmer out of prison and locked away in a state mental hospital. On September 10, 1991, at his pretrial hearing, Dahmer pleaded not guilty by reason of mental disease or defect. Under Wisconsin law, a person is not responsible for criminal conduct if at the time of the offense that person was suffering from a mental disease and lacked either the capacity to distinguish right from wrong or to conform his conduct to the law. Therefore, if convicted, Dahmer would be committed to a state mental hospital for no specific term but instead would be held until a judge or jury concluded that he no longer posed a danger to the community.

Criminally insane patients cannot be committed for longer than the maximum prison terms for their crimes, in this case, life. A 1988 *Milwaukee Journal* study of criminally insane patients found that the average confinement was five years for patients committed for first-degree murder. Patients such as Dahmer, who were involved in particularly brutal or highly publicized cases, usually were confined much longer, the study showed.

Although not confined to any sort of treatment facility in the past, Jeffrey Dahmer was under the care of psychiatrists during his probation for assaulting the brother of Konerak Sinthasomphone in 1988. A psychiatric treatment professional who met Dahmer observed, "For some men their only means of expressing things is through sex. Men express their feelings very poorly, according to the common lore. The crimes may reflect anger first—sex is only the medium for that." The doctor said Dahmer disclosed nothing and was very guarded about his formative childhood years.

A psychologist who worked with inmates for the Wisconsin Department of Corrections said Dahmer had an illness that was likely transmitted through heredity, if newspaper reports of Joyce Flint Dahmer's alleged mental illness were true. The psychologist noted that Lionel Dahmer's self-described strict religious leanings could indicate rigidity about other matters, such as sexual morality, and probably had great difficulty accepting his son's sexual preference. "Most parents don't handle it too well when their kids diverge from the norm," the psychologist said.

The psychologist talked about Dahmer's confessions. "There may be some psychological dynamics to his confessions. There could be some relief in being caught. Whatever pain he had is finally over. Or there could be some charge for him for all of this confessing."

He described Dahmer as a formidable liar who used untruths to blanket and protect parts of his life. "Sometimes the man has lied so often that the lie becomes the truth. He tells the lie so often, he starts to believe it himself."

After his conviction for sexual exploitation of a child in 1989, court-appointed psychiatrists prescribed at least two drugs for Dahmer, lorazepam, an antianxiety drug, and doxepin, an antidepressant. He also had an old prescription for Halcion, a drug akin to Valium, which he gave to Konerak Sinthasomphone's brother in 1988. Psychiatrists often prescribe antianxiety drugs, similar to barbiturates, to treat what they regard as major mental disorders. The drugs are intended to chemically control anxiety, nervousness, tension, and sleep disorders. The antidepressants cause frequent effects like drowsiness, lethargy, and difficulty thinking. The drug Halcion has come under fire for allegedly causing aberrant behavior in some of its users.

Several psychiatrists probed Dahmer's mind after his pleas of not guilty and not guilty by reason of mental disease or defect on September 10, 1991. A two-part trial was scheduled: the first phase would determine if Dahmer had committed the killings, and the second would determine if he was insane at the time. Despite his insanity plea and what Boyle called his client's depressed condition, Boyle had already established early on that Dahmer was mentally competent to go to trial and to assist in his own defense.

A number of the families were eager to talk to me after Dahmer made his plea in court in September 1991. They felt the not guilty plea was a disgrace.

"I was mad as hell," said Carolyn Smith, Eddie Smith's sister. "The man's just got it too good. Everywhere I turn it's just like everything's catered for Dahmer, and to have him just turn my life upside down. Well, it's just not right."

Inez Thomas, mother of David Thomas, rejected the claim of insanity. "I think he knew exactly what he was doing and how he was going to do it. There's nothing wrong with Jeffrey Dahmer."

Jeffrey Dahmer's court appearances had the air of a movie premiere. At his initial entrance, cameras clicked incessantly, and we reporters furiously scribbled in our notebooks whenever he uttered anything in response to a question from Milwaukee County Circuit Judge Frank T. Crivello. Dahmer spoke in a monotone, his voice devoid of any inflection.

Many serial killers like the publicity, the idea that they've become famous rather quickly, Fox said. They do lots of interviews, and they glorify and elaborate on what they've done. The preen in court.

"Dahmer does not seem to be the type," he added. "Most serial killers are very much into power and control, and this feeds their ego. Dahmer was more on the shy side and not wanting to be on the cover of *People* magazine."

Many people came to court to see if they could sense any underlying evil in Jeffrey Dahmer by looking at him. I remember being filled with a strange sense of anticipation as I waited in the courtroom to see what a serial killer looked like. I was shocked to see that he looked just like an ordinary fellow. I had thought the pupils of his eyes might do spirals. What he had done was awful, but I could not get over how ordinary he looked. The times I saw him up close, I saw nothing there. He did not appear crazed, like mass murderer Charles Manson, nor did he exude the charm of serial killer Ted Bundy. There was just nothing to him.

His appearance declined in his three subsequent pretrial court appearances, and he looked more disheveled each time I saw him. At his last pretrial court date, he wore a faded orange T-shirt and bright orange cloth pants that flopped over his blue tennis shoes and brown socks. His complexion had turned pallid and he had neglected to shave.

From all my delving into Dahmer's background, I tried to construct my own portrait of him. He was a loner, lost in fantasies from an early age, who did not fit in with his schoolmates and would act the fool for them. He drank to excess and was desperately lonely, abandoned by those who were supposed to love him. His favorite movie was *The Exorcist*, filled with satanism, although it was not clear whether he worshipped the dark forces of evil. He apparently recognized that something was wrong with him because he showed up at a clinic at the Milwaukee County Mental Health Complex, near the end of his string of killings, but left after waiting fifteen minutes.

Some in Milwaukee's gay community told me they believed that Dahmer had not really "come out" publicly and had serious problems accepting his homosexuality.

The only thing in which he had any sense of pride was his job, and when he lost that, he may have lost the last vestige of normality in his life.

He conveyed to probation officer Donna Chester that he generally did not trust people, but when he had to be around his fellow workers, he tried to disappear into his fantasy world whenever possible. That world eventually became much more important than the real world and ultimately took its place.

I wondered if Dahmer would open up to the court-appointed mental health professionals who tried to figure him out. His

motivation became the only part of the Jeffrey Dahmer story I
could not pin down to my satisfaction.

While psychiatrists and psychologists were trying to get into
Jeffrey Dahmer's head to discover his motivations, one man
claimed he already knew what they were.

Writer Brian Masters, author of *Killing for Company*, one of
the most revealing portraits of a serial killer taken from his own
words and psyche, posed the question to serial killer Dennis
Nilsen, a British civil servant who confessed to killing fifteen
men. He asked Nilsen to analyze the Jeffrey Dahmer case and
offer his interpretation from his own unique perspective (in a
sort of journalistic *Silence of the Lambs*) for *Vanity Fair* magazine,
in September 1991. I met Masters at the Dahmer trial and asked
him what he learned from Nilsen.

Nilsen, convicted in 1983, had gone to pubs and gay bars,
taken people home with him, and killed them. He often waited
until they were drunk and sleepy, then strangled them with a
tie. Nilsen would wash the body, sit it in a chair, and often
masturbate next to it, according to Masters.

Nilsen kept the bodies under the floorboards, and when the
space became too crowded and the stench overpowering, he
dismembered the bodies and burned them in the back yard.
When he lived in an apartment, he sliced the bodies into two-
inch strips and flushed them down the toilet, then boiled the
heads. Nilsen was caught when the plumbing backed up.

Masters went to interview Nilsen at Her Majesty's Prison Al-
bany on the Isle of Wight in August 1991. Nilsen told Masters
that he objected to the portrayal of Hannibal Lecter in the
movie *Silence of the Lambs* as a potent figure. "My offenses arose
from a feeling of inadequacy, not potency. I never had any
power in my life," Nilsen told Masters. The same was said to
be true of Dahmer, who, from all accounts, including that of
Nilsen, was as appalled by his own acts as we were.

There were further striking similarities between the two men.
Nilsen also had a run-in with the police when he picked up a
boy who later fell asleep in his apartment and woke to find
himself being photographed, Masters reported.

"I had always held within me a fear of emotional rejection

and failure," Nilsen said. "Nobody ever really got close to me. There was never a place for me in the scheme of things. My inner emotions could not be expressed, and this led me to the alternative of a retrograde and deepening imagination. I had become a living fantasy on a theme in dark endless dirges.

"The loner has to achieve fulfillment alone within himself," he added. "All he has are his own extreme acts. He is abnormal and he knows it. Loneliness is a long, unbearable pain. I felt that I had achieved nothing of importance or of help to anyone in my entire life. I would think that if I drank myself to death my body would not be discovered until at least a week after (or longer). There was no one I felt I could call upon for real help. I was in daily contact with so many people, but quite alone in myself."

The similarities to Dahmer were uncanny. When I read the *Vanity Fair* article, it was as if I was allowed to peek into what Dahmer must have felt. When journalists spend an inordinate amount of time investigating one subject—in my case, Jeffrey Dahmer—we become hungry for any morsel that fills in the blanks. If I could not interview Jeffrey Dahmer myself, I would learn about him from someone like him.

Probation officer Donna Chester's later notes detail Dahmer's feelings that his life had no purpose. His anguish over his deeds came through often in statements from Gerald Boyle and indicated that he knew he was in trouble before he was caught. Nilsen, too, was afraid of abandonment, and neither had been touched much as children. Shari Dahmer told reporters that Jeffrey Dahmer could not embrace or touch.

Nilsen explained his fantasy life: "I made another world, and real men would enter it, and they would never really get hurt at all in the vivid, unreal laws of the dream. The need to return to my beautifully, warm, unreal world was such that I was addicted to it, even to the extent of knowing of the risks to human life. The pure primitive man of the dream world killed these men. These people strayed into my innermost secret world and they died there. I'm sure of this.

"I was engaged primarily in self-destruction. I was killing myself only, but it was always the bystander who died," Nilsen told Masters.

As to Dahmer's necrophilia, Masters speculated, after his interview with Nilsen, that Dahmer may have "wanted to gaze upon, and touch, a body which did not resist his attentions. It is like the game of 'playing dead,' a pretense children used to explore and touch one another's bodies without fear of reprimand.

"I remember being thrilled that I had full control and ownership of this beautiful body," Nilsen said of one of his victims. "I was fascinated by the mystery of death. I whispered to him because I believed he was still really in there."

Dr. James Fox added to the picture. "Basically, these people feel they are victims. The motive is simply revenge, but it's revenge at people who had nothing to do with them."

Shortly after his confession, Dennis Nilsen wrote a passage that evidenced the remorse that he, and probably Jeffrey Dahmer, felt: "The details of this case are horrible, dark, and alien. I must be a really terrible, horrific man. I am damned and damned and damned. How in heaven's name could I have done any of it?"

Jeffrey would likely not have stopped. He got good at what he was doing, and he developed a taste for it.

"What was in his head?" is a question that continues to haunt me.

Professionals have speculated that the public really does not want to know what makes a Jeffrey Dahmer tick.

13

Gaping Wounds

The Aftermath in Milwaukee

Jeffrey Dahmer is a prime and frightening example of what can happen when someone repeatedly falls through the cracks of the system. He evaded police, judges, the probation system, and his father's and neighbors' observations of his behavior. But what we want to know is if he slipped through because the police did not care or because the city's agencies handling Dahmer's case were overworked.

Milwaukee was plenty angry about it, as evidenced by an extensive search by citizens and law enforcement professionals for explanations and scapegoats. Blame was laid everywhere. People said the police didn't do their jobs, the probation officer failed to detect a killer, and Jeffrey Dahmer's neighbors ignored their civic duty by not reporting the stench in their building to officials. Leaders from the gay, Laotian, and black communities cited prejudice on the part of the police department and intolerance by the white heterosexual population. Others held Jeffrey Dahmer's parents accountable for the deaths, by doing nothing when the signs of a troubled young man were easily apparent. In turn, the union representing the Milwaukee police expressed its outrage over the public criticism of police, not only by citizens but by public officials.

A *Milwaukee Journal* editorial running the day after the discoveries asked, "Might [Dahmer] have gotten the help he needed if mental illness were not still so stigmatized?" The editorial board wrote that "society needs better ways of detecting people prone to violent behavior, of treating them, and of keeping incorrigibles locked up. If society invested more in crime prevention, maybe the old question 'Do you know where your children are?' would not now have such a chilling ring."

Should the judge have realized that Jeffrey Dahmer would never get treatment for his alcohol and sexual problems? Would a visit by the probation officer to Dahmer's apartment have revealed his secret? In hindsight, it's easy to criticize. But Dahmer was not that different from others on probation—he did have a job and he showed up for his appointments. His success in luring seventeen victims to his apartment shows Dahmer's skill at deception. Still. . . the fact that Jeffrey Dahmer killed seventeen people while he was supposedly under court supervision leaves an undeniable feeling that the system didn't work.

The National Coalition on Television Violence as well as D.A. E. Michael McCann cited TV violence, slasher-type movies, and pornography as contributing factors in the Dahmer case, explaining that young people see murderous movie characters like Freddy Krueger from *Nightmare on Elm Street* as heroes. The Coalition also said that some movies were how-tos for budding killers.

Professor James Fox rebutted the charge. "I share their concern about this type of entertainment. But I don't want to let the implication rest that Jeffrey Dahmers are created by the

media. These people do enjoy violent pornography. Serial killers are not created by what they see. When they're not doing
it themselves, they like watching it. That's the kind of entertainment they like because it's already in their personality. We
should have more controls over the kind of media we have for
the general population, but to blame serial murder on television
and the movies is a little extreme."

In Milwaukee, some community leaders used the Dahmer
murders to flex their political muscle, while others were genuinely enraged. Walter Farrell, professor of educational policy
and community studies at the University of Wisconsin–Milwaukee and a prominent member of the black community, had been meeting with black leaders since the serial
murder case began. "People are venting their frustration," Farrell said. "They're very angry. It seems clear that Dahmer was
not targeting just males and homosexuals, but black males or
males of color."

Farrell agreed with members of the minority community that
police tend to treat them differently than members of the white
community. "I do think that had Konerak been white and Dahmer been of color, there would have been a different response.
I do believe that would have occurred and would have elicited
some different instincts from the officers who were called to
the scene."

Queen Hyler, an activist and cofounder of the Milwaukee
chapter of the anticrime group Stop the Violence, said, "We've
lost so many, and I've attended so many funerals of black men.
We've been fighting a battle to save our young black males, and
to have this kind of horror, it's just unthinkable."

Outrage over police conduct in the case prompted State Representative Gwen Moore to hold a press conference in front of
Dahmer's apartment building and to ask the Attorney General's
office to "step in and investigate the training policy and procedures which may have contributed to a diminished police
response to victims in this particular crime. Mothers are suffering, families are suffering, because of the negligence of the
police department."

Criticism of perceived police attitudes toward minorities and
homosexuals grew louder and angrier with the revelation that

officers had had contact with Dahmer and the fourteen-year-old Laotian boy who later became his victim.

Shortly after Dahmer was charged with the murders, Milwaukee Mayor John O. Norquist announced the formation of a citizens' blue ribbon panel to study police community relations. Believing they would not get a fair shake, a group of black leaders formed their own "black ribbon" commission.

Norquist heightened the fury of white police officers by announcing at a press conference in August 1991, that racial insensitivity was a factor when police left the fourteen-year-old Konerak Sinthasomphone with Dahmer. "I understand the rage that exists, especially in the area most devastated by this killer," Norquist said. "The desire to lash out and fix blame is strong, but we must remember, one man killed these victims."

When Milwaukee Police Sergeant Lenard Wells, president of the League of Martin, an organization of black police officers named for Dr. Martin Luther King, Jr., came forward and agreed with Norquist, the police department became a house divided between black and white officers. Wells said racism should have been addressed years before the Dahmer case. "In terms of the effects of the case and the seriousness of it, if you put it on a scale of one to ten, I would rate racism and homophobia in the department as an eight," Wells said. "It goes directly to how you interact with people of color and people of different interests and values than your own."

Wells felt that the department failed to train officers adequately to deal with people of different race and sexual orientation, despite the league's repeated calls for such sensitivity training.

Officers at the police academy receive sixteen hours of sensitivity training during their twenty-week program before going out on the street, but Wells discounted those sessions, saying they "stink," because they do not go into problems in the black community in enough depth. Milwaukee's black community agreed, and they held numerous rallies in front of the Oxford Apartments, claiming officers at the scene May 27 would have investigated more thoroughly if Dahmer had been black and the boy had been white instead of Laotian.

"This is a two-thousand person force, and it's just filled with many, many diligent, talented, and concerned officers," explained M. Nicol Padway, president of the Milwaukee Fire and Police Commission. "It is also a force comprised of a broad mix of personalities and philosophies and personnel. There is no guarantee there will always be the level of sensitivity that you would like."

Sergeant William Wade, vice president of the League of Martin, said he felt racist attitudes on the part of police officers do not stem internally from the Milwaukee Police Department. "A lot of this, I think, they grew up with it. You would think [white officers] would realize that [blacks] are not all the same, and they would treat us as individuals. But for some unknown reason, some officers, even after years of exposure to this, will still treat black people the same way—like we're all crooks.

"Someone in the black community should have Chief Arreola's ear," Wade recommended. "Somebody out there should be able to keep him a little bit better informed."

Most black officers believe that, in contrast to former police chief Harold Breier, Arreola has reached out to the inner-city community. However, the department remains a reflection of Breier, a rigid, law-and-order Chief for twenty years until his retirement in 1984.

Breier, a strict disciplinarian, ran the department through the troubled days of enforced busing and the 1967 Milwaukee race riots. When asked about busing, Breier, typically brash, said busing spreads crime from the black neighborhoods into the predominantly white communities: "We have bused crime all over the city. The south side now has black crime."

He publicly answered charges that he was a racist: "Are you a racist because you tell the truth? I figured I do what I thought was right and the hell with everything else."

His supporters, many of whom have risen to management positions in the department, credited him with keeping Milwaukee's crime rate low while other cities, like Detroit, were crime-ridden.

Breier was also a sexist. Women have worked in the Milwaukee Police Department since 1922, but although they went through the same training as their male counterparts, they were restricted to investigating sexual assault and child abuse cases.

Until 1975 they were not placed on street patrol or allowed to take promotional exams. Breier opposed women being on street patrol, saying, in 1984, "I think it's a tough job for a woman. I don't know that I'd like a woman as a backup if I were going to a bank robbery in progress." The Milwaukee Police Department is far behind other, similar-size cities in its promotion of women and named its first female captain only in 1990.

The department's critics cite the Breier years as fostering the racism and sexism that still exists. Breier was chief during two cases of alleged excessive force by police that enraged the black community. In July 1981, rape suspect Ernest Lacy died in police custody. Lacy, who was black, fought violently when three white officers tried to arrest him. Two other white officers pulled up in a paddy wagon and placed Lacy inside. The officers did not know that Lacy had stopped taking medication for mental problems. He lay motionless on the floor of the wagon. When the wagon arrived at the scene of the assault so the victim could identify Lacy, officers discovered he was dead.

Breier's investigation found no wrongdoing by the five white officers, and an inquest into the death revealed no grounds for criminal charges. The Lacy family filed a complaint with the Fire and Police Commission; after lengthy hearings, one officer was fired and the other suspended without pay for periods ranging from forty-five to sixty days for failure to render aid. The Lacy family also brought a civil case for damages which the city settled out of court for $600,000.

A second case alleging police brutality surfaced three months later, when a suspect fleeing from police during a high-speed chase was badly beaten by the officers who had chased him. The suspect, James Schomperlen, who was white, was beaten in front of numerous witnesses, and pictures of his bruised and swollen face appeared prominently in the media. The case highlighted issues of brutality in the police department. Breier found three of the officers guilty of misconduct in public office and fired them. One was eventually reinstated when he appealed his termination.

The Lacy and Schomperlen cases brought police department racism and brutality to the forefront, and black community leaders still referred to both cases when discussing police conduct with Jeffrey Dahmer on May 27, 1991.

In February 1991, several months before the Dahmer murders were discovered, Chief Arreola appeared on a radio talk show and said the department "in the past has enjoyed the reputation of being a racist organization." White officers responded by creating their own lobbying group, Law Enforcement Officers Combat Against Reverse Discrimination, LEOCARD, which black officers immediately branded as a white supremacist organization.

Arreola, who had been in charge of the police in Port Huron, Michigan, a suburb of Detroit, was the first Chief to come from outside the department; that alone raised officers' objections to him before they even met him. Robert Ziarnik, Arreola's predecessor, resigned in 1989 after five years as Chief, citing his unwillingness to succumb to political pressure from City Hall as to how he should run his department.

"Some said maybe it'll be good that he [Arreola] is from the outside," said police union vice president Gary J. Brazgel. "We don't have all these kiss-ass buddies from all these years. You know, the people in 'the club.' This might help."

But Arreola upset his men early on. Lenard Wells remembered, "Arreola made a promise to the troops that he never kept. He told them that he was going to visit with them, go to every district station, and they waited and they never got that visit. It was like he divorced himself from the backbone of the department: the patrol officer."

Officers also were infuriated when Arreola failed to go to the hospital when an officer died in the line of duty. "A lot of guys will never forgive him for that," said Bradley DeBraska, president of the Milwaukee Police Association, the police officers' union. "When one of us dies in the line of duty, it should be the one time when we put aside all differences and become united. Him not showing up was a terrible slap in the face."

Arreola gained favor with some factions of the community when he talked publicly about the need to dispel long-standing discriminatory policies. He has instituted community-based policing, trying to make officers more responsive to the neighborhoods they patrol.

Former Chief Breier said of community-based policing, "There's no substitute for strong law enforcement. First, a police officer doesn't have the training to take care of all the social ills of the city. And second, he should be so busy maintaining law and order that he doesn't have time for all that crap. When I was Chief we were relating to the good people, and we were relating to the other people too—we were throwing those people in the can."

Breier's philosophy is widely shared within the department, by both blacks and whites. Cops know that the idea of walking the beat is conceptually sound, but there aren't enough officers to answer the emergency calls that come in at a furious rate.

Arreola has sought to hire more minorities and promote them to supervisory ranks. The minority communities see him as a positive sign that the department is changing, but the department is still a microcosm of a racially segregated city. Of the sixteen aldermanic districts, two inner-city districts are over 90 percent black, while three other districts, all on the far south side of the city, are less than 1 percent black. More than half of Milwaukee's blacks live in three inner-city aldermanic districts, and more than half of its Hispanics live in two aldermanic districts on the near south side.

Milwaukee has the largest disparity in the ratio of unemployed whites to unemployed blacks in the country. It also has the lowest median income for black families, the highest percentage of single-parent families, the highest rate of births to black teenagers, and the second highest percentage of black men who are in prison.

The inner-city districts have the lowest incomes in the city and a high percentage of housing stock in either substandard condition or vacant and boarded. The inner-city districts also report the highest crime rates in the city and have the most contact with the Milwaukee Police Department.

The police department mirrors the composition of its constituency. As of October 1991, of 237 supervisors with the rank of sergeant and above, 21 were black men, 9 white women, 7 Hispanic men, and one Asian man; the rest (84 percent) were white men. Of 1,306 police officers, 895 (69 percent) were white men, 113 white women, 163 black men, 31 black women, 84 Hispanics, and no Asians.

When the Dahmer murders were widely publicized, the most volatile issues in Milwaukee proved to be the police conduct with Dahmer and the Sinthasomphone boy and the fact that most of the victims were black. The minority communities believed the Dahmer case was glaring proof that the police, predominantly white, are primarily interested in helping whites and consider all blacks to be criminal elements.

While some praised Arreola for meeting with members of the black community when Dahmer was in the news, others had a different view. John Wesley, a fifteen-year black veteran of the department, said, "If the Chief comes to a meeting in the black community, we should not look at this as some sort of great endeavor. He's the Chief and he serves blacks inside the inner city. The police should be there. You should demand that they be there."

On August 8, 1991, the Reverend Jesse Jackson came to town. The presence of a nationally-prominent figure like Jackson helped to cement the idea that the city's healing could not be achieved by Milwaukee alone. The former presidential candidate and longtime civil rights leader said, "This is an opportunity as well as a challenge, while America is watching, to maybe address America from Milwaukee."

Judging by the response of black leaders and residents, Jackson's visit successfully focused attention on the need for a unified response to the issues raised by the Dahmer case.

"There is a lot of brokenness in the community, broken hearts, broken dreams, and broken relationships," Jackson said, speaking to the crowd of almost two thousand people in front of a local Baptist church. "Yet in all of this brokenness, the leadership will have to pick up the pieces and turn to each other and rely on each other."

Jackson stressed the underlying reasons for the victims' vulnerability—substandard education, unemployment, crime, drugs, racism—all prevalent throughout the country and exacerbated by a lack of investment in America's cities.

Before Jackson's arrival, the mood of the city was so racially charged that every official action regarding the black community was criticized as racist. On July 30, 1991, local elected officials announced that a national victim assistance task force would come to Milwaukee to work with residents and community groups that were providing help to relatives of Dahmer's victims. Based in Washington, D.C., this nonprofit group, the National Organization for Victim Assistance (NOVA), trained residents to help families of the victims and provided services to community groups that helped the families. The team sent to Milwaukee included mental health professionals, clergy, law enforcement officials, and victim services workers.

State Representative Gwen Moore, whose constituency included Milwaukee, said an outside group was needed because no local organization had sufficient credibility among all the affected communities to handle the matter. Moore considered it a positive step in healing the community. But within days of her announcement, the Wisconsin Association of Black Social Workers issued a press release decrying NOVA's appearance in Milwaukee.

"We are deeply disturbed, offended, and outraged about the use of NOVA to provide grief counseling and training. Our specific displeasure is the use of an outside non–African American group to deal with African American problems and concerns," the association said. "There are a number of reputable, credible African American psychotherapists and psychologists in Milwaukee whose training and profession is to deal with individuals who are experiencing stress in their lives and are unable to cope with stressful situations. Once again, the perception is that we as African American professionals lack the skill, knowledge, and ability to address and deal with our own people and community. The question is when will the insults end?"

No matter what steps any group took to try to get the community back together, the efforts were met, more often than not, with fury. The Milwaukee police wives' support organization sprang into action when the community turned against the police department after the May 27 incident was made public. The wives started Operation Blue Ribbon, which distributed thousands of blue ribbons for people to wear or tie around trees and lampposts in front of their homes. The ribbons and, subsequently, T-shirts that read SUPPORT THE MILWAUKEE POLICE were intended to show support for police officers but were perceived by the victims' families as a slap against them. Other T-shirts in fashion at the time read DUMP ARREOLA, with a picture of the Chief inside a red circle with a slash through it. There were also buttons made with the same insignia.

The wives appeared at a routine public Fire and Police Commission meeting, hoping to express their concern over the firing of the two police officers. Soon enough, a shouting match erupted between the wives and the victims' families. Arreola's supporters chanted his name while others booed him when he took the podium to speak on business unrelated to the Dahmer case. Little three-year-old Brittany Olsen, fired officer John Balcerzak's niece, held up a placard over which I could barely see her blond hair and big eyes. The sign read: "JOHN BALCERZAK IS . . . A GOOD MAN, A GOOD POLICEMAN, A GREAT UNCLE, AND WE LOVE HIM." One activist carried a placard that said "DIVIDED JUSTICE: MILWAUKEE POLICE ASSOCIATION, LEAGUE OF MARTIN, LATINO POLICE UNIONS, WOMEN POLICE UNIONS."

The two sides heckled each other throughout the meeting. As I stared around the room, rimmed with officers there to control the crowd, one television reporter turned to me, shaking his head and whispering, "There's bad karma in here. You can feel it."

When a voice from the anti-Arreola faction would yell "Bring back the cops," someone from the other side would yell "Tell your wife to behave," a reference to the large number of police wives who organized anti-Arreola rallies. What would ordinarily have been an uneventful meeting was transformed into theater.

After the meeting, I asked Linda Kuspa, who started the police wives' support group, when the whole situation became a race issue. "When the Chief and the Mayor announced to the public that there was racism in the Milwaukee Police Department, that was it," Kuspa said. "There was no longer any mention of Dahmer. It was the police who killed all the people. I knew right then it was going to be bad and that the community activists would take those statements and run with them."

Kuspa started the wives' support group to try and deal with all the women's outrage. Kuspa and her husband Mike, a Milwaukee police sergeant, have been married for twelve years. "The wives started talking to each other about the kind of confrontations we were having with people at our jobs, people who would ask why the police gave that poor little boy back to a killer, and lecturing us about how irresponsible cops were," Kuspa explained. "These are our husbands they're talking about, the people we share our lives with and love deeply."

Kuspa and several of the wives agreed to meet at someone's home, but when Kuspa discovered fifty women wanted to get together to talk about their feelings, she held the meeting in a church hall.

And the media were there.

"The reporters wanted to come in, but I said we needed to talk to each other," Kuspa remembered. "They were really pushy and said we were keeping them out, but all we wanted was just to talk about our feelings with each other."

Operation Blue Ribbon began that night. A few days later, Kuspa planned a vigil in support of the police. The group was growing.

"It was never meant to be an official organization or to be an activist type of thing," Kuspa said. "I wanted the public to be aware of what was not being reported in the Dahmer case, like the younger picture of Konerak Sinthasomphone being used by the media when there was another one that made him look more his age. And I wanted lay people to understand the procedures the officers go through when they make arrests. Nobody knew what went on behind the scenes."

The wives held a "Deer Hunters' Widows Party" in late November 1991, a social occasion for women whose husbands were off hunting for the weekend. The press came again. When a reporter asked for a comment, Kuspa merely answered, "We just want to start laughing again."

Kuspa said her message, though simple, proved difficult for people who do not know police officers to understand. "It's not just the police officers who are responsible for the safety of the community," she said. "We can't constantly blame the police for problems in the community. These cops have so much knowledge that people should stop them and ask what they can do, how the citizens can help keep kids off the streets and out of trouble. I just wish people knew what their jobs were."

I know the heartache of living with a police officer. It was gut-wrenching to watch the person I loved most in the world being torn apart each day he went off to a job he used to love. It was even harder being the reporter covering the story, putting the cops in the news, and then going home to a cop at night and listening, through the tears and the outrage, to how the people he was there to help taunted him.

Instead of being a conflict of interest, it made me a better reporter because I had truly seen both sides of the story—something we reporters are frequently accused of not doing. As a citizen, I understood the community anger, but as someone who shares her life with a police officer, I realized the media did not want to present the cops' point of view. It would be like siding with the enemy. I finally understood why the police always seem to hang out with each other. Nobody else is willing to walk in their shoes.

As the case continued to inflame the community, extremist factions began to appear. During a rally for the police officers held at a rented Milwaukee hall, unbeknownst to the officers inside, a white supremacist organization put flyers on cars in the parking lot that read "The Church of the Creator supports the White police of Milwaukee." The police had no connection to the group. Nonetheless, the leafleting generated further outrage.

The officers needed some way to express their anger at Arreola's premature suspension and subsequent firing of Officers Joe Gabrish and John Balcerzak. Anti-Arreola sentiment ran deep within the Milwaukee Police Department. Cops wore their DUMP ARREOLA T-shirts under their uniforms and pinned under their coats the buttons with Arreola's picture encircled in red and slashed through. One cop told me if I was ever covering a story and he got shot, I should stall the Chief at the scene until his buddies could cut off his DUMP ARREOLA T-shirt from underneath his blue uniform.

Arreola issued a memorandum prohibiting officers from wearing the T-shirts and buttons on or off duty and threatening disciplinary action if they did. That's all the cops needed. DUMP

ARREOLA T-shirts became de rigueur. Buttons were hidden under uniform ties, inside hats, under coat lapels.

Cops began to feel the backlash in the street in the weeks after the firings. "Kids were saying, 'Get away, he'll kill you,' just to be funny," one cop told me. "I went to answer a burglar alarm, and the woman at the house said to me, 'You're not one of those crazy cops that let that little boy get killed, are you?' It was awful. I became shorter with people than ever before. I think I'd rather be a street sweeper."

Another officer said he took a couple of assignments and then hid the rest of the night. "It was the first time in eight years I hid from people. But every time I went out on a call or drove my squad car, people yelled horrible things at me."

A white officer with thirteen years on the force told me about the day he was called to a domestic-violence situation at a house in the inner city. "I went in the house and this black guy was holding a knife at the throat of his girlfriend's four-year-old daughter and he was screaming at the girlfriend to get him some drug money she owed him. I stood there and eventually talked him out of the knife. The little girl ran to her mother, who was crying and screaming, 'Thank you for saving my baby, Officer' to me. Now, the girl and her mother and the guy were all black, but when I walked out of the house with the guy in handcuffs, the neighbors were screaming at me, 'You motherfuckin' pig! Why don't you leave the brothers alone and go kill some Oriental kid? It was one of the worst days I've had on this job," he said, wiping his eyes with the back of his hand.

According to James Romanesko, senior editor at *Milwaukee Magazine*, although the Dahmer case ignited the controversy, the issue of how well Arreola was serving Milwaukee had begun boiling months earlier. "His problems go beyond the police union's no-confidence vote and whether he was right or wrong in the firings. The questions about Arreola go right to his management style, his ability to lead, and his effectiveness as police chief of a major city."

Arreola's early supporters now call the Chief a disappointment and worry that he has surrounded himself with ambitious commanders who may be looking out for themselves instead of the Chief, Romanesko added.

Bradley DeBraska, president of the union that represents Milwaukee police officers, had never been afraid to say exactly what he thought about the Chief. When the suspensions of the three officers were announced on July 26, 1991, DeBraska countered with the first of many public attacks on Arreola.

"In his rush to find a scapegoat for the recent tragedies, the Chief has suspended three Milwaukee police officers, knowing full well that the community would interpret the suspensions as his conclusion that they had failed to perform their duties," DeBraska said. "Even Jeffrey Dahmer gets a trial before he is convicted."

On August 7, 1991, DeBraska and Robert Kliesmet, president of the International Union of Police Associations, AFL-CIO, announced the results of a vote taken among the Milwaukee membership. An overwhelming 85 percent of the 1,570 sworn police officers voted no confidence in Arreola's ability to run the department, and over half rated his performance as Chief of Police "poor."

None of the union's activities seemed to upset Arreola. But he had to take notice when DeBraska sent a letter to the membership on September 10, 1991, reminding officers about the need to adhere to proper police procedure. The letter essentially advocated a work slowdown, although DeBraska publicly denied it. It talked about the need for complete and thorough investigations, including calling a supervisor to any scene where there is any question involving procedure. DeBraska also wrote that "officers must be sure to check the squad car from front to rear, top to bottom, inside and out, under the hood, inside the trunk, all the equipment, and the cleanliness of the interior and exterior." The process, if done to the letter of the rule, could take up to twenty minutes before the officers could go out on the street.

What followed was predictable. The busiest cars in the districts, the ones that formerly took fifteen to twenty assignments a night, were taking five. Two officers on a normally busy squad went to investigate a call from a woman whose car's side rear window had been smashed and who needed a police report for insurance purposes. Usually police direct citizens to go to a district station to file a report with a clerk if no one is injured, but these officers were conducting a "complete and thorough" investigation. The woman saw nothing, but the officers went house to house and interviewed everyone on her block to see if they had witnessed any suspicious activity.

Detectives in the department's Criminal Investigation Bureau received twenty-page reports from officers on minor crimes, causing a backlog of paperwork, and "Blue Flu" rumors ran rampant. Officers would come to work and find the computers were backed up two hundred assignments because of "complete and thorough" investigations.

Officers insisted that the Chief's actions had made many of them afraid to use the discretionary judgment they were given when sworn in.

Even the local college newspaper joined the fury when the *University of Wisconsin–Milwaukee Times* published a sort of tote board that posted, "The number of days since Milwaukee Police Chief Arreola should have resigned," with a number below it that changed weekly.

Arreola declared, "I think that I can lay that responsibility [of how Milwaukee officers were perceived after the Dahmer incident] at the foot of the union because they created such a furor. To the world, they said we cannot be held accountable. To the world, they said that a police officer's judgment cannot be questioned."

While Arreola lost the support of much of the rank and file, minority community leaders in Milwaukee generally praised the Chief for moving quickly to discipline the officers. The leaders also criticized the way Milwaukee police deal with complaints made by minority residents.

"The Chief made the right decision and we support him 100 percent," said Queen Hyler, president of the local chapter of Stop the Violence. "Chief Arreola is the only Chief who has made an effort to work with everyone in this city and assure every citizen of the same protections under the law. I sincerely believe that he is trying to make an effort in Milwaukee."

The Reverend LeHavre Buck, executive director of the Harambee Ombudsman Project, a community service organization, said that Arreola's actions against the officers were proper and procedurally correct and may have forstalled the possibility of civil violence.

"He showed the community that there is a possibility for something to be done about this," Buck said. "We as citizens have dealt with a lot of negligence, blatant disregard of the value of human life, poor follow-up on missing children, lack of following police procedure, and disrespect for the rights of people who do not speak English. Everybody's in rage and mourning here. It's taken a toll on people. People are very edgy toward everything and everybody right now. So, hopefully, maybe we'll get some justification out of it—whatever that is. I don't know how you get justification out of losing your son, but it will be interesting."

Michael McGee, a militant black Milwaukee alderman known for his controversial views and solutions to problems in the black community, said, "If you're white, [the police] usually perceive that you have a lot of right on your side. There's lot of ineptness, but I think that's just related to their insensitivity to the black community."

Black community leaders held rallies so that residents could gather and vent their outrage over the police handling of the Dahmer case. Many members of Milwaukee's black community felt that it took something like the Jeffrey Dahmer murders for them to be heard, that the case exposed the festering mistrust between whites and blacks in Milwaukee.

Mistrust was not exclusive to the black community. Milwaukee's gays and lesbians believed antigay bias on the part of the police allowed Dahmer's murder toll to mount. The furor among gays began when the term "homosexual overkill" was used by officials to describe the murders.

"People just exploded over that," remembered Terry Boughner, editor of the gay newspaper *Wisconsin Light*. "It was the red flag that went up and was followed by a tremendous amount of anger and ridicule. Nobody countered with Ted Bundy committing heterosexual overkill. We immediately thought, Here comes something involving the gay community and we're going to get blamed for that. There is a lot of anger rooted in the fact that the gays and lesbians think the people in the straight community think they're scum."

Boughner said the effects of the case on the gay community would not be that drastic. "For those who hate us [homosexuals], it's simply going to confirm their prejudices. For those who are knee-deep in their own homophobia, they wish it would all go away. The bar people, they'll go on."

Club 219 became the most famous numbered club since Studio 54, and it also has become quite the tourist attraction. When the media covered the gay bar where Dahmer sought out many of his victims, Club 219 experienced an influx of straight people, media, yuppies; even tour buses stopped out front so passengers coud take snapshots.

Owners of businesses that catered to the gay community said they have felt no long-term ill effects, save for a few eggs pelted at the Club 219's front windows. Bar owners told Boughner their business is up since the case was in the news.

"In times of crisis, people want to be together," Boughner said. "This whole thing will not make the gay community more cautious. Where can gays and lesbians in this town go? People will say, 'It happened to him, it won't happen to me,' or, 'It happened at 219 so I can go to another bar.' "

Scott Gunkel, president of the Lambda Rights Network, a gay rights organization in Milwaukee, explained the outrage in the gay community. "The police could have followed so many angles, it's almost unbelieveable. It's like a bad B-movie, that they didn't do anything. I've had a number of reports of incidents where both parties, if they're male, go downtown [to jail] even though one of them is obviously being victimized and not retaliating at all. Or where they're harassed or they're simply just left alone, and police say, 'Well, they're two guys, they'll punch it out.' "

Gunkel is a bartender at Club 219. "I see quite a bit of violence within the community and from outside the community. Mostly the police take their time getting there when there's trouble. I believe they wait to see if the altercation leaves the scene first." Gunkel said the average police-response time for a fight at a gay bar was about twenty minutes, sometimes longer, as opposed to five minutes elsewhere.

Antigay sentiment was not limited to Milwaukee. A group called the Oregon Citizen's Alliance offered posters that read:

"Free Jeffrey Dahmer (All he did was kill homosexuals)." Sales were brisk.

The National Gay and Lesbian Task Force issued a statement, on July 29, 1991, calling the case a grisly example of how hatred destroys the lives of gay people and people of color. "Such vague and dangerous terms [e.g., "homosexual overkill"] falsely equate killing with homosexuality. When, for example, has the term 'heterosexual overkill' been used to describe the serial killing of women by a male perpetrator? By confusing victims with perpetrators, media and police statements have unwittingly fostered an atmosphere of intolerance that has led to a dramatic increase in antigay harassment and threats in Milwaukee and perhaps elsewhere as well."

Police and owners of gay bars confirmed that harassment of gays outside the bars and vandalism to the establishments had increased in the wake of the revelations about the Dahmer case.

Some people argued that the different community factions which focused on the police were overlooking the truly blameworthy parties: probation agent Donna Chester and Judge William Gardner.

In *Milwaukee Media Focus*, the editors wrote that they were outraged by the media's minimal attention to Chester and Gardner. "As a result of this lax coverage, the probation department and Judge Gardner both escaped the kind of community wrath that would later be directed toward the police."

Some community outrage proved downright bizarre.

An advertisement in the August 9, 1991, *Des Moines Register* read:

"Milwaukee . . . July 1991 . . . They were drugged and dragged across the room . . . their legs and feet were bound together . . . Their struggles and cries went unanswered . . . Then they were slaughtered and their heads sawn off . . . their body parts were refrigerated to be eaten later . . . It's still going on."

It's not what you think. The ad was placed by an animal rights group that compared meatpackers to Jeffrey Dahmer.

"The ad is not just tasteless, it's an obscenity," said Dave Mehlhaff, spokesman for the National Pork Producers Council. "For them to try to capitalize on this shocking tragedy in Milwaukee we think is sick and demented."

But the group defended its decision to use the Dahmer case in its campaign. "What we hope to accomplish is to point out that abuse is abuse regardless of the species," said Kathy Guillermo, of People for the Ethical Treatment of Animals. "We hope it will jolt a few people into realizing that what happened to those people is no different than what happens to animals."

The Milwaukee papers refused to carry the ad, but we all reported on the story and included the copy from the ad.

And in Ohio, the Reverend Donovan Larkins, spurred by the Jeffrey Dahmer case, announced plans to step up his practice of staging bonfires to burn books and paraphernalia he considered satanic or pornographic.

The media reported everything odd that concerned the Dahmer murders, but most members of the minority community said coverage of the racial issues raised by the case was long overdue.

All the publicity focused on Milwaukee adversely affected one community group or another. The case and the continued references to Dahmer's homosexuality tarnished the entire gay community for the acts of one deranged man and damaged many people's already limited perception of the gay community.

Milwaukeeans have traditionally been proud of their city, especially its safe streets. Before Jeffrey Dahmer became a national figure the people of Milwaukee wanted to dispel the image of their city that was synonymous with beer and beer bellies, bratwurst, bowling, and Laverne and Shirley. We have Jeffrey Dahmer to thank that the first thing people mention when they hear "Milwaukee" is no longer two television characters who were brewery workers but rather a serial killer.

Publicity about Milwaukee was extremely widespread. Several Milwaukee County officials on business in Poland when Dahmer's crimes were discovered, were told the news by a local Polish official.

Milwaukee has a rich German heritage—15 percent of the population—and the work ethic to match. It is largely a blue-collar town where bowling is a popular activity and going out for a fish dinner on Friday—a "fish fry"—is a ritual. Long a beer-brewing capital, the malt beverage is still the most-requested fare at the corner tavern, and as for beer bellies, Milwaukee has been named as one of the top cities in the country whose residents are overweight.

Eventually, the city government decided that the beer-bellied, friendly image was provincial, and Milwaukee worked to promote its cultural offerings and festivals around the country. Milwaukee has come far in its goal, evidenced by its ability to attract top performers to our venues, drawing crowds with a state-of-the art sports facility and increasing convention business. The city's ballet, symphony, and repertory companies have received critical acclaim around the country.

But as Milwaukee struggled to throw off the old images, we realized that big problems come with the big-city image. The state of Wisconsin, specifically Milwaukee, has become a welfare magnet, since neighboring states have drastically cut their welfare benefits. In 1991, Milwaukee's record year for homicides, police say the victims and perpetrators are not local but from Illinois, Michigan, and Indiana. They flock to Wisconsin because of our lucrative welfare benefits.

Tourism was up before Jeffrey Dahmer made the news, and residents were devastated that our latest image was "Home of serial killer Jeffrey Dahmer."

All of Milwaukee felt victimized by Dahmer. People felt angry and depressed. Part of our collective bewilderment over what happened stemmed from our fear of the unknown, which made us wonder, If someone as apparently nondescript as Dahmer could be so dangerous, what about the others around us? What do we really know about other people?

Residents were also infuriated by the idea that their police department was eager to serve only white heterosexuals. Anger and fear regarding the police surfaced in light of the discovery that they had dismissed the situation between Dahmer and Konerak Sinthasomphone as a domestic squabble, and people began to listen for the first time to the black and gay communities. It appears that massive calls for changes in the police department will be addressed under Police Chief Philip Arreola.

There are those who say it took a serial killer to bring to light problems that sorely needed addressing. Before, whites would read the yearly homicide tallies in the paper, believing the deaths are a problem in the black community and they are unaffected by it. In the wake of Jeffrey Dahmer, people who lived comfortable, shielded lives had to take notice of festering problems in the black and gay communities, two groups many here did not want to admit they shared a city with.

Milwaukee continues the struggle to rebuild its sense of community after citywide crisis. Life is not as gentle here as it used to be when I grew up in Milwaukee. But then, no one's life is gentle anymore. If you lived here in the summer of 1991, you know that we were all forced to look at ourselves and our attitudes about race and sex. No one enjoyed the view.

14

The Living Victims

Friends called me from all over the country to rib me about my hometown, and the national media interviewed me about what it was like to live in Milwaukee. I thought, This must be how people in Dallas felt when President Kennedy was assassinated.

The year 1991 was the most violent year ever for the city. A record 168 people were homicide victims, fifteen of them killed by Jeffrey Dahmer. Milwaukee's murder rate, skyrocketing even before the Dahmer tragedy, earned the city the dubious distinction of being called "The New Murder Capital" by *Newsweek* magazine. In the last five years the homicide rate has increased 126 percent, and 75 percent of those murdered were black.

I see the effects of the Dahmer case being the public's realization that our problems are bigger than the budgets we allocate to solve them. The police will be doing their jobs with more sensitivity. The dubious notoriety Milwaukee has received in connection with Jeffrey Dahmer may force us to look at ourselves.

Milwaukee is rapidly losing its sense of itself. It used to be that you could find anywhere from two to four generations of the same family living there, often in the same neighborhood. But the younger people are moving out, and their elders often follow, as more affordable senior-citizen housing becomes available in the suburbs.

Milwaukee had traditionally been a safe city, where people from all over the state would come for festivals, fairs, and ball games. The increasing number of murders certainly served as a deterrent to visitors, but as County Supervisor Dan Cupertino put it, Jeffrey Dahmer was "the icing on the cake" so far as it concerned Milwaukee's reputation as a place of increasing crime.

For those who live in Milwaukee's affluent suburbs, the Jeffrey Dahmer case became a gruesome event that could only happen in the city. "That's why we moved away from there," suburbanites told me. "That sort of thing doesn't happen out here."

Most people here were scarred by the events of the summer of 1991. Some watched their neighborhoods turned into tourist attractions. People drove past victims' homes and took photographs. Dahmer's apartment building became a bona fide circus in the days after his arrest: expensive imported cars filed slowly past while their passengers craned mini-cams out the window to get film footage for their home movie collection. Some curiosity seekers even parked their cars and posed for snapshots in front of the building. Clergy came and prayed over the building, television newspeople did their stories before it, and politicians used it as a backdrop for numerous press conferences and rallies.

Other places associated with heinous crimes have experienced similar events. In 1957, authorities found human organs in frying pans and human carcasses hanging in Ed Gein's home in Plainfield, Wisconsin, making him the state's heretofore most famous criminal. The character, 'Buffalo Bill' in the movie *Silence of the Lambs* was based on Gein. Shortly after his arrest, arsonists burned his house to the ground.

John Wayne Gacy's suburban Chicago property was sold by

sheriff's auction in 1984; the only bid came from the savings and loan that held the mortgage. Today, it is an empty lot.

After James Huberty fatally shot twenty-one people at a McDonald's in San Ysidro, California, in 1984, the McDonald's Corporation razed the restaurant and erected a memorial in its place.

It is not clear what will happen to the Oxford Apartments. Some have proposed selling the building (appraised at $531,000) and using it as a homeless shelter; others urge that it be torn down and a memorial erected. Neighborhood residents find it a source of pain and most want it razed.

"Someone who thinks they're doing something positive for society may burn the building down," mass murder expert James Fox said. "It's a constant reminder of something negative."

One couple from Hartford, Wisconsin, said they would like to buy the building and convert it into a museum of criminal artifacts. They expressed interest in Dahmer's apartment furniture and the shirt he was wearing when he was arrested. They said they would donate any money from paid admissions to the museum to the families of Dahmer's victims'. The families told me they would refuse any money from a museum that would glorify a man who took their loved one's life.

As of this writing, the American flag flying in front of the building is still at half-mast.

Our collective mental health has suffered. Even people who did not live in the neighborhood experienced negative effects from the Dahmer murders. Mental health officials said children were having nightmares, asking to sleep with parents and refusing to eat meat as stories of the murders invaded their world.

John Palmer, executive director of Human Services Triangle, a Milwaukee County counseling agency, said the damage to young minds could be lasting. Palmer said that in the days following the discoveries in Dahmer's apartment, parents had been bringing their children to his agency for counseling because of fear sparked by the killings. "Their sense of community has been destroyed. Their sense of the future and the terms of life have been changed," Palmer said. He felt that problems were more likely to develop in children who lived in Dahmer's neighborhood.

Leslie Fedorchuk of Helpline, a twenty-four-hour crisis hotline, said they had received hundreds of calls from people whose fear was brought on by the Dahmer case. "There's a lot of reaction to what's been in the media, but a lot of people don't have friends to talk to, so the anxiety just sits there," she said. "I think there's a whole group of people out there for whom this is very personal. People called up to sat that something similar happened to them and this has reawakened the memory of it."

Most mental health professionals I spoke with harshly criticized the television stations for breaking into children's programming to give updates on the case. When asked if parents should raise the issue with their children, family therapist Steve Petrie said, "You've got to know your kids. If they are kids who keep things to themselves, I'd surely talk about what is going on with them, what's going on today. I'm not so sure I would directly say: 'Did you hear about the guy who is cutting people up?'

"That scares me," Petrie added. "You don't want to cause alarm. You want to help children reduce their concern as much as possible."

The psychological effects on our fear and anger will pass with time. A much more difficult problem concerns the effect Jeffrey Dahmer had on the community. We try to be optimistic that the Dahmer case brought Milwaukee's problems into the open so they can be analyzed, discussed, and solutions put in motion, but none of that is possible as long as mainstream heterosexual whites shut out other groups.

"The community has banded together in the case of the Gainesville murders," observed Fox, referring to the murders of coeds at the University of Florida. "The reason is those kids were mainstream, middle class, young, white, and everybody around identified with them. That's where the difference lies with the Jeffrey Dahmer case. Most Milwaukeeans do not identify with gays and blacks. You will not have the unified public response that you found in Gainesville."

A unified response is difficult because the case demands a

focus on the problems of institutional racism, fear and hatred of gays, lenient judges, faulty bureaucracy, urban decline, government budget cuts, and media supersaturation.

State Representative Gwen Moore said she hopes good will emerge from all this, with improved relations between the currently warring factions of the city: police officers, minorities, and elected officials. "Once a community goes through a crisis like that, it's never the same," she said. "Hopefully, the community is never the same for the better."

But other officials said the change in Milwaukee is not necessarily positive. "Like it or not, Jeffrey Dahmer is setting Milwaukee's agenda," said Alderman John Kalwitz, referring to the vigils, marches, rallies, investigations, suspensions, finger-pointing, legislative proposals, demands for resignations, and consuming media coverage that have followed the killings. "Almost everything we do or want to do is impacted upon by this tragedy."

The case has resulted in upheaval in the police department, a rising coalition of protest from inner-city churches, gays, Asians, neighborhood activists, as well as public and private efforts. "At some point, nobody was mad at Jeffrey Dahmer anymore," Gwen Moore said. "Everybody was mad at somebody else. It really elucidated the kinds of division that exist within the community, black versus white, homosexual versus heterosexual, the community versus the police, the police chief versus the police union. That's what was so painful about it here."

Most dramatically, the effect of the Dahmer case has been to underscore two of our most pressing problems: growing alarm over violent crime and minority resentment of police.

An even wider chasm than before this incident exists between Police Chief Philip Arreola and his officers, resulting in low morale.

Mayor John O. Norquist's Citizen Commission on Police-Community Relations, or the Blue Ribbon Commission, created as a result of the Jeffrey Dahmer case, held public hearings to help gauge the mood of the community toward their police department.

Ten years ago, a study of the Milwaukee Police Department concluded, "No department can hope to effectively serve the community as a whole when a significant portion of its population [blacks] is substantially alienated from it."

The Blue Ribbon Commission released its findings in October 1991. Not much has changed in ten years. The commission recommended that police department recruiting efforts include the Southeast Asian community, gays and lesbians, as well as Hispanics, Native Americans, and blacks. They also suggested using psychological tests as part of the police officer applicant-evaluation process. They said supervisors must be accountable for monitoring the behavior of officers, for noting and correcting any inappropriate behavior patterns, and for reinforcing excellent behavior.

When rating the relationship between police and the citizenry, the report found great racial polarization between whites and blacks as well as, to a lesser extent, between Hispanics and whites. The report cited widespread belief among blacks that police use more force when restraining and arresting minority suspects and that they treated minorities worse than whites.

State Representative Gwen Moore said, "It's up to us in the community to make sure these recommendations don't get filed away or gather dust on a shelf."

The report looked good on paper, but the street officers and supervisors told me all the mending at this juncture is moot. Police work in Milwaukee has been irrevocably altered, and most cops feel too beleaguered as a result of the scrutiny directed toward them to work with the enthusiasm they once had.

The officers on street patrol feel that their discretionary powers have been usurped and that the Chief's office has no confidence in their ability to make appropriate decisions. Cops are relentless cynics to begin with, and Jeffrey Dahmer turned them into pessimists. Officers take retirement as soon as they are eligible, and many who recently joined the force are circulating their résumés. The middle management of the department remains young, and whole shifts of inexperienced officers are working the streets because the officers with more time on the job just do not care to go the extra mile to help the rookies learn their jobs.

Chief Arreola has become the enemy in the eyes of his men while earning points in the community. The question is whether he can survive without the support of the rank and file.

For those of us who have covered the department for years, Jeffrey Dahmer will probably have no lasting effect on the way we do our jobs. We will continue to be hypocrites in that we judge people by standards we ourselves could not be held to. We will continue to look for the sensational, and management will continue to cite the need for sensitivity in our coverage. *Sensitivity* became the buzzword of 1991, and several of the local media have begun sensitivity training for their staffs. Several of the black reporters at the *Journal* laughed when they heard this and wondered aloud how you teach someone to be sensitive.

The Dahmer case did elicit some sensitive behavior. Paramount Pictures pulled local advertisements for the upcoming movie *Body Parts* and local theater owners decided not to show the film. The movie was not about multiple murders or dismemberment, but Paramount officials said the title was "an unfortunate coincidence." The first week of the discoveries in Dahmer's apartment, one local television station chose not to air an episode of "Phil Donahue" which featured Donahue touring some of New York City's most popular transvestite bars. The station felt the timing was problematic.

The Dahmer case had an immediate effect on one longstanding Milwaukee custom. For many years, Milwaukee citizens have erected haunted houses for charity. But after sweating through a summer of Dahmer stories, Milwaukee was not in the mood for a blood-and-guts Halloween. In 1991 organizers of some of the leading haunted houses took special care not to construct exhibits that would further frazzle an already unnerved city. The Dahmer case forced many of them to redo some past feature attractions, such as a butcher shop that displayed severed body parts.

Other effects on the area include renewed discussion in the state legislature to bring back the death penalty. The legislature had outlawed capital punishment in 1853, although efforts to restore it resurface periodically. Wisconsin Governor Tommy G. Thompson said the Dahmer case "shows we have to have prison beds to lock up people who are unfit for society." With that, Thompson recommended 115 more probation agents to alleviate overworked caseworkers such as Donna Chester.

Some politicians, rather than institute the death penalty for homicide, favor the idea of a law against dismembering human bodies. The proposed dismemberment legislation would designate mutilation, disfiguring, or dismembering a corpse as a separate crime, punishable by as much as twenty years in prison and a $10,000 fine. An additional ten years in prison and a $10,000 fine could be imposed for hiding a body.

The Jeffrey Dahmer murders spurred some divisive political campaigns for the 1992 local elections, when the community was still split over wrenching racial controversies. Gregory Gracz, a candidate for mayor, charged that Mayor John O. Norquist has "driven a wedge" between whites and blacks when he alleged that racism was evident in the actions of the police officers who returned Konerak Sinthasomphone to Dahmer. Politicians used the Dahmer case when announcing their campaign plans to pull the city together. Political analysts have said that any attempt by white candidates to use blatantly divisive tactics would set race relations back a long way, especially with the repercussions of the Dahmer case so fresh.

The feelings of the relatives of the victims are inestimable compared to the emotions experienced by reporters or to those who simply lived in the same city. But to varying degrees, all the participants in the case of Jeffrey Dahmer were victims in some way, and we all carry the scars.

15

Day of Reckoning

The trial of Jeffrey Dahmer had the air of a movie premiere, complete with local celebrities, groupies who hounded for autographs, and a full-scale media onslaught—of which I was a part. I had covered the case since the early morning hours of July 23, 1991, and by late January 1992, my interest in Jeffrey Dahmer was greater than ever. While other reporters felt mounting burnout, I was fascinated by each day of the proceedings. I knew that I would finally learn even more about the man who had held my curiosity for the past six months.

I worked as a reporter for the *Milwaukee Journal* until September 1991, when I left to write this book. I was soon hired as a consultant by WISN-TV (Channel 12), the ABC affiliate in Milwaukee, that won numerous awards for it's Dahmer trial coverage. After the trial, I was hired full-time as the crime reporter there. My function was to cover any breaking news on the Dahmer case and provide commentary and analysis for a nightly news special during the trial. I had often envied television for its immediacy. It was more difficult to cover the story for Channel 12 because I had to stop using words to describe events and rely instead on pictures. But all told, when it came to the daily trial coverage, you couldn't beat the visuals—the sounds and the faces that *were* the Jeffrey Dahmer trial.

Interest in the Jeffrey Dahmer story had lessened by mid-September. The last real news concerned the firing of the two police officers, John Balcerzak and Joe Gabrish, and the suspension of Richard Porubcan. Dahmer stories were scarce in the local newspapers and on the TV news, but that didn't mean we weren't all looking for the one angle no one else had discovered. We in the media knew that once we were together in the controlled environment of the trial, we would all obtain basically the same information and there would be little chance for scoops or exclusives.

The first pretrial stories began to trickle out in early January 1992, when we learned Dahmer, who had been charged with committing fifteen murders in Wisconsin would probably change his plea from not guilty to guilty. In a letter to Milwaukee County Circuit Judge Laurence Gram, Gerald Boyle wrote that Dahmer would still stand trial on the insanity issue. We wondered if we would still hear all the details of Dahmer's crimes since he was now admitting the murders and would no longer be tried for them.

By the time the trial was over, we all had more details than we could stand.

The pretrial hearing on January 13 was a preview of things to come. Judge Gram's courtroom in the Milwaukee County Safety Building, just a few blocks from the Ambrosia Chocolate Co. where Dahmer worked, had been altered to increase security for the trial. Gram was not pleased with the new barrier that bisected his courtroom, but he was keenly aware of the need for security for the worst murderer in the state's history.

The courtroom was swept for bombs by a dog trained to sniff for explosives, and everyone allowed into the courtroom was searched and checked with a metal detector. There was no room for modesty as sheriff's deputies unceremoniously removed hair spray from the women's bags and looked inside tampon containers.

In the courtroom, an eight-foot-high barrier was constructed from bullet-resistant glass and steel, designed to isolate Dahmer from the gallery. While I'm sure the $15,000 wall was a good security device, it was a nightmare for reporters. The structure may as well have been soundproof. When some of the witnesses with quieter voices took the stand, most of the reserved media seats in the courtroom were empty as we watched the proceedings on television in the media center three floors below.

The media center for the Dahmer trial could be compared to the Rashid Hotel in Saudi Arabia for reporters covering the Gulf War. It was the nerve center. Dan Patrinos, media coordinator for the trial and supervisor of the art and photography departments at the *Milwaukee Sentinel*, received seat requests from news organizations across the country as well as from Japan, England, and Australia. Preference was given to the local media, and a "pool" system was instituted, meaning several reporters would sit in on any process in the judge's small chambers and then report back to the others. Television images and still photographs from the courtroom proceedings were made available to any station or print media that wanted them. There are those who say we have no professional ethics to begin with, but it is a given that it is grounds for lynching by reporters if you hold back some nugget of information from the pool and use it for yourself.

While hundreds of news organizations applied for courtroom seating, only 100 seats were available: 23 for reporters, 34 for the victims' families, and the remaining 43 for the general public. On January 13, all the media seats were filled as we waited for our first look at Jeffrey Dahmer since August, his last court appearance. Only twenty relatives of the victims were present. The seats allotted for the public were empty: it seemed the locals had had enough of Jeffrey Dahmer for a while and chose to watch the proceedings, which were being carried live, at their homes. That would change as the trial came to a close, and people came in droves for one last look.

Reporters grew quiet when Dahmer entered the courtroom, wearing a blaze orange prison-issued jumpsuit, blue tennis shoes, and brown socks. We craned forward and peered over the steel crossbars of the security shield to look at him. I had not seen Jeffrey Dahmer since his last court appearance in September 1991.

Since then, I had delved into his private life to write this book and I was almost anxious to see him after my extensive research.

I looked at him differently this time, with some sense of how he grew up, but not of how he became a monster.

Judge Gram denied Gerry Boyle's motion for a change of venue and his motion to have the jury picked from outside Milwaukee, citing the implausibility of finding anyone in the state who hadn't heard some pretrial publicity.

As expected, Dahmer changed his plea to guilty, which angered the victims' families. They feared they would never learn what had actually happened to their loved ones once they had entered Jeffrey Dahmer's lair.

"I want to know what happened to my brother from the minute Jeffrey Dahmer met him to the minute he killed him," Eddie Smith's sister, Carolyn, told me after the hearing. "I want to know every detail."

I wondered aloud if that would really serve a purpose, to know all the gory details.

Carolyn answered, "It wouldn't be any worse than when I go to the chiropractor and I see the skeleton in the office and it trips me out."

Dorothy Straughter, the mother of Curtis Straughter, another victim, said to me, "The way my imagination has been running, I'd rather know the truth."

And Shirley Hughes, mother of Tony Hughes, said, "We get up in the morning with this and we lay down with this at night. I want to know everything."

The families agreed that the truth could not be much worse than their own assumptions and the nightmares that had haunted them since July 23, 1991.

They got their wish, starting January 27, 1992.

The victims' families were not the only ones anxious to know more as hundreds of reporters converged on Milwaukee for the Jeffrey Dahmer trial. As I drove to the Milwaukee County Safety Building, I felt excited about being part of a major news event. I suppose it's observations like that that make reporters appear cold and unfeeling, but for so much of the proceedings reporters, like other people, wanted to be present at the most sensational trial Wisconsin has ever seen.

The media center was set up in two rooms on the second floor of the building; the trial was in room 578, three floors above. The media center became our home and we began to interact as a family. The small yellow room had long tables with chairs crowded behind them along each wall and one down the center of the room. A separate room housed wire-service reporters and print reporters from *Newsweek* and the Associated Press to people from England and Australia. In addition to Milwaukee's four local TV stations, one which carried the trial live, there was a barrage of Chicago television and radio stations crowded into the yellow room. Editing machines were stacked three high, and hot lights burned constantly. After having been a print reporter all my life, I had to learn to walk around the room in a sort of half-crouch to avoid walking into someone's camera shot.

When one woman from the Milwaukee Convention and Visitors Bureau heard that a pack of journalists from all over the world was in town, she headed over to the Safety Building and handed out bags of get-to-know-Milwaukee goodies, such as coupons and information about the city. She told me she wanted us to see the good side of the city and not this nasty place where someone had murdered fifteen people. She made everyone's newscasts.

The first three days were uneventful as we trudged through jury selection. District Attorney E. Michael McCann and defense attorney Gerald Boyle sat at a large round table in the judge's chambers, away from television cameras. Along with trial Judge Laurence Gram, they interviewed prospective jurors.

It was slow going those first few days as we sat around the media center, waiting for the pool reporter to come down for a briefing. To bide our time, we interviewed each other for stories, our favorite subjects being journalists from abroad, and we gathered information on the latest laptop computers and technical gadgets.

The briefings from the chambers by the pool reporter were some of the lightest moments of the trial. Associated Press reporter Lisa Holewa described a woman who said she could not serve on the Dahmer jury because she raised exotic birds and they would die without her. Even Dahmer, sitting in a corner of the judge's chambers, laughed. The woman was excused. "The bird lady" was nearly everyone's lead story that day. Some prospective jurors asked to be excused because, as one woman put it, "I don't think I have the stomach for it."

If you were looking for the drama and fast-paced excitement of TV's "L.A. Law," the Dahmer trial was not the place to find it, although the TV show "Entertainment Tonight" saw fit to cover us covering the trial. I have to agree the spectacle of all of us crammed into that room was indeed entertaining.

I was lucky enough to be the pool reporter the second day of jury selection. Deputies ushered me into the judge's chambers, and I took a seat slightly behind the defense attorneys, who were at the large round table. I looked toward the corner of the room, and there sat Jeffrey Dahmer, just a few feet away from me. Three deputies were in the room, so there was never any security risk, but to be so close to him made me swallow hard. He had changed into brown pants, a tan jacket, and a beige shirt with no tie. Yellow-tinted glasses rested atop his nose but he didn't use them for reading; he simply stared at the floor or out the window behind my head the entire time. Prospective jurors never looked at him. Dahmer briefly looked up at me when I walked into the room and then returned his gaze to the floor. He will not likely remember one of the many reporters he saw during his trial, but this reporter can still remember looking a serial killer straight in the eye.

What I also remember about Jeffrey Dahmer was that he was an attractive man when he laughed. The tabloid newspaper, *Weekly World News*, carried a cover headline that read, MILWAUKEE CANNIBAL KILLER EATS HIS CELLMATE. Before prospective jurors were brought in the room, Boyle held up the newspaper and we all laughed, especially Jeffrey Dahmer. I could see how so many were taken in by him.

I listened as Gerry Boyle warned prospective jurors that the trial would include testimony about human carnage, cannibalism, mutilation, sex with dead bodies, "everything you can possibly imagine." We had a further hint of what was to come after Dr. Frederick Fosdal, one of the state-appointed psychiatrists, leaked information to a Madison, Wisconsin, newspaper that Dahmer had performed crude lobotomies on some of his victims.

By the end of the day, January 29, twelve jurors and two alternates were picked—six white men, seven white women and one black man.

The victims' families were outraged that only one black man was on the jury. They were furious about a lot of things, including the fact that reporters had the first row of seats in the courtroom and they had the second row.

One day some of the families staged a protest over the seating arrangements and that two seats were permanently reserved for Dahmer's parents. The victims' families' seats would be given up if they were not in the courtroom when proceedings began.

The protesting families carried signs in the hallway likening the situation to "White's Only" signs of the fifties. I discovered the D.A. had already granted their wish for better seats the night before the scheduled protest (a protest apparently staged for the media's benefit).

Ironically, during the protest, all the victim's families' seats in the courtroom were empty as the trial went on.

I talked to a member of the local chapter of the national organization, Parents of Murdered Children, during the trial. She often goes to court with the families of murdered children to offer moral support and she said that she has never seen families requesting the special treatment they did in the Dahmer case. In addition to special seating requests, the families wanted free meals and a special place to eat. Some even asked for clothing allowances for court attire.

The insanity defense was difficult from the outset for Gerald Boyle. Because Dahmer had changed his plea to guilty on January 13, the case was no longer about his guilt or innocence. What was left was whether he was legally responsible for his crimes. Under Wisconsin law, the burden of proving insanity lies with the defense. Throughout the trial, Boyle claimed

Dahmer suffered from a sexual disorder, making this the first trial in Wisconsin history where someone used an alleged sexual disorder to try to escape responsibility for murder.

Mike McCann's job was to show the jury that Dahmer was not insane under the definition, only evil.

The parade of psychiatrists and psychologists for both sides proved baffling and, at times, boring. The key to Boyle's defense was to make the jury understand what he meant by mental illness, and then to apply that definition to his client.

A subtle point confused many people. The doctors were being asked not only whether Dahmer was mentally ill, but also whether, at the moment the crime was occurring, his mental illness had become so severe as to prevent him from understanding or appreciating what he was doing.

The case turned into a battle of the doctors.

The leading defense psychiatrist, Frederick S. Berlin, is an expert on sexual disorders at Johns Hopkins Hospital in Baltimore. California-based psychiatrist Park Elliot Dietz, hired by the state, also has expertise in this area; he had testified for the state in the case of John Hinckley, who shot President Ronald Reagan in 1981. Both men served on the committee that helped update the section on paraphilias in the American Psychiatric Association's widely-used *Diagnostic and Statistical Manual*. As we listened we learned more about what other people like to do for sexual pleasure than we cared to know.

Paraphilias are characterized by recurrent, intense sexual urges and sexually-arousing fantasies involving nonhuman objects, children, or other nonconsenting persons, or the humiliation of oneself or one's partner. Necrophilia, or sex with a corpse, falls under the heading of paraphilia and played a central role during expert testimony in the case of Jeffrey Dahmer.

No one in the state of Wisconsin had ever been found not guilty by reason of insanity solely on the basis of a paraphilia.

In his opening statement, Gerry Boyle tried to prepare the jury for what they would hear about all these "illnesses" in regard to his client: "Jeffrey Dahmer wants a body. A body. That's his fantasy. A body," Boyle began.

New information emerged when Boyle told a story about Dahmer at the age of fifteen. Dahmer became obsessed with the idea of killing and having sex with a jogger he saw every day in front of his Bath, Ohio, home. He sawed off a baseball bat and rode his bike to find the man, but the jogger never appeared again. "Thanks be to God, that man never jogged that way again," Boyle said.

Dahmer's attorney continued. "He started masturbating on a daily basis and the object of his fantasies were thoughts concerning young boys of his age. Even as an early teenager, he started becoming interested in bones of dead animals. He would take them home, he would bleach them, he would study them. None of the interests that he had were known to his family."

Throughout the trial, Dahmer's father and stepmother, Lionel and Shari Dahmer, sat in the back of the courtroom, holding hands and stared bleakly at Boyle. Sometimes Shari took copious notes or filed her nails. Across the aisle sat the families of Jeffrey Dahmer's victims.

Boyle told of the time when Dahmer brought home the head of a fetal pig he had worked on in a biology class: he removed the skin and kept the skull in the same fashion he would later preserve his human trophies. Soon, he became obsessed with the idea of killing a hitchhiker.

Boyle then talked about the night he met the man who would be the first victim in a thirteen-year killing spree. "One night, to the regret of the world at large . . . the horror scene starts. He is driving around and he sees a hitchhiker, and the hitchhiker doesn't have a shirt on, and Jeffrey Dahmer wants his body—his *body*," Boyle explained.

After Dahmer killed Steven Hicks, he masturbated on the dead body and had sex with it. He cut the body open, just as he had sliced open animals during his childhood. He was fascinated by the insides of bodies, with their intricate, bright colors. In fact, it was later revealed that Dahmer's preference was to have sex with the viscera of his victims.

Boyle contended that Dahmer's crimes were not racial. "Mr. Dahmer's obsession was body form, not color. He wanted a body."

The defense attorney said Dahmer did not know how his next victim, his first in Wisconsin, Steven Toumi, died in 1987.

Dahmer will not be charged in that murder because of lack of evidence.

The two had drunk quite a bit of strong rum, and they passed out. When Dahmer woke up, he was lying on top of Toumi and Toumi was dead. Toumi had bruises on his body and his chest was caved in.

Boyle confirmed the cannibalism we had only speculated about before the trial. "He ate body parts so that these poor people he killed would become alive again in him. He played with heads, he painted them, colored them, the skulls of these poor people."

As his killings intensified, Jeffrey Dahmer's actions became even more outlandish. "It got so bad that he started doing surgical experimentation so as to keep them from dying because he wanted them for his purposes. He wanted to create zombies, people who would be there for him."

Dahmer enjoyed watching *The Exorcist III* and was fascinated with Satan. He fancied himself as the evil emperor in *Return of the Jedi*, who had absolute control over his subjects. He even purchased yellow-tinted contact lenses so that he could more closely resemble the emperor in the movie.

After that statement I figured those would be two movies video stores could not keep in stock. Sure enough, when I checked later for a story, video store owners said they were flooded with requests for both movies.

It was also revealed that Dahmer took various body parts to work with him at Ambrosia Chocolate, where he was employed on a work-release program from midnight to eight A.M. during the ten months he was confined to the House of Correction in 1989. He kept Anthony Sears's head in his locker, along with other body parts.

Boyle tried to give the jury some relief after his opening statement by apologizing to them that the details of the case were so gruesome, but, he added, "It isn't going to get any worse than this."

Boyle was right, it didn't. However, his descriptions were repeated ad nauseum.

When McCann addressed the jury, he portrayed Dahmer as a selfish man who killed people only to suit his own sexual preferences. He said Dahmer's drugging men at the gay bath-houses was calculated and no more insane than men using al-cohol to convince women to have sex with them. He tried to show that Dahmer carefully planned the deaths of his victims by choosing people without a car so he would not have to dis-pose of it.

We also learned that Dahmer would have preferred a live person because he liked to hear the heartbeat. He would have restrained from killing them if they would have stayed for a couple of weeks. McCann ended his statement by talking about Dahmer's ability to function under intense pressure when of-ficers arrived in his apartment the night of May 27, 1991. McCann tried to show Dahmer's recognition of right from wrong and his self-control under stress. The District Attorney recalled the many instances when Dahmer failed to cooperate with or lied to counselors he was seeing in connection with his earlier conviction on sex charges.

"You can hold a sick person responsible for his conduct when that sick person has rejected help," McCann said. "This guy knows how to con the system. Now don't let him con you."

The witness lists from both sides were lengthy, but in the end only a few from each were called. The lists included the man who cleaned Dahmer's carpeting in his apartment building, the hardware store employee who sold him equipment he used to dismember his victims (these two were later called to the stand), his pharmacist, and any police officer who had ever had contact with him.

Milwaukee Police Detectives Dennis Murphy and Pat Ken-nedy took the stand and read the 160-page confession. Some of the victims' relatives wiped tears from their eyes as previously unknown details of their loved one's deaths were read. Dorothy Straughter, mother of Curtis Straughter, groaned and wept and finally left the courtroom after Murphy read that Dahmer had saved the skull, genitals, and hands of her son after he killed him. I listened intently as I learned details of the case I had not heard before.

The confession was a litany of sexual deviance. The jurors did not appear squeamish as Murphy and Kennedy read the graphic details of Jeffrey Dahmer's crimes.

Starting in the eighth grade, he started to masturbate daily while fantasizing about boys his age. At about the age of fourteen, he first came up with the idea of using corpses for sexual purposes.

He told police that although he was not physically or sexually abused, he remembers his home being filled with tension because his parents were "constantly at each other's throats." He felt guilty for his parents' marital problems because his mother, Joyce Flint, had told Jeffrey that she had severe postpartum depression and suffered a nervous breakdown after she gave birth to him.

Dahmer told police he used to drive around with a friend who liked looking for dogs walking along the road and hitting them. Murphy read a part of the confession that said his friend once hit a beagle puppy and Dahmer never saw such a look of terror when the dog flew across the hood and hit the windshield. Downstairs in the media room there was a collective "Oh, no!" when we thought about this helpless puppy. It was ironic that there we all were, writing about bizarre sexual practices, cannibalism, and the murder and dismemberment of human beings, but the first outburst from the media was over this puppy.

The night Dahmer killed Hicks in 1978, he was nearly caught when he was stopped by police at three A.M. and ticketed for driving left of the center line. Officers shone flashlights into the car and asked Dahmer what was in the several garbage bags on the back seat. Steven Hicks's dismembered body was inside. Dahmer told them he was taking garbage to the landfill. When asked by Kennedy and Murphy why he remembered Hicks's name and no other victim's, he replied, "You don't forget your first one."

He did not get rid of Hicks's body until returning from Army service in Germany two years later.

He left Ohio for a warmer climate and in 1981 moved to Miami Beach, where he got a job making sandwiches at Sunshine Subs. He stayed only a few months, but while he was there he was befriended by a woman from England. She had long, curly, thick black hair, and he thought her name was Julie. She was in the United States illegally and wanted Dahmer to marry her so that she could stay in this country. He was never attracted to her physically, but they did go out to dinner and for long walks on the beach. She wrote to him after he left Miami, but he never answered her letters.

When he lived with his grandmother in West Allis, Wisconsin, he tried to control his urges by going to church and finding religion. But in 1985, when Dahmer had gone to the library, a young man passed him a sheet of paper that read, "Meet me in the bathroom. I'll give you a blow job." Dahmer never went, but his control started falling apart. He hid in a Milwaukee department store all night and stole a male mannequin, took it home, and related to it in a sexual way. His grandmother discovered it, and he had to throw it away. He even dabbled in the occult for a time, saying, "I suppose I related to the satanic beliefs."

He became obsessed with the idea that if he could keep someone with him, somehow the person would never leave. He thought of drugging people for control, because he was so desperate to have somebody who would not leave him. This led him to read the death notices in the paper one day, and he came upon a notice of an eighteen-year-old man's death.

He went to the funeral parlor while the deceased was in his coffin. He tried to figure out how he could steal the body or rob the grave. He even called taxidermists and inquired about stuffing and preserving animals, to give him more insight on his plan of "preserving" humans so he could keep them with him.

In 1986, he received a prescription for Halcion, a hypnotic drug, after duping a doctor into believing he was having trouble sleeping. Once he had the pills, he could go on to the next phase of his plan, which was to experiment with drugging people.

Dahmer could not get an erection if his partner was awake, only after he was unconscious. He liked it when they were unconscious because then they could not have anal sex with him. He wanted to perform sex on them but did not want to cater to any of his partners' desires. He did not want others to have control.

The victims' relatives were gratified when they heard in court that Dahmer himself was the victim of a bizarre sexual attack. On Thanksgiving Day 1989, he woke up in a strange apartment and found himself hog-tied and suspended from the ceiling. Dahmer told police he drank too much and blacked out before waking up in the unfamiliar apartment. His legs were tied together, his arms were tied behind his back, and he was hanging by hooks and ropes from the ceiling. The man was sexually assaulting him with a candle. I heard laughter from several family members seated behind me in the courtroom.

"When he realized what was happening, he began screaming and swearing at the suspect," Murphy said. After the man let him down, Dahmer left but never called police. "He stated he chalked this up as an experience he had to incur because of his high-risk life-style. He stated that this time he was the victim."

When Dahmer returned to the House of Correction, he passed several inches of a piece of candle during a bowel movement.

As for his cannibalism, he ate the body parts of people because he believed they would come alive in him. Detective Murphy said Dahmer experimented with different types of kitchen seasonings to make the cooked human flesh taste better. While working at a plasma center in Milwaukee, he took home a vial of blood and drank it; he did not like the taste. He kept meat patties in his freezer that were actually strips of human flesh and muscle.

In January 1982, Dahmer bought a .357 Magnum revolver which he used for target shooting. Lionel Dahmer took it away when he found out about it from Catherine Dahmer, Jeffrey's grandmother. Jeffrey said it was one of the few objects he owned that brought him pleasure.

The letter Dahmer sent to Judge William Gardner in 1989, asking for early release from prison where he was serving his sentence for sexually assaulting Konerak Sinthasomphone's brother, was actually written by a fellow inmate who "appeared to be knowledgeable in such matters," Dahmer said. Dahmer rewrote it in his own hand and signed it. It worked.

Most of the details of the murders after he moved into apartment 213 at the Oxford Apartments at 924 North 25th Street in Milwaukee remained unchanged during the reading of the confession. However, there were some revelations.

Dahmer saved a penis from one victim and painted it flesh-colored so it would look natural. He often left his dead victims lying around the house naked so he could have oral and anal sex with them at will. He was always completely naked when he dismembered his victims—not for erotic pleasure, but because the job was messy and he did not want to get body fluids on his clothes.

When he performed makeshift lobotomies on his victims, Dahmer would first drug them to knock them out, and then drill a hole in the head and with a syringe injected muriatic acid into the brain. Some died instantly. However, Jeremiah Weinberger managed to walk around for nearly two days after being injected with the acid.

Dahmer disposed of his victims in twenty-gallon plastic garbage bags. He confessed he felt a sense of loss when he killed them, but also excitement about what he did. He told Murphy that as he disposed of the bodies and looked at the bags, he felt the victims' lives were such a waste because they were reduced to a few bags of garbage. He said he felt remorse after each murder, but the feeling did not last.

Would-be victim Tracy Edwards's credibility was impaired by Dahmer's confession and later by Edwards himself when he took the stand. Dahmer said he did not remember doing most of the things Edwards had described on numerous television talk shows. He said Edwards never opened the refrigerator and Dahmer never threatened him with a knife and did not say he planned to cut out his heart. A number of psychiatric experts told me that people like Jeffrey Dahmer do not announce their intentions in advance.

As to his feelings about the crimes, Dahmer said that while he enjoyed keeping the bodies of his victims, their presence in his apartment caused him to feel thoroughly evil. "I have to question whether or not there is an evil force in the world and whether or not I have been influenced by it," Dahmer told police. "Although I am not sure if there is a God, or if there is a devil, I know that as of lately I've been doing a lot of thinking about both, and I have to wonder what has influenced me in my life."

Murphy also quoted Dahmer as saying, "That's what happens when you think you're not accountable to anyone. My moral compass was so off."

Tracy Edwards was the first civilian witness to take the stand. Edwards was the only person who ever saw Dahmer right before he was going to kill, but his testimony often proved faulty. Shortly after Dahmer's arrest in July 1991, Edwards started doing the national talk-show circuit. Each time he was interviewed, his story became more detailed and more outlandish. What he said when he was paid to appear on national television was markedly different from what he told police had happened in Jeffrey Dahmer's apartment in July. Edwards, who praised the police for rescuing him that night, sued the Milwaukee Police Department for its alleged insensitivity in dealing with him. A federal judge tossed the suit out of court.

Edwards testified that Dahmer was "going out of himself" and "rocking back and forth and chanting." Edwards said he agreed to go to the apartment to pose for photographs, and that when the two got back to the apartment Dahmer placed a brown bag holding a six-pack of beer they had bought on the kitchen table, not in the refrigerator. That would become important later, when McCann tried to trip him up for telling a talk-show host that when he opened the refrigerator to get a beer, he saw the head.

He testified that after Dahmer slapped a handcuff on him and threatened him, Edwards hit him and ran out the door. Edwards said he found the police, who joined him going back to the apartment. On talk shows he said the police would not come back with him, and he said nothing about that when he testified in court.

When McCann cross-examined Edwards, the would-be victim was obviously nervous. He stammered through his answers and looked constantly at his attorney, seated behind Boyle.

Edwards had told television interviewer Geraldo Rivera that there were eight locks on the door and he "luckily" opened the right one. McCann produced a photograph of the apartment door taken the night of Dahmer's capture. It showed a door with one deadbolt and a small push-in lock on the doorknob. McCann pressed him on why he didn't testify about all the gory things he said he saw in the refrigerator on national television. Edwards claimed he tried to block it all out.

"I didn't think anybody wanted to know," Edwards said, to explain why he never told police in his original statement on July 23, 1991, that he saw any body parts in the apartment. McCann had shattered Edwards's testimony. Ironically, I learned that the day before he testified, Edwards had again appeared on "Geraldo" and told yet a different story.

Expert testimony was the most difficult part of the trial to cover because it got so complicated. From each expert, I culled a couple of nuggets that lay people could understand, and sometimes the expert revealed a new piece of information.

Defense witness Dr. Frederick S. Berlin—a heavy-set man with a tuft of curly black hair—testified for two days that Jeffrey Dahmer had a sick obsession with dead bodies that he couldn't control and that caused him to kill. "He has fantasies and urges about having initial sexual contact with someone while they're alive," Berlin testified. "He then fantasizes and imagines continuing sexual acts and intimate relationships in a transition state that's sort of between life and death; at times he's called it a zombie-like state." Berlin went on to explain that Dahmer acted on the fantasy, continuing to "relate to the body of the person after death."

Berlin emphasized that Dahmer's feelings and urges were not voluntary: "Nobody would ever decide to have this kind of affliction. He's discovered that he's afflicted with these recurrent, erotically-aroused fantasies and urges of the most sick sort."

"In my medical opinion," Berlin added, "Mr. Dahmer was out of control and was becoming progressively more out of control; and it wasn't going to be he who was going to stop it, it was going to have to be stopped by some outside force, which is exactly how it inevitably was stopped."

Under McCann's cross-examination, Berlin became extremely agitated and engaged in a yelling match with the prosecutor.

McCANN: Doctor, you spent far less time than any of the other experts [with Dahmer], didn't you?

BERLIN: It's not the amount of time spent. It's the quality of time. I did everything within my power to make certain I wasn't getting a biased view of this case.

MCCANN: The way to do that is to talk to the defendant himself, not what the police wrote, not what counsel wrote, not what the neighbors said, but to talk to the defendant himself.

BERLIN: You are very naive. You think you can get the answer from him! He's biased. I'm sorry for yelling. You're attacking my professional and personal credibility and my integrity.

Dahmer sat between two of Boyle's assistants, Wendy Patrickus and Ellen Ryan, at the defense table. He wore a suit for the first time and seemed unaffected as Berlin testified to his deepest sexual secrets and mental problems. Several jurors dozed during Berlin's testimony, which became quite tedious. He covered every analogy to Dahmer's compulsion, from bestiality to Betty Ford's drinking.

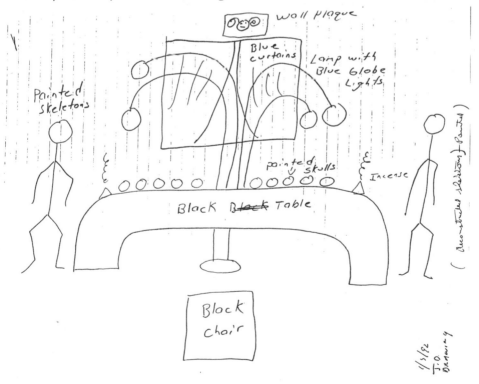

The most interesting expert proved to be Dr. Judith Becker, a clinical psychologist from Tucson, Arizona, and professor of psychology and psychiatry at the University of Arizona. She was a member of Attorney General Edwin Meese's Commission on Pornography and dissented from the group's finding of a link between pornography and violence.

She spoke in a quiet, almost inaudible tone. Hired by Boyle, Becker revealed that Dahmer had elaborate plans to build a temple or shrine that featured his victims' remains, in hopes of "receiving special powers and energies." Dahmer drew a sketch to show Becker the table that would feature skulls, painted skeletons, incense burners, and mood lights. "He was going to be getting some kind of power that would help him socially and financially," she said.

Dahmer purchased the base of the temple, a black table, before going to jail for sexual assault in 1989. He planned to buy a black chair to sit on in front of the table. He planned to line up the skulls of ten victims on the table and position one full skeleton on each end of the table. Incense would be burning on the table, and everything would be illuminated by four blue overhead globe lights, Dahmer explained to Becker. Blue curtains and a wall plaque, perhaps depicting a goat, would form the backdrop of the shrine.

Dahmer had also purchased a statue of a griffin, a mythical animal with the body and hind legs of a lion and the head and wings of an eagle. The griffin is commonly used in satanic worship. Dahmer told Becker he bought it because it represented evil, which is how he felt.

Becker characterized Dahmer as consumed by the mental disease that led him to kill uncontrollably because of his obsession with the dead. Like Berlin, Becker concluded that Dahmer appreciated right from wrong, but was so obsessed by necrophilia that he "did not have substantial capacity to conform his conduct to the requirements of the law."

Becker was able to offer new details of Dahmer's childhood and adolescence.

BECKER: At four years Jeffrey had a double hernia operation, and he remembered experiencing terrible pain in his groin area, so much so he asked his mother if his genitals had been cut off.

BOYLE: Why would this aspect be of interest?

BECKER: In relation to the offenses that Jeffrey committed and the fact he experienced pain there . . . and the fact he slit open the abdomens of the 15 men . . . that he murdered.

Becker related another story from Dahmer's childhood. "He remembered taking some tadpoles to his teacher, and Jeffrey stated that he liked this teacher. However, he was upset when he learned this teacher had given the tadpoles to a boy in his class, who was Jeffrey's best friend at the time. Jeffrey went to the friend's house and stated that he took motor oil and poured the motor oil into the container of tadpoles in which they were housed to kill them. Jeffrey viewed his teacher as a kind person, but he felt that she had rejected him by giving away the tadpoles."

Becker told of a fishing incident when Dahmer went to catch some bluegills in the pond behind his Bath, Ohio, home. "Jeffrey remembered his father showing him how to cut open a fish to clean it. He remembered the egg sac caught his eye. It was the color of it, bright orange . . .

"Jeffrey, for the most part in relating material, was pretty monotone and pretty flat. When he talked about cutting the fish open and seeing the inside of the fish, he became somewhat more animated, somewhat more alive, in a sense."

Becker felt Dahmer's fascination with the colors of the insides of the fish was related to his later fascination with the look of the viscera, or insides, of his victims. Dahmer told Becker he cut every victim open in the abdomen.

At age five, Dahmer recalled persuading a playmate to stick his hand into a wasps' nest, telling him it was populated by ladybugs. The boy was stung. Becker said that act was significant because Dahmer understood his friend would be hurt.

Dahmer talked to her about the cannibalism. "He tried tasting the flesh and the heart," Becker related. "He bought a meat tenderizer, tenderized the heart, and ate it and the muscle meat. It gave him a sexual thrill while eating it. He felt that the man was a part of him and he internalized him. He reported having an erection while eating it."

Dahmer told Becker that he performed a sexual act with every victim's body after death, something he did not tell police. Dahmer also told her that he felt as though "a nuclear explosion" had occurred within him after he was charged with the slayings and that he considered killing himself while shaving before court.

Dahmer also told her that holding the skulls of some of his victims frequently brought him sexual gratification. "According to Jeffrey," Becker said, "the head represented the essence of the person. I asked him if he spoke to the heads, and he said he might have."

When Becker asked about his fascination with body parts, Dahmer said, "Maybe I was born too late. Maybe I was an Aztec." (Dahmer believed Aztecs preserved parts or all of the dead.)

McCann's assistant, Assistant District Attorney Carol White, failed to shake Becker's testimony; she could not be rattled like Berlin.

During this second week of the trial, we in the media started to wonder what the jurors were doing with their free time. The jurors were sequestered, kept away from family and friends. They were shown nonviolent and comedic movies like *City Slickers*, *King Ralph*, and *Home Alone*. They were allowed no television, radio, or newspapers, for fear of exposure to news coverage of the trial.

Dr. Carl M. Wahlstrom, a Chicago psychiatrist and the last of Boyle's experts to testify, said Jeffrey Dahmer was cunning, dismembering bodies to conceal his crimes, and capable of going long periods without killing.

Wahlstrom said, "He didn't like killing, and he wanted to keep the victims alive in a zombie state. He talked about not liking it and drinking at times to overcome that dislike. [He had] a bizarre, grandiose delusion that he could actually do a crude brain operation that would make people forget their memory and identity. . . . And . . . he went out [and got] one after another, even though these [operations] were failing, and [he] continued to try and do such a delusional type of activity."

After the defense rested, a court-appointed psychiatrist from Milwaukee, Dr. George Palermo, testified that Dahmer suffered from a serious personality disorder which needed to be treated, but said he was not psychotic or legally insane. "He is an organized, nonsocial lust murderer, who killed in a methodical and shrewd manner," Palermo said. "He is driven by obsessive fantasies of power over others."

Palermo added he had expected to come face to face with a crazy person when he met Dahmer because of the number of people he had killed. "I was shocked," Palermo recalled. "He's a likable fellow. Whatever he has done, he's still a human being." He said he found Dahmer's speech clear and his answers coherent. He felt Dahmer was amiable and intelligent.

Palermo said Dahmer had lied for years and was lying still. He doubted Dahmer's claim that he planned to build a temple from the bones of the bodies and did not believe he ate the flesh of any of his victims. He testified that Dahmer had embellished the facts and made them more ugly than they already were. He also doubted Dahmer drilled holes in any of the victims' heads while they were still alive.

In a rare show of emotion, Dahmer scribbled on a piece of paper after Palermo testified that Dahmer's weight ballooned to 290 pounds from smoking so much marijuana. We were later told that he wrote the note for Boyle saying he was angry because Palermo's claim was untrue.

The prosecution's witnesses consisted of a parade of people who testified about their contact, no matter how cursory, with Jeffrey Dahmer. McCann called the guy who cleaned the bloodstains from the carpeting at Dahmer's apartment, the man who sold him the large blue barrel, and the hardware store employee who sold him the boxes of muriatic acid. McCann also called Dahmer's coworkers to testify that the man they remembered never seemed to be hearing voices, had unconnected thoughts, or was incoherent. McCann also called Ronald Flowers, whom Dahmer invited to his grandmother's home but later decided not to kill.

Flowers testified that he went to Dahmer's grandmother's home after he had car trouble outside Club 219. Flowers remembered little except that Dahmer offered to help him out

with "his own car." Dahmer did not drive. He told Flowers that
his car was at his grandmother's house, and they had to take a
cab to get there. When the two got to the house, Dahmer fixed
coffee and slipped a sleeping potion into Flowers's cup. Flowers
woke up at a local hospital, not knowing how he got there.
Flowers reported the incident to the police, but there was in-
sufficient evidence to charge Dahmer at the time.

"When he handed me the cup of coffee, his eye contact was
solid and he didn't divert it at all. It was almost as though he
was waiting for something," Flowers testified. "I was thinking
to myself, What is he waiting for?"

Dahmer decided not to kill Flowers because his 250-pound
body he could not easily dispose of.

Flowers recognized Dahmer a year later, but Dahmer said he
did not recognize him. " 'Maybe we could go for a cup of coffee?' " Flowers testified Dahmer said to him at this second meeting. Flowers stared Dahmer down when he got off the witness
stand.

The next witness was the brother of Konerak Sinthasomphone, whom Dahmer sexually assaulted in 1988, for which
Dahmer went to prison in 1989. The boy testified that he went
to the apartment to have pictures taken for money but drank
a drugged drink and later woke up in the hospital.

One witness who testified was a surprise; we of the media
had never heard of him. The man told the jury he and a friend
accompanied Dahmer to the Ambassador Hotel (where Dahmer would murder Steven Toumi) in the spring of 1987, after
meeting him at the gay bar C'est La Vie. Dahmer prepared
drinks for the man and his friend, but when his guests drank,
Dahmer stood up and stripped off all his clothes. He lay there
outstretched, with his hands behind his head, and talked about
his days in the Army, the man said. The man and his friend
eventually passed out. When they awoke the next morning,
Dahmer was gone and they found signs that they had been
sexually assaulted.

Another witness was Jeffrey Connor, a friend of victim Anthony Sears. Connor testified that he and Sears met Dahmer at
a gay bar in March 1989. He drove Dahmer and Sears to the
grandmother's home, and Connor never saw Sears again. "I

felt that he was a very nice person. He seemed very kind," Connor said of Dahmer.

The prosecution asked all the witnesses who had been picked up by Dahmer the same series of questions concerning whether or not Dahmer seemed crazy when they encountered him. They all answered no.

After the men described their brushes with Dahmer, Frederick Fosdal a psychiatrist from Madison, Wisconsin, took the stand. Fosdal stopped short of calling Dahmer's disorder, known as necrophilia, a mental disease under the state's insanity law. In addition to a disorder, he called it a "maladjustment," and even referred to it once as Dahmer's "unhealth." Fosdal also said he had never seen a sexual disorder that rendered someone unable to conform his conduct to the law. Fosdal revealed for the first time that Dahmer kept the bodies in the bathtub when he didn't have time to dismember them and frequently showered with them.

Dahmer's cannibalism and his belief that this would make his victims part of him was not delusional thinking and did not suggest he was psychotic, Fosdal said. "It was just a symbolic gesture," he said.

After Fosdal, McCann called two of Dahmer's former bosses from Ambrosia Chocolate, who said that while Dahmer was in the midst of his killing spree, he went about his job without raising any suspicions.

"I had no problems with Jeffrey," said Walter Boening, Dahmer's former supervisor. "Jeffrey was always polite."

And Melvin Heaney, plant superintendent, remembered when Dahmer was arrested for the sexual assault of the Sinthasomphone boy in September 1988. "He told me that he had gotten into a problem, that he had propositioned a young lady that he thought was of age and he later found out she was a minor."

Neither knew anything about the skull Dahmer supposedly kept in his locker. On cross-examination, the defense asked each man how much time he actually spent with Dahmer, hoping to show that the periods would be too brief for the witnesses to get to know him.

Police Lt. Scott Schaefer took the stand for the prosecution and decribed arresting Dahmer at Ambrosia in September 1988. "He was very nervous," Schaefer recalled. "He was very concerned with his employer not knowing why he had been taken into custody." Dahmer told Schaefer he had wanted to have sexual contact with the Laotian boy, but he didn't want to push it.

The manager of the Unicorn Bathhouse in Chicago testified that Dahmer visited the bathhouse ten times between April 1990 and February 1991 without incident.

It was a full courtroom gallery during the testimony from Milwaukee police officers John Balcerzak and Joe Gabrish both of whom had been fired.

There were no surprises from either on the stand. Their future rested on what would come out in court regarding the Konerak Sinthasomphone incident May 27, 1991. They said they conducted a full and proper investigation and believed they took the appropriate action. They portrayed Dahmer as a master manipulator who thoroughly convinced them that Konerak was his friend.

Sopa Princewill, manager of the Oxford Apartments, was next to testify. He had received complaints about the smell (almost every tenant complained about it), and determined it was coming from Dahmer's apartment. Three times Princewill confronted Dahmer about the odor wafting throughout the building. He helped Dahmer clean his refrigerator and recalled for the court that all he saw in the refrigerator was "some kind of meat." Apart from the smell, Princewill said Dahmer's apartment "was probably the neatest apartment I've ever seen," compared with others in the building.

The carpet cleaner Dahmer hired testified about a large, two-foot-by-three-foot dark stain in the bedroom that wouldn't come out. Dahmer told him it was chocolate. He thought it was blood or wine.

Finally, Dr. Park Elliot Dietz settled into the witness chair for two days. We carefully watched to see if McCann would be able to have admitted into evidence the hours of videotape Dietz shot of Dahmer as he examined him. We never got the chance to see it.

Dietz revealed that Dahmer had another close call when

someone reported to police that the odor in the apartment hallway indicated that someone had died. Dahmer, having taken too long to dismember a body, left for work with the job half done and returned home to find police had kicked in a neighbor's door down the hall from his apartment. "Mr. Dahmer said he found that experience frightening and finished the dismemberment task quickly that morning," Dietz said.

Dietz, a noted psychiatrist, has been quoted widely on his belief that a defendant may be considered to know right from wrong if he tries to avoid getting caught by such acts as hiding the bodies of victims. A clinical professor of psychiatry and biobehavioral sciences at the University of California–Los Angeles School of Medicine, he was the prosecution's star witness.

Dietz quoted Dahmer: " 'It's a strange situation to be in. I mean I was so intent on having a great deal of control and shaping my own destiny, and now it's all out of my hands. You can't keep running from the truth forever. Eventually you have to face the consequences. It may take years, but eventually you do.' "

Dahmer always knew that what he was doing was wrong, Dietz said. Evidence was plentiful that Dahmer acted rationally and in his own self-interest for example, he always used a condom when engaging in sex with a corpse, Dietz testified.

Dietz felt Dahmer's sexual attraction to viscera might date to his freshman year in high school, about the time he began to masturbate frequently. He was fascinated when dissecting animals in school and had thoughts about the animal parts while maturbating. "Then it becomes sexualized," Dietz said. "If it enters his mind enough times while he masturbates, it becomes a sexy thought."

During the whole trial, the testimony had desensitized so many of us in the media, that we made jokes to keep our sanity while we covered the biggest story of our careers. But when McCann and Boyle gave their closing arguments, the case suddenly became very human.

I felt myself choke up during McCann's closing. We all did. After holding up a colored photograph of each victim, saying to the jury, "Don't forget Richard Guerrero," "Don't forget Anthony Sears," and so on for each of the fifteen victims, he questioned characterizing the drugging of the victims as an act of kindness: "Is that a kindly act or a cowardly act to drug them before he killed them?" an emotional McCann asked the jury. "That was no favor."

Then, in a short speech that sent family members rushing from the courtroom in sobs, McCann spoke as if inside the thoughts of the victims: "Don't kill me by drugging me, come at me with a knife and a gun. Let him have his knife, and I'll confront him with my bare hands!" he screamed.

For Boyle's part, he drew for the jury a powerful visual image of what he referred to as the "Jeffrey Dahmer human being." It was a chart showing the initials J. D. inside a circle; radiating from the circle, like spokes of a wheel, were the horrifying aspects of his life. Boyle read them off rapidly:

"Skulls in locker, cannibalism, sexual urges, drilling, making zombies, necrophilia, disorders, paraphilia, watching videos, getting excited about fish eggs, drinking alcohol all of the time, into a dysfunctional family, trying to create a shrine, showering with corpses, going into the occult, having delusions, chanting and rocking, picking up road kill, having obsessions, murders, lobotomies, defleshing, masturbating two, three times a day as a youngster, going and trying to get a mannequin home so he could play sex with a mannequin, masturbating into open parts of a human being's body, calling taxidermists, going to grave yards, going to funeral homes, wearing yellow contacts, posing people who are dead that he killed for pictures, masturbating all over the place.

"This is Jeffrey Dahmer," Boyle said, toning his voice down. "There isn't a positive thing on this."

Boyle called Dahmer "a runaway train on a track of madness, picking up steam all the time, on and on and on. And it was only going to stop when he hit a concrete barrier or he hit another train. And he hit it, thanks be to God, when Tracy Edwards got the hell out of that room."

But McCann countered during his rebuttal closing argument, "He wasn't a runaway train, he was the engineer!" McCann said the case was about sexual urges. We all have them and we must control them. But Dahmer chose not to, McCann said.

By the end of the trial, we were all completely confused as

to what actually constituted a mental disease. We assumed the jury would be puzzled too.

Judge Gram tried to clarify the issue in his instructions to the jury:

"You are not bound by medical labels, definitions, or conclusions as to what is or is not a mental disease.

"You should not find that a person is suffering from a mental disease merely because he may have committed a criminal act or because of the unnaturalness or enormity of such act or because a motive for such act may be lacking.

"Temporary passion or frenzy prompted by revenge, hatred, jealousy, envy, or the like does not constitute a mental disease.

"An abnormality manifested only by repeated criminal or otherwise antisocial conduct does not constitute a mental disease.

"A voluntary state of intoxication by drugs or alcohol or both does not constitute a mental disease.

"A temporary mental state which is brought into existence by the voluntary taking of drugs or alcohol does not constitute a mental disease."

With that, the jury was sent to deliberate Friday afternoon, February 14.

After five hours they returned to the court where we held tense as Judge Gram read the verdict: "Count one, Did he suffer from a mental disease? Answer, No." And so it went for fifteen counts, as the respective family members began to sob and scream and hug each other. Guilty and sane on all fifteen counts. Only two jurors dissented. In a criminal case, a jury's decision would have to be unanimous, but in an insanity case, the law allows for a 10-2 vote.

It was over.

We go on to other stories, perhaps none as dramatic. But for the families it goes on forever. In the hour before Jeffrey Dahmer's sentencing, the relatives were given a chance to express their feelings. Again, emotions, even for the grizzled media, were high as the relatives of the victims unleashed their anger toward the man who stole from them.

I was not prepared for the impact on me of what are officially called "victim impact statements."

J. W. Smith, brother of Edward Smith, quoting statements gathered from Eddie's family:

"From Michael, another brother. 'I'm sure Edward was a friend to Jeffrey Dahmer, as he was to us. I have these pictures in my mind that are running continuously. How can anyone comprehend or come to accept that never again in this life will Edward be?'

"From John, another brother. 'Jeffrey Dahmer has erased a million future memories for me, of my closest brother.'

"From me. Our dad is gone and now so are you. I never had the chance to say good-bye to either of you. You are unique and I love you.'

"From Maia, a sister. 'I wanted to see justice done and no dollar amount can bring my brother back. If you feel any remorse, let's change the Son of Sam law to the Jeffrey Dahmer law.' (The Son of Sam law, first enacted in New York State, was meant to prevent convicted murderers from profiting from their crimes, through publication of their stories as books or movies.)

"From Josephine Helen, our mother. 'Let me tell you briefly about Edward Warren Smith on a more personal level. Ed was raised in a Christian home where he learned how to be a loving, trusting, respectful human being. Eddie inherited all the blessings that a family structure had to offer. The greatest of these blessings was love.' "

Stanley Miller, uncle of Ernest Miller:

"There is no place in a civilized society for anyone who shows no regard for life. To Jeffrey Dahmer: You have become a hero to a few, but you have become a nightmare to so many more. I'm not for the death penalty, but you are a perfect candidate. To the Dahmer family: I know that there are some dark days for your family, but the morning will come and you will make it through."

Shirley Hughes, mother of Anthony Hughes:

"I would like to say to Jeffrey Dahmer that he don't know the pain, the hurt, the loss, and the mental state that he has put our family in. Tony thought you was his friend. He knew you. [*Quoting from a poem written by a friend of Tony's*] 'My friend, what is it that you've given me, what is it that you're doing to me? I'm helpless. Is that a thrill to you to know that I can't fight you back and that the hardest struggle in my life is fighting to keep my eyes open with the hope of seeing the dawn of a new day? You have total control over me. Mom, I'm gone, my hope, my breath, my want to live have been taken away from me unwillingly.

" 'But, yet I'm not far away. When you get cold, I wrap my arms around you to warm you. If you get sad, I softly grab your heart and cheer you up. If you smile, I'll smile right along with you. When you cry, take one teardrop and place it outside your window ledge, and when I pass by I'll exchange it for one of mine. Two fingers and one thumb, Mom.' "

Shirley Hughes held up the sign-language symbol for I love you.

Dorothy Straughter, mother of Curtis Straughter:

"You took my seventeen-year-old son away from me. You took my daughter's only brother away from her. She'll never have a chance to sing and dance with him again. You took my mother's oldest grandchild from her, and for that I can never forgive you. You almost destroyed me, but I refuse to let you destroy me. I will carry on."

Janie Hagen, sister of Richard Guerrero:

"You are a diablo, el puro diablo, [*continuing in Spanish and then translating*] the devil, the pure devil that walked our streets and was loose. So, Your Honor, please, I beg you, don't let this man ever walk our streets and see daylight again."

Inez Thomas, mother of David Thomas:

"That was my baby boy that you took away from me. You took away his two-year-old child's father. She sits in the window asking, 'Where is Dada?' She called him Dada. 'Where is Dada? When is Dada coming?' And I think that is a sad thing for a child to see, to go through all of her life not to know her father. I want to thank the jury for seeing this man for what he is, a sneaky, conniving person."

Donald Bradehoft, brother of Joseph Bradehoft:

"We lost the baby of the family, and I hope you go to hell."

Marilyn Sears, mother of Anthony Sears:

"I just wanted to know just why, you know, why it would be my son? Just keep this man off the streets, please."

Rita Isbell, sister of Errol Lindsey:

"Whatever your name is, Satan. I'm mad. This is how you act when you are out of control. [*Voice rising*] I don't ever want to see my mother have to go through this again. Never, Jeffrey! [*Screaming*] I hate you motherfucker! I hate you!"

Then Isbell charged the defense table and lunged for Dahmer. He sat perfectly still as deputies rushed to protect him. Some of the family members were angry because they had wanted the relatives to maintain their dignity, but others told me Rita Isbell expressed what they had all felt for so long.

The Jeffrey Dahmer trial was the most expensive in Milwaukee court history, with total costs soaring to more than $120,000. Daily security cost $5,400 a day, including 24-hour protection of the 14-member sequestered jury. Trial costs included $65,000 for the prosecution's expert psychiatric witnesses, $8,000 for the Medical Examiner, and $5,400 for jurors' fees (a juror receives $16 a day for sitting on a trial). A typical felony trial costs $400 a day.

The costs were staggering; much of the testimony was nauseating. Surely something has to be learned, something good must come of it.

District Attorney E. Michael McCann feels we should recognize the danger of fantasy and that thinking about anything is a definite precursor to doing it.

Attorney Gerald Boyle hopes that anyone with any kind of serious problem who watched the trial will discover help exists.

Most of all, I was astonished at how normal this man looked and sounded. As I sat with other reporters in the courtroom the day Jeffrey Dahmer was sentenced, I heard him read his statement to the court calmly and eloquently, and I wondered how easily I could have been conned.

His apology, covering a thirteen-year bloodbath, ran four typewritten pages:

Your Honor:
It is now over. This has never been a case of trying to get free. I didn't ever want freedom. Frankly, I wanted death for myself. This was a case to tell the world that I

did what I did, but not for reasons of hate. I hated no one. I knew I was sick or evil or both. Now I believe I was sick. The doctors have told me about my sickness, and now I have some peace.

I know how much harm I have caused. I tried to do the best I could after the arrest to make amends, but no matter what I did I could not undo the terrible harm I have caused. My attempt to help identify the remains was the best I could do, and that was hardly anything.

I feel so bad for what I did to those poor families, and I understand their rightful hate.

I now know I will be in prison the rest of my life. I know that I will have to turn to God to help me get through each day. I should have stayed with God. I tried and failed and created a holocaust. Thank God there will be no more harm that I can do. I believe that only the Lord Jesus Christ can save me from my sins.

I have instructed Mr. Boyle to end this matter. I do not want to contest the civil cases. I have told Mr. Boyle to try and finalize them [sic] if he can. If there is ever money I want it to go to the families. I have talked to Mr. Boyle about other things that might help ease my conscience in some way of coming up with ideas on how to make some amends to these families, and I will work with him on that.

I want to return to Ohio and quickly end that matter [his first murder, that of Steven Hicks] so that I can put all of this behind me and then come right back here to do my sentence.

I decided to go through this trial [he could have pleaded guilty and gone straight to jail] for a number of reasons. One of the reasons was to let the world know these were not hate crimes. I wanted the world and Milwaukee, which I deeply hurt, to know the truth of what I did. I didn't want unanswered questions. All the questions have now been answered. I wanted to find out just what it was that caused me to be so bad and evil. But most of all, Mr. Boyle and I decided that maybe there was a way for us to tell the world that if there are people out there with these disorders, maybe they can get help before they end up being hurt or hurting someone. I think the trial did that.

I take all the blame for what I did. I hurt many people. The judge in my earlier case tried to help me, and I refused his help and he got hurt by what I did. [A reference to criticism directed at Judge Gardner, for letting Dahmer off easy.] I hurt those policemen in the Konerak matter, and I shall ever regret causing them to lose their jobs, and I only hope and pray they can get their jobs back because I know they did their best and I just plain fooled them. For that I am so sorry. I know I hurt my probation officer, who was really trying to help me. I am so sorry for that and sorry for everyone else I have hurt.

I have hurt my mother and father and stepmother. I love them all so very much. I hope that they will find the same peace I am looking for.

Mr. Boyle's associates, Wendy and Ellen, have been wonderful to me, helping me through this worst of all times. I want to publicly thank Mr. Boyle. He didn't need to take this case. But when I asked him to help me find the answers and to help others if I could, he stayed with me and went way overboard in trying to help me. Mr. Boyle and I agreed that it was never a matter of trying to get off. It was only a matter of which place I would be housed the rest of my life, not for my comfort, but for trying to study me in the hopes of helping me and learning to help others who might have problems.

I now know I will be in prison. I pledge to talk to doctors who might be able to find some answers.

In closing, I just want to say that I hope God has forgiven me. I think He has. I know society will never be able to forgive me. I know the families of the victims will never be able to forgive me for what I have done. But if there is a God in heaven, I promise I will pray each day to ask them for their forgiveness when the hurt goes away, if ever.

I have seen their tears, and if I could give up my life right now to bring their loved ones back, I would do it. I am so very sorry.

Your Honor, I know that you are about to sentence me. I ask for no consideration. I want you to know that I have been treated perfectly by the deputies who have been in your court and the deputies who work the jail. The deputies have treated me very professionally and I want everyone to know that. They have not given me special treatment.

Here is a trustworthy saying that deserves full acceptance: "Christ Jesus came into the world to save sinners— of whom I am the worst. But for that very reason I was shown mercy so that in me, the worst of sinners, Christ Jesus might display his unlimited patience as an example for those who would believe in him and receive eternal life. Now to the King Eternal, immortal, invisible, the only God, be honor and glory forever and ever."

—1 Timothy 1:15–17

I know my time in prison will be terrible, but I deserve whatever I get because of what I have done.

Thank you, Your Honor, and I am prepared for your sentence, which I know will be the maximum. I ask for no consideration.

He got none. Jeffrey Dahmer was sentenced to fifteen consecutive life terms, or 957 years, in prison.

APPENDIX A

Serial Murderers in the United States

(*Source:* Dr. Ron Holmes, Southern Police Institute)

Years	Victims	Name	Location	Victim Traits
	6+	Alonso Robinson		
1900	12	Joseph Briggen	California	Hired hands
	41	Billy Gohl	Washington	Sailors
	14–49	Belle Gunness	Indiana	Suitors, husbands
	3–8	Louise Peete	California	Men and women
	3*	Mary Eleanor and Earl Smith	Washington	Men
	11	Tillie Klinek	Illinois	Husbands and suitors
	15	James Watson	Northwest U.S.	Suitors
	15–50	Harry Powers	West Virginia	Suitors, children
to	10*	Raymond Lisenba		
	12	Joseph Mumfre	Louisiana	Italian grocers
	unknown	Mads Sorenson	Indiana	Husbands and suitors
	17–20	Gordon Northcott	California	Children
	17–20	Sarah Northcott	California	Children
	4	Clarence Robinson	California	Children
	31–100	Jane Toppan	Massachusetts	Patients
	27	Amy Archer-Gilligan	Connecticut	Men and women
	15	Anna Hahn	Ohio	Elderly male patients
1940	20	Earl Nelson	Several states	Female landladies
	21	Carl Panzram	Connecticut	Varied
	100*	H. H. Mudgett	Illinois	Varied
	15–200	Albert Fish	New York	Children
	12+	Johann Huch	Illinois	Wives
1940	10	Jake Bird	Washington	Females
	6	Mack Edwards	California	Children
to	11	Nannie Doss	Oklahoma	Husbands, family members
	4	Harvey Glatman	California	Women

*Current unsolved murder cases.

220

Years	Victims	Name	Location	Victim Traits
	5	Anjette Lyles	Georgia	Husbands and three women
1959	9	Melvin Rees	Maryland	Young women
	3*	Bill Heirens	Illinois	Women
	10*	Richard Biegenwald		
	3–20	Martha Beck	New York	Women
1959	3–20	Ray Fernandez	New York	Women
	5*	Edward Gein	Wisconsin	Women and children
1960s	13	Albert DeSalvo (Boston Strangler)	Massachusetts	Women
	4–5	Jerry Brudos	Oregon	Young women
	3–6	Richard Marquette	Oregon	Women
	5*	Charles Schmid		
	7	Posteal Laskey	Ohio	Women
	7	John Collins	Michigan	College women
	5	Janice Gibbs	Georgia	Family members
	10*	The Zodiac* Killer	California	Men and women
1970s	12	Edmund Kemper	California	College women, mother
	100*	Harvey Carignan	Oregon, Washington	Young women
	5⁺	Erno Soto	New York	Young black males
	3*	Audrey Hilley	Alabama	Husband, women, police officer
	25	Juan Corona	California	Farm workers
	6	David Berkowitz (Son of Sam)	New York	Women
	Unknown	Richard Macek		
	Unknown	Vernon Butts		
	Unknown	Vaughn Greenwood		
	6	Richard Cottingham	New York	Patients
	36–400†	Ted Bundy	10 states	Women
	13	Herbert Mullin	California	Varied
	33	John Wayne Gacy	Illinois	Young men
	39	Gerald Eugene Stano	Florida	Women
	10–22	Angelo Buono ("Hillside Strangler")	California	Women
	10–22	Kenneth Bianchi ("Hillside Strangler")	California, Washington	Women
	27*	Dean Corll	Texas	Men
	27*	Wayne Henley	Texas	Men
	32	Wayne Kearney	California	Men
	8*	Henry Lucus	Several states	Men and women
	35*	Ottis Toole	Several states	Men and women
	13–21	William Bonin	California	Men
	7	Carlton Gary	Georgia	Elderly women
	18	Paul Knowles	8 states	Men and women
	100*	Joseph Fisher	Several states	Men and women
	3	Joseph Kallinger	Pennsylvania	Son, young boy and a woman
	6*	Gary & Thaddeus Lewington		
	15*	Patrick Kearney		
	14	Manuel Moore	California	White adults
	14	Larry Green	California	White adults
	14	Jessie Cooks	California	White adults

*Current unsolved murder cases.

†During an interview on death row in Florida, Bundy admitted that the number of his victims could be as high as 400.

Years	Victims	Name	Location	Victim Traits
	14	J. C. Simon	California	White adults
	4	Velma Barfield	South Carolina	Husband, mother, two women
1980s	7–50	Douglas Clark	California	Prostitutes
	3*	Carol Bundy	California	Prostitutes, boyfriend
	3–5	Betty Lou Beets	Texas	Husbands and one man
	8	Mary Beth Tinning	New York	
	10*	David Carpenter	Texas	
	15*	Coral Watts	Several states	
	6	Richard Chase	California	Women and children
	4	Richard Angelo	California	Patients
	10	Gerald Gallego	California, Nevada	Men and women
	1–14	Randy Woodfield	California, Washington, Oregon	Women
	10	Christine Gallego	California, Nevada	Men and women
	10	Robert Long	Florida	Women
	17	Robert Hansen	Alaska	Prostitutes
	5–8	Gary Bishop	Utah	Young boys
	2–28	Wayne Williams	Georgia	Young boys, girls, 2 adult men
	15	Richard Ramirez ("Night Stalker")	California	Varied
	8	Christopher Wilder	Several states	Young women
	2–12	Joseph Franklin	Several states	Young black males
	6–8	Terri Rachels	Georgia	Patients
	46	Gene Jones	Texas	Patients
	7	Christine Palling	Florida	Children and elderly man
	11–28	Sherman McCrary	Several states	Prostitutes
	11–28	Carl Taylor	Several states	Prostitutes
	48*	The Green River Killer*	Washington	Women
	48*	The San Diego Killer*	California	Women
	3	Beoria Simmons	Kentucky	Women
	54	Donald Harvey	Kentucky, Ohio	Hospital patients
	9	Calvin Jackson	New York	Hotel guests
	4*	Gary Heidnik	Pennsylvania	Women
	8*	Alton Coleman	Several states	Women
	8*	Debra Brown Coleman	Several states	Women
	8	Robin Gecht	Illinois	Women
	8	Edward Sprietzer	Illinois	Women
	8	Andrew Kokaraleis	Illinois	Women
	8	Thomas Kokaraleis	Illinois	Women
	25*	Leonard Lake	California	Men and women hikers
	25*	Charles Ng	California	Men and women hikers
	16–61	Randy Craft	California	Men
	10	Arthur Shawcross	New York	Prostitutes
	6*	Lawrence Bitteger	California	Women
	6*	Roy Norris	California	Women
	3–25	Bobbie Sue Terrell	Florida	Nursing home patients
	8–9	Dorthea Puente	California	Boarders
	5–17	Anthony Joyner	Pennsylvania	Nursing home patients
	7*	Jeffrey Feltner	Florida	Patients
	12*	Richard Diaz	California	Patients
	6	Robert Bedella	Kansas City	Young males
	3	Jane Bolding	Maryland	Patients
	7	Priscilla Ford	Nevada	Men and women
	7	Troost Avenue Killer*	Missouri	Women and prostitutes
	9	The Tied Up Murders*	Missouri	Women and prostitutes
	10	The Avenue Mutilator*	Missouri	Women and prostitutes
	4	The Downtown Killer*	Missouri	Women and prostitutes
	5	The Main Street Killer*	Missouri	Prostitutes

*Current unsolved murder cases.

Years	Victims	Name	Location	Victim Traits
	100+	Richard Kuklinski	New York, New Jersey	Hitman
	6	Wayne Nance		One man, five women
	3	Judias Buenoano	Florida	Husband, boyfriend, son
1990s	6	Richard Berdella	Missouri	Street people
	7	The Gilham Park Strangler*	Missouri	Women and prostitutes
	14	Miami, Ohio Killer*	Ohio	Women
	5	Gainesville Killer*	Florida	Women and one man
	3	Westley Dodd	Oregon, Washington	Young boys
	9	Ray & Faye Copeland	Missouri	Farmhands
	17	Jeffrey Dahmer	Wisconsin, Ohio	Men
	3	Oscar Bolin		Women
	3+	Leslie Warren		Women
	7	Aileen Wuornos	Florida	Men
	6+	"Thrill Killer"	California	Store clerks
	18+	Joseph Akin	Georgia	Hospital patients
	7	Robert Foley	Kentucky, Ohio	Men and women
	6+	Michael St. Clair		Men and women
	6+	Dennis Reese		Men and women
	20+	Scott Cox	Oregon	Women
	3	Kevin Garr	Virginia	Women
	4	William Green	Texas	Men and women
	7	Michael Lefthand	North Dakota, Wisconsin	Men
	7	Manny Pardo	Florida	Drug dealers
	5	Cathy Wood	Michigan	Nursing home patients
	5	Gwen Graham	Michigan	Nursing home patients
	6	"Newark Killer"	New Jersey	Black women
	4+	George Putt	Georgia	Men and women
	20+	Gerald Schaefer		Men and women
	3	Sean Sellers	Oklahoma	Grocer, woman, stepfather

*Current unsolved murder cases.

APPENDIX B

The Victims

Date disappeared	Victim, hometown	Age	Race	Criminal record
June 18, 1978	Steven Hicks, Coventry, Ohio	18	White	Minor property crime; marijuana possission
Sept. 15, 1987	Steven Toumi, Ontonagon, Mich.	28	White	—
Jan. 16, 1988	James Doxtator, Milwaukee, Wisc.	14	American Indian	Car theft; prostitution
March 24, 1988	Richard Guerrero, Milwaukee, Wisc.	25	Hispanic	Extensive record—theft, robbery, armed burglary, prostitution
March 25, 1989	Anthony Lee Sears, Milwaukee, Wisc.	24	Black	Shoplifting; fraudulent use of credit card
June 14, 1990	Edward Warren Smith, Milwaukee, Wisc.	28	Black	FBI has file on Smith
July, 1990	Ricky Lee Beeks (numerous aliases), Milwaukee, Wisc.	33	Black	Extensive record—rape, theft, criminal trespass, disorderly conduct, prostitution
Sept., 1990	Ernest Miller, Milwaukee, Wisc.	24	Black	—
Sept., 1990	David Thomas (13 aliases), Milwaukee, Wisc.	22	Black	Extensive record—shoplifting, battery, attemped armed robbery, resisting an officer
Feb., 1991	Curtis Straughter, Milwaukee, Wisc.	18	Black	Sexual assault
April 7, 1991	Errol Lindsey, Milwaukee, Wisc.	19	Black	Arson; battery with a knife; injury by conduct regardless of life
May 24, 1991	Anthony Hughes, Milwaukee, Wisc.	31	Black	—

Date dis-appeared	Victim, hometown	Age	Race	Criminal record
May 27, 1991	Konerak Sinthasomphone, Milwaukee, Wisc.	14	Laotian	Prostitution
June 30, 1991	Matt Turner, Flint, Michigan	20	Black	Juvenile record in Michigan
July 5, 1991	Jeremiah Weinberger, Chicago, Ill.	23	Hispanic	—
July 12, 1991	Oliver Lacey, Milwaukee, Wisc.	23	Black	—
July 19, 1991	Joseph Bradehoft, Minnesota	25	White	Domestic assault; property damage